PENGUIN BOOKS

THE HEART OF INDIA

Mark Tully was born in Calcutta and educated in England. He worked for the BBC in South Asia for twenty-five years and now works as a journalist in New Delhi. Among the many major stories he has covered are the Bangladeshi war, Mrs Gandhi's State of Emergency, the execution of Zulfikar Ali Bhutto, the Russian occupation of Afghanistan and Operation Blue Star – when the Indian army launched an attack on the Golden Temple, the holiest shrine of the Sikhs. This operation and the Punjab problem were the subjects of his first book, *Amritsar: Mrs Gandhi's Last Battle*, which he wrote with his colleague Satish Jacob. In 1987 he made the much-applauded radio series *From Raj to Rajiv*, which traced the story of India's forty years of independence. His second book accompanied this series. *No Full Stops in India* is also published by Penguin. His most recent book, *Lives of Jesus*, is published by Penguin/BBC Books, and accompanies the BBC series of the same name.

In 1992 Mark Tully was awarded the Padma Shri by the government of India, a rare honour for a foreigner. This puts him in the unusual position of being decorated by the Queen of Britain and the President of India.

I would never have written these stories without
Gillian Wright, who worked with me from the plans
for the first visit to Uttar Pradesh until the
last 'i' was dotted

MARK TULLY

———

THE HEART OF
INDIA

PENGUIN BOOKS

PENGUIN BOOKS

Published by the Penguin Group
Penguin Books Ltd, 27 Wrights Lane, London W8 5TZ, England
Penguin Putnam Inc., 375 Hudson Street, New York, New York 10014, USA
Penguin Books Australia Ltd, Ringwood, Victoria, Australia
Penguin Books Canada Ltd, 10 Alcorn Avenue, Toronto, Ontario, Canada M4V 3B2
Penguin Books (NZ) Ltd, Private Bag 102902, NSMC, Auckland, New Zealand

Penguin Books Ltd, Registered Offices: Harmondsworth, Middlesex, England

First published by Viking 1995
Published in Penguin Books 1996
7 9 10 8 6

Printed in England by Clays Ltd, St Ives plc

CONTENTS

INTRODUCTION

When I ended my long career as the BBC's correspondent in Delhi, many people I met in India were surprised that I was not returning to live in Britain. They imagined I would follow the pattern of the British civil servants and police officers who spent their most active years ruling India and then returned to Dorset, Devon or Cornwall to enjoy their well-earned retirement. But the idea of leaving India never crossed my mind. I would have looked back on my life as wasted if, after spending nearly thirty years working in India, I had no desire to remain once my BBC career was over. The roots I had put down were not so shallow that I could pull them up as soon as the job which brought me here had ended.

At least four generations of my mother's family before me spent their working lives in India. Most of them went 'home' to retire, and I can well understand why. In the first place, they were positively discouraged from 'staying on'. Britain ruled India, but it did not colonize it. The British Raj did not encourage settlers. Settlers might set a bad example and 'go native', destroying the carefully nurtured image of the difference, and hence the superiority, of the British race. The Raj, it was thought, depended on that image of superiority to enable it to rule so many with so few. Philip Mason was a member of the Indian Civil Service, the 'steel frame' which held the Raj together. In his memorable book *The Men Who Ruled India* he described the Indian Civil Service as 'a corps of men specially selected, brought up by a rigour of bodily hardship to which no other modern people have subjected their ruling class, trained by cold baths, cricket, and the history of Greece and Rome, a separate race from those they ruled, aloof, superior to bribery, discouraged from marriage until they were middle-aged, and then subject to long separations'.

But I wasn't sent to rule India – the Raj was over long before I could offer myself for the Indian Civil Service. Even if the opportunity had been there, I am sure I would never have been accepted. I wasn't very good at the Spartan life of my public school, I was a careless writer of Latin and Greek prose and I was bored by cricket. I was sent to write and broadcast about India, and an independent India too. That meant I couldn't keep aloof. I had to become involved; I had to become part of India – at least that was the way I saw it. Some have argued that I became too involved, that my reporting was prejudiced by my affection for India. For my part I have never been able to understand why British journalists who are open Francophiles, overt admirers of America or enthusiasts for some other Western country which they report are not likely to be accused of being partisan, but correspondents who identify themselves with countries whose cultures are not European or American are regarded with the gravest suspicion.

I soon realized that it was not going to be difficult to get involved in India. From the first day I arrived I was surrounded by friends – the friends my predecessor introduced to me, the staff of All India Radio, many of them much senior to me, the members of the Press Club, my new neigbours. Many are still good friends to this day. It's through them that I became involved in their country. Now, when I am asked why I'm staying on, I reply, 'Because of my friends.'

That, of course, is only part of the truth. I'm drawn to India by its beauty, particularly its natural beauty. Recently I was beside a camp fire in the Great Himalayan National Park, watching the snow-covered mountains glitter in the sunset. A week later I was in Kerala, in the extreme south, sitting in my bathing trunks, looking out over the Arabian Sea as the sun slid like a great red dome below the horizon. There are the smells of India too, which evoke such nostalgia. There is the dry scent of early summer in Delhi as the blue jacarandas, the scarlet gulmohars and other trees come into flower, the sweet smell of the queen-of-the-night and the freshness of the first scent of pine trees in the foothills of the Himalayas after a long, hot and dusty drive across the plains. There are the folk songs and the classical music with the *raagas* that start with such austerity and end in ecstasy. There are the great epics and the love poetry. There's the art of the Pradhan tribe in Central India which occupies the whole of one wall of my flat. There's the colour of the festivals, the solemn dignity of the courtyards of the great mosques filled with line after line of worshippers bowing their heads in prayer and the colourful informality of the *pujari* performing the evening rites in a Hindu temple. There's the sound of priests singing the Sikh scriptures carrying across the water of the sacred tank in which the Golden Temple stands. There are the great monuments of India. I have never known anyone to be disappointed by the Taj Mahal or the forts of Rajasthan. There are fresh-cooked *parathas* for breakfast in the open-air *dhabas*, or restaurants, along the Grand Trunk Road, and there's the delicacy of a vegetarian *thali*, or tray, in Gujarat.

All these keep me in India, but they are not the whole. It would need a poet to describe what India means to me, and I am no poet. I can only say that I'm not alone among foreigners in believing there's nowhere like India, and no people like Indians. I am perhaps more unusual for a foreigner in that I have been accepted as a part of India.

I am unique in the privilege I have enjoyed of having my reports carried for many years by the Indian-language services of the BBC, services listened to in villages all over India. I have been the correspondent in what I believe will turn out to have been the heyday of BBC radio in India. I started my career with the transistor radio which brought cheap and easily portable sets to Indian villagers. I ended it just as television was beginning to have an impact on BBC radio audiences. During my time the government-controlled All India Radio allowed no rivals, so those who wanted independent news on radio had to tune into international stations. Now there are signs that the government is loosening its stranglehold on the electronic media. This will mean more rivals for the BBC too. Of course, BBC radio has a big future in India, but my successors will not have it as easy as I did. There is also BBC World Service television, but I have found that radio builds up a more intimate relationship between a broadcaster and the audience. Perhaps because of that intimacy, I have been shown great affection in India, although my reports were by no means always what the listeners wanted to hear.

These stories may seem a poor way to repay that affection. They do not paint an idyllic picture. But Indians do not expect uncritical acclaim. They do not deny reality. So I hope the stories will be accepted as what they are intended to be – a tribute to the Indian villager.

Mahatma Gandhi said, 'India lives in her 700,000 villages, obscure, tiny, out-of-the-way villages ... I would like to go and settle down in some such village. That is real India, my India.' Madhukar Upadhaya, a friend of mine who reports for the BBC, celebrated the 125th anniversary of Mahatma Gandhi's birth by repeating one of his great symbolic protests against the British, the Dandi salt march. Madhukar walked for twenty-two days, covering 241 miles and visiting all the villages through which the Mahatma had passed. He ended his journey on the coast where the Mahatma defied the government by making salt without paying tax on it. On his return Madhukar said to me, 'The old village ways are dying out and nothing is replacing them.' But the best-known writing about modern India has for the most part ignored the plight of the villagers who are losing their old moorings and not finding new ones. Writers have concentrated on urban, middle-class India. I hope these stories will do something to restore the balance.

I am a journalist, so I decided the best way to write about the Indian villager was to go into the villages and towns of the eastern half of Uttar Pradesh to look for stories and then report them. However, I soon realized that it would cause grave embarrassment, and in some cases even danger, to many of those who told me their stories if I revealed their names. When I sat down to write I found that merely changing the names of the characters was not enough; the stories would have to be more heavily disguised. Then I let my imagination loose, and the stories took on new and unexpected shapes. That's how what started as journalism became fiction. But the stories are realistic. Each one has been read by a friend who knows the places, the people and the traditions described. Each friend has certified, 'Yes, it could have happened like that,' at the same time making invaluable suggestions about details.

I chose the eastern half of the vast state of Uttar Pradesh for many reasons. First and foremost, it's a part of India of which I am particularly fond. It's the heart of the Gangetic plain and, for me, the heart of India. There are many places of pilgrimage in India but none quite like Varanasi, with its *ghats* on the banks of the Ganges and its temples. Centuries ago the Buddha preached his first sermon near Varanasi. Tulsi Das wrote the best-known version of one of the two great Hindu epics, the Ramayana, sitting on the *ghats* at Varanasi. It tells the story of the God-King Rama, who is believed to have been born at Ayodhya in eastern Uttar Pradesh. Lucknow is where I count the eastern half of the state as starting and was the capital of the Nawabs of Avadh until the British removed Wajid Ali Shah from his throne. The city remained the centre of a Muslim culture renowned for the gentleness of its manners and the beauty of its poetry. In modern times Allahabad was the home of the Nehru family who ruled India for so many years after Independence. Three of the Prime Ministers who were not members of the Nehru family came from eastern Uttar Pradesh.

Prem Chand, one of India's most highly acclaimed short-story writers, lived near Varanasi and wrote about the villages of eastern Uttar Pradesh during the Independence movement. While I was writing these stories, I met a journalist in Varanasi, and during what I thought was an informal conversation I mentioned that I was a great admirer of the legendary Munshi Prem Chand, although at the same time I made it clear that I could not aspire to his greatness. Within hours there was a story on the United News of India wire, which reaches the remotest corners of the country, saying, 'Mark Tully aims to be the modern Prem Chand.' That prompted an editorial in the august *Times of India* headlined 'Munshi Mark Tullyji'. Fortunately, the *Times of India* did say that I had 'confessed my limitations'. The editorial ended with the hope that 'Munshi Tullyji's modern decameron will mirror the emergence of new forces with their impact on traditional lifestyles and democracy itself.'

I do not know whether the *Times of India* will judge these stories to live up to its expectations, but it is true to say that I also chose eastern Uttar Pradesh because I wanted to write stories about the impact on traditional village life of the changes taking place in India. I felt that too many changes had already taken place in western Uttar Pradesh, which has been heavily influenced by the prosperity and modernity of Delhi. Not enough change has taken place in Bihar to the east. In the villages and towns where I looked for my stories I found the old ways still surviving but the modern coming in fast.

One last reason I must mention for choosing eastern Uttar Pradesh is Hindi. Although two other languages, Avadhi and Bhojpuri, are widely spoken in the area, Hindi is almost universally understood, and that's the only Indian language I can manage.

My earlier book, *No Full Stops in India*, was didactic in purpose. It was a plea for Indians to promote economic growth which would protect their country's ancient culture, not merely to ape what I believe is the sterile materialism of the modern Western culture which now threatens to dominate the world. These stories are not didactic. I have not written them systematically to make a series of predetermined points. I hope they will make a good read. This time I leave the reader to judge the impact of modernity on ancient India. But I do hope they will at least convince some that the caste system is not entirely static, that the less privileged castes are on the move and that Indian village women are not always silent sufferers of male oppression.

Gillian Wright travelled with me wherever I went. There would have been no stories to tell if it hadn't been for the villagers who welcomed us into their homes, insisted on giving us food and, of course, tea and answered inquisitive questions. In many other parts of the world I would have been told to mind my own business. It would be invidious to mention any by name unless I mentioned them all. I must also thank those to whom I turned for advice on the stories, in particular the Lucknow-based journalist Ram Dutt Tripathi and his wife Pushpa, the Naqvi family of Mustafabad, the Ansari family of Yusufpur-Mohammadabad, I.B. Singh of Lucknow and Hiralal Yadav and his son Shyam Kishore Yadav, both members of the Uttar Pradesh State Legislature. I must also thank the government of Uttar Pradesh for many inexpensive nights in their rest houses.

THE BARREN WOMAN OF
BALRAMGAON

The water in the drain in front of the small temple of Shiva was normally a dismal muddy brown, but today it was a bright, cheerful purple. The dog stretched out on the temple platform had scarlet and yellow patches added to the brown and white the gods had given him. The temple platform itself was stained with green and scarlet. It was Holi in the village of Balramgaon – the spring festival when everyone and everything is smeared with coloured powder or dowsed with dyed water. The Yadavs who dominated the village had just finished singing a *faag*, or special Holi song, in honour of Shiva and were now moving on to their next destination, the house of the primary-school teacher.

The men chattered excitedly to each other as they walked. One young man, whose hair had been stained even blacker than usual, said, 'Now we've got to sing a *faag* of Krishna. After all, that's what Holi is about: Braj, the home of Lord Krishna.'

Another, wearing a cotton cap with 'Happy Holi' embroidered on it, laughed and said, 'Yes! Let's celebrate Krishna. He stole the clothes of the milkmaids while they were bathing at Vrindavan. Let's celebrate that.'

An old man with a yellow stain on his white beard coloured green, did not approve of that remark. Wagging his finger, he said, 'We Yadavs don't want anything like that on Holi. We don't get drunk and run off into the fields with other men's women. That's work for the Bhangis and Chamars.'

'More's the pity,' the young man replied.

The ragged group walked on past empty houses with *char-*

poys turned up on the verandas. No one was going to laze on them today. Children wearing only tattered underpants, their faces smeared with an assortment of colours, ran about with water-pistols shaped like fishes and plastic plungers fixed in bottles of noxious-looking coloured liquid, spraying anyone who didn't manage to get out of their range. Two old farmers hobbled along with the help of long bamboo staves. Only the cows and sleek black buffaloes tethered in front of the houses were unmoved by the excitement of the festival.

The schoolmaster's brick house, plastered with pale-brown mud, stood in a small grove. Two tall *neem* trees provided shade for his small courtyard. Yellow oleanders were in flower, as were red cannas and purple bougainvillaea. Holi was the season for flowers, especially red flowers that were used to make the colouring smeared everywhere. The schoolmaster stood on the veranda to greet the *faag* party. He embraced each man three times, saying, 'Holi greetings,' and then asked them to sit down. Sweet pastries known as *gujias* and salty snacks were produced. Cigarettes, *bidis* and matches were passed round on a metal tray.

The *faag* party sat under the thatched eaves of the veranda. They were divided into two groups. Chote Lal Yadav, who had seen more than eighty Holis, put his hands on the shoulders of two men and lowered himself gingerly. Everyone looked towards him. He raised his arm, pointed at the men opposite and started singing:

'My snake-lord is sleeping – Krishna, run away from here.
My snake-lord's a killer – Krishna, go there and he'll bite.
My snake-lord is sleeping here –
Sweet child, run from Kali's lair.
Hah, hah, hah, hah!'

The refrain was taken up by the rest of his group, singing at the top of their voices to make themselves heard above the frenzied beat of the drums, the clashing of tambourines and the clanging of cymbals.

Then the other group repeated the refrain, leaning forward and pointing aggressively at their opponents to give the impression that they were singing even louder. Chote Lal Yadav's jaw sagged as he sat, silently waiting for the chance to come back at them. When it came he led his group in singing:

> 'Said child Krishna, "Go and wake him.
> It's him I've come to nail.
> I'm going to kill your snake-lord
> And play within his lair."'

When the first song was over, Ram Lakhan Yadav, a man of about thirty who had been sitting at the back, taking no part in the *faag*, rose and picked his way through the singers towards the gap between the two groups where the percussionists were sitting. He was carrying a pair of cymbals.

Chote Lal Yadav said, '*Arre bhai*, sit down, we don't need any more cymbals. Two are quite enough. If you too come in now, we won't be able to make ourselves heard above all the banging and clashing.'

A young man, Hoshiar Singh, sneered, 'Get out of here, Ram Lakhan. Holi's the season for cutting the crop – and where's your crop? Don't you know how to plough? Something wrong with the seed? Didn't you irrigate the field? What's the problem? People like you bring us bad luck. We'll have poor crops this year if you play Holi with us. Wait until your house produces some children before trying to play those cymbals.'

Ram Lakhan pulled the young man to his feet and punched him in the face. Before a full-scale fight could develop the singers were on their feet, pinning back the arms of the two men. Ram Lakhan was frog-marched off the veranda and given a parting kick to see him on his way.

In the small inner courtyard of the house next to Ram Lakhan's his wife was standing against the wall watching women pressing the pastry for *gujias* into moulds and frying *papadums* and *kachoris*. A child darted to the pile of freshly cooked *gujias* and stuffed one into his mouth. His young mother caught him up in her arms, hugged him and said, 'What will we do if you go on like that? The men will be very angry if there are not enough *gujias* for everyone who comes to the house today. They will smack you if I tell them what the problem is.'

There was a tussle going on in another corner between one of the brothers of the house and his younger sister-in-law. She was trying to stop him pouring a pot of coloured water over her, but let go of the pot for one moment to prevent the border of her sari from slipping off her head and found herself drenched with yellow dye.

Ram Lakhan's wife thought, 'I have no brother-in-law to play Holi with, no children to hug. I look like all these women here. I've got the same gold nosepin, the same bangles, the same silver anklets. I wear the red *sindoor* of a married woman in my hair. But really I'm nothing like them because I have no children, and there's no family in our house.'

Rani and Sima, two of the younger wives of the family, came over to her. Rani asked, 'Why don't you have any colour on your face or your sari? Doesn't anyone play Holi with you?'

Sima giggled and said, 'Nobody plays Holi with a barren woman. It brings bad luck.'

Ram Lakhan's wife stared silently at the ground.

Sima poked her in the ribs and asked, 'Have you been sitting under our mango trees? They should be flowering now, but they aren't, and people say that if a barren woman sits in a mango grove, the trees won't flower.'

Both giggled like the schoolchildren they really were, and Rani said, 'Come on, we are wasting our time. Her mouth is closed as tight as her womb.'

Ram Lakhan's wife walked around the edge of the courtyard, her head turned towards the wall, until she reached the front door. No one noticed her going. It was as if she had never come to play Holi with her neighbours.

The Yadavs of Balramgaon paid calls on each other until late that night. Ram Lakhan wondered whether he should call on the man who had insulted him. It was said to be particularly important at Holi to go to the homes of people you were not on speaking terms with, but he couldn't face the possibility of another insult, so he stayed inside his room. When his wife came to the door and announced that food had been cooked, he said, 'How can I eat food when all day I have had to eat the insults of my own *biradari*? You eat. I'm not coming out.'

Ram Lakhan's wife went back to the corner of the courtyard where she had her kitchen and tried to eat a little herself, but she too had no appetite. She did not have the energy to wash the pans in which the vegetables had been cooked. She squatted against the wall, looking up at the cloudless night sky, bright with a full moon and countless stars, and thinking of her own noisy family home where a new child had always just arrived and her great-grandparents seemed set to live for ever. What a stark contrast to this silent, lonely house where only she and Ram Lakhan lived. The family she had married into had a tradition of dying young, and Ram Lakhan had been an only child.

The silence was broken by a shout from her husband's room. 'Come here, you. I want to talk to you.'

She covered her head, stood up, walked slowly across the courtyard and stood in the doorway. Her husband shouted, 'Come in,' but did not get up. He ordered her brusquely to squat on the floor at the end of the *charpoy* on which he was lying.

Turning on his side and looking towards the wall, Ram Lakhan said in a surly voice, 'Because of you, my Holi has been terrible. Everyone else joking about red colour for a woman's monthly blood, fertility, Krishna and the milkmaids, and I've had to eat insults about your infertility. I've had to eat blows too, and I've been kicked up the backside. They wouldn't even let me take part in *faag* in case I brought bad luck to their crops.'

His wife said, 'Do you think mine has been any better? Do

5

you think I haven't eaten insults? The two youngest daughters-in-law next door, just children, they spoke to me as though I was some old hag, some servant they could behave with as badly as they liked. Now I come home only to be ill-treated by you.'

'What do you mean? It's my right to speak to you as I like. Now not only do I get no respect in the village, I don't even get it at home. My own wife answers me back. Am I a man or just a pair of pyjamas? I am not going to endure another Holi like this one. Either you produce a child this year, or I will send you back home and take another woman.' Rani started to sob quietly. 'Don't start crying again. You always try that one and then you turn my mind, and I am lost. This time I really mean it. There must be something you can do.'

'I'm crying because it's so sad. We live much better than most others in this village. You know how to speak to me so well at night, whereas other women tell me how rough their men are sometimes, but still it's no good because we can't produce children.'

Ram Lakhan was easily moved by his wife. Perhaps because of their loneliness they had become very close. She was certainly not just a cook and a housekeeper. She had a fair complexion and green eyes, rare in Belramgaon. As a child she had carried brass pots of water on her head every day. Balancing them had given her a lithe hip movement which could still arouse Ram Lakhan when he watched her walking.

He sat up, swung his feet over the end of the *charpoy* and started to undo her hair. It flowed down her back – shining and black. He ran his fingers through it and said, 'I don't want to lose you. I know that you are much better than any other man's wife in this village, but we can't go on like this. Something has to be done.'

His wife scrambled up on to the *charpoy* and pulled him down beside her, saying, 'This is the only way to produce babies.'

After making love the couple lay on their backs, looking up at the fan wobbling hazardously on its stem as it stirred the warm night air. Rani said lazily, 'I've heard that it's not always the woman who is infertile. It can be the man, and then there are some medicines to help with that. I have been to the family-planning clinic, and they say there is no reason why I can't have children. Perhaps it would be a good idea if you went to see a doctor.'

'But you know there's nothing wrong with me. I've just shown you again that there's no shortage of seed in me. The doctors don't know everything. It's obvious that it's you who are barren.'

Rani, realizing that there was no point in trying to persuade him any further, turned on her side, saying, 'Well, then, all that's left is praying to the gods for the gift of children.'

The gods did not oblige, but the Pradhan didn't like quarrels among the Yadavs as they threatened to divide his community, which was the source of his political strength. Unless all the Yadavs voted together he would not be re-elected. So he called Ram Lakhan and Hoshiar Singh to his house. He said to Ram Lakhan, 'Fights sometimes happen in every community, but why did you have to have a fight on Holi of all days?'

Ram Lakhan replied, 'He insulted me. He said I couldn't join the *faag* because I was childless and that would bring bad luck to everyone. He was obscene too, making lewd remarks about my not knowing how to sow my seed.'

'Is that true?' the Pradhan asked Hoshiar Singh.

'Well, I meant it only as a joke. Everyone makes jokes about that sort of thing on Holi. There was no need for his brain to get so hot. He should have been able to take it.'

'No man should be asked to tolerate insults to his wife, whether she is barren or not. In the old days I would have called a meeting of the caste council and asked them to impose *hookah pani bund* on you to teach you how to behave and what jokes are proper and what are not. Now, unfortunately, the rules are more lenient. If we are to hold the community together, we can't be too strict. I suggest that you apologize and let it be known in the village that you were in the wrong.'

Hoshiar Singh clasped his hands and said, 'All right, Pradhanji, I have nothing against Ram Lakhan. I don't know why I lost my head. Perhaps it was the *bhang*. I have to admit that I had drunk a glass and that was wrong too.'

The Pradhan laughed and said, 'All right, we will overlook that too this time. Young men will be young men. Now embrace Ram Lakhan, and let's hear no more about it.'

So Ram Lakhan's honour was restored, and he was able to rejoin the group of Yadavs who gathered at the Pradhan's house each evening to discuss everything from village gossip to national politics. The elders still passed a hookah round; the younger men smoked *bidis*, or cigarettes. There was no liquor – the Pradhan strongly disapproved of that because drinking also led to quarrels.

One evening they were discussing the rice crop. It looked as if it would be particularly good that year. The Pradhan said, 'Now that we have a Yadav Chief Minister in Lucknow there's been no problem over bank loans to buy seeds, no shortage of fertilizers, and we have even been able to see that the water reaches our canal, so we have every reason to be thankful.'

A farmer who, by virtue of his years, was rather less respectful to the Pradhan than most of the Yadavs, wagged his finger angrily at him saying, 'Satpal, what are you talking about? You, the Pradhan of my *biradari*, are praising the politicians for a good harvest. In my days the young men would have gone to give thanks to Guru Gorakhnath at the *mela* in the temple at Gorakhpur, but nowadays the politicians think they are gods, and people like you only encourage them by giving them credit for everything. It's shameful. If the Chief Minister came here, you wouldn't just touch his feet, you'd lie down on the ground in front of him. Where's your pride as a Yadav?'

Hoshiar Singh, anxious to re-establish himself in the Pradhan's favour, said, 'Old man, you don't understand these times. Our Pradhan has to be a politician too, otherwise we would get nothing. Everything comes from *sifarish*, and if you don't have contacts, you can't do *sifarish*. The days of the gods are over. We have to live on this earth, on the soil of this village.'

But the Pradhan was not so pleased by this defence as Hoshiar Singh had hoped. He was himself a religious man, and so he didn't want anyone to commit the sin of hubris on his behalf. At the same time he wanted to avoid a split between the elderly and the young in his community. He turned on Hoshiar Singh and said, 'You fool. Don't show disrespect to the gods or to your elders. That's the whole trouble nowadays: the young have no respect for the past. You think everything started from the time you first went to the barber for a shave. I think some of you should go to Gorakhpur this year to show your respect for God and put an end to this arrogance. I would suggest that you go, Hoshiar Singh, and you can take Ram Lakhan with you, so that he can pray for help with his problem – and you make sure there's no fighting this time.'

Hoshiar Singh and Ram Lakhan were left with no choice, so they and three other young Yadavs spent a cold night on the train to the town of Gorakhpur in the middle of January. When they reached the shrine of holy man Guru Gorakhnath they found there was a large, crowded and noisy fair outside the temple gates. The young men decided to see what it had to offer before going on to fulfil their more solemn purpose. At the entrance of the fair barbers sat waiting to shave the heads of young children brought to pay their respects to Guru Gorakhnath. A man was having his luxuriant moustache trimmed. He held a mirror in one hand to make sure the barber didn't cut it back too far but at the same time toned down its arrogant assertion of manhood sufficiently to avoid insulting the god he had come to worship.

In the fairground they found the usual mixture of sacred and secular which goes with almost all Indian religious occasions. There were women sitting cross-legged on the ground behind piles of orange, bright-red, shocking-pink and bilious-green powder. There were stalls selling calendars with pictures of the gods. A few young women, revealing the smooth brown skin between their blouses and their lowslung saris had somehow found their way into this pantheon.

Bharat photographers offered the opportunity of portraits set against various backgrounds. They could make it appear that customers had been photographed at the Kaaba in Mecca, in a Hindu temple or at the architecturally much admired new Baha'i temple in Delhi. They could also give the impression that they had been sitting with the film star Sri Devi in a room filled with all modern conveniences. Outside balloons and bubbles blown by the sellers of bubble mixture floated in the air. A vendor of flutes repeated monotonously the same few notes in the hope of persuading customers that it was not too difficult to play his instruments. All the rich variety of Indian cuisine was on offer. The young Yadavs made their way to a café and ordered white crunchy sweets called *khaja mithai*. Hoshiar Singh said, 'After this let's see the side-shows, so that we can enjoy ourselves, before we go to the temple to keep the Pradhan happy.'

As they made their way towards a giant wheel crowned with the Indian flag, they passed an exhausted mother reclining against the white cotton bags in which she had brought pots, pans and all the other necessities of a long family outing. She held a baby in her lap, and two small girls tugged at her *sari*, impatiently urging her to spend more of the family's scant resources. An old man was snoring peacefully, the urge to sleep having triumphed over the discordant music blaring from the side-shows and other entertainments. A young couple were investigating the contents of their tiffin carrier.

The Yadavs had a ride on a gigantic swing, shaped like a Viking boat. They took pot-shots at prizes with air-guns whose sights had been deliberately distorted. They stared at a tent advertised as 'Saajan Disco Dance Party'. It was topped by a ten-foot cut-out of a lady whose scant pink sari had slipped down to her buttocks and revealed almost all of her legs. Ram Lakhan refused to countenance entering that tent, so they went on to a freak show which promised a snake with the head of a woman but decided that it hardly fitted in with the sacred purpose of their visit. Then they came across a young man standing by a tricycle van. He was surrounded by a crowd of men. They guffawed as he bellowed through his megaphone, 'Sand-lizard oil! Rub it on and you'll feel the difference. Put your cock in at Kanpur, you'll take it out at Gorakhpur. One bottle only ten rupees, and what a surprise you'll give the ladies!'

One of the crowd shouted, 'How do we know?'

'I've told you. Try for yourself. Have you ever seen the Qutab Minar tower in Delhi, hundreds of feet high and built of solid stone? How do you think they got that up in those days, years ago when they didn't have scaffolding? They didn't. They built it flat along the ground, rubbed sand-lizard oil on it and it stood up all on its own. Sand-lizard, the oil for men. It's only ten rupees a bottle, ten rupees a bottle. Roll up, roll up. Ten rupees a bottle, to put bone in your prick. Do you want a cock, or would you like a spade? Do you want to screw, or do you really want to make the grade?'

One man was pushed forward by his friends, handed over a ten-rupee note and hurriedly shoved a bottle of oil into the pocket of his *kurta*. That broke the barrier of reserve. The salesman crammed ten-rupee notes into a shabby black bag, while his assistant handed out the bottles.

Hoshiar Singh said, 'I'll give it a go,' and pushed his way through the crowd surrounding the salesman. As he handed over a ten-rupee note he asked whether there was any medicine to produce children.

The salesman produced a packet from the cupboard fixed to his cycle-rickshaw, saying, 'With these pills you can get milk out of a bullock and puppies out of a barren bitch.'

Hoshiar Singh handed over another ten-rupee note, went back to his colleagues and gave the packet to Ram Lakhan, saying, 'Don't be angry. You never know. They might work.'

Ram Lakhan was not amused, but he didn't want to draw attention to himself. So he took the pills and walked away, saying, 'I've had enough of this. There's a long queue to get into the temple. If we don't stop fooling around, we won't get to see Guru Gorakhnath today.'

The queue was moving slowly across the park towards the white temple with its three tall *shikaras*, or towers. The devotees were penned between two wooden fences to keep them in line. As the Yadavs joined the queue a well-dressed man was arguing with the sub-inspector in charge of the police party, whose job it was to ensure that everyone joined the queue and no devotee crossed the rope barrier and walked straight up to the temple. The man protested, 'I'm a government servant. I am allowed to go straight into the temple.'

The sub-inspector growled, 'No one is allowed past this barrier. Those are my orders.'

'But you can't expect a man in my position to stand in a queue like this, especially as I have my wife and children with me.'

'There are plenty of wives and children in the queue. Get in line or get out.'

The Yadavs stopped to join the crowd which was gathering to witness this altercation. Hoshiar Singh said, 'You have spoken exactly right, Inspector Sahib. These government servants, they think they are the owners of India. They need to be shown something.'

Then, turning to his friends, he asked in a loud voice, 'Have you seen his wife?'

'What do you mean?' another Yadav replied.

'Look at the gold around her neck, look at the gold on her arms, look at the gold on her fingers. A government officer doesn't need to come to this festival. He takes enough bribes to afford to go to Tirupati where you offer gold and jewels. He's come here only because he's mean. He's heard that Guru Gorakhnath will listen to your prayers for just a bag of rice.'

The crowd roared with laughter. The civil servant walked off as quickly as the small modicum of decorum he retained would allow, leaving his wife to drag their two young children away as best she could. The police sub-inspector said, 'Bastards. Shameless people. They think everyone is going to touch their feet, and then, when they are challenged, they don't have the courage to face up to it. Anyway you certainly made an owl out of that one.' Then, turning to face the crowd, he said, 'I'm going to take this lot to the top of the queue, just to show that I am the law around here. Even bastard government servants have to listen to me.'

So the Yadavs found themselves being led through the park to the pillared portico of the temple. No one dared to object to the sub-inspector when he inserted them at the front of the queue. Behind them stood a group of farmers wearing brightly coloured turbans and speaking a dialect from the Rajasthan desert the Yadavs couldn't understand. There were also men wearing side-caps set at jaunty angles, who had come across the near-by border with the Himalayan state of Nepal. Ram Lakhan said, 'I thought this was a local festival for people like us from the east, but people seem to have come from everywhere.'

Hoshiar Singh replied, 'I have heard that Lord Gorakhnath was a very powerful *yogi*. That's, I suppose, why people come here from all over India. Look behind you. There are some Bengalis wearing *dhotis* so long that I can't understand why they don't trip over them. People know that a *yogi* is much more likely to do their work than that bastard government officer I saw off. That's why they have faith in Lord

Gorakhnath. Maybe he will do your work too,' he said to Ram
Lakhan.

'I thought you'd given the Pradhan an assurance that you
would not tease me about that any more. Now you first go and
buy me those pills, and then tell me what I have to ask from
Lord Gorakhnath. I don't want another fight. Why don't you
leave me alone?'

'All right, all right. I accept. I only thought it might help.
We all have problems, after all, and I will certainly ask Lord
Gorakhnath to solve mine.'

'You ask him to solve yours and leave me to ask him to
solve mine.'

The priests controlling the temple were anxious that devotees should not spend too much time in front of the image of
Guru Gorakhnath because the more pilgrims who passed
through the temple the more wealth they contributed. So the
queue moved forward through the temple hall at a steady
pace, and Ram Lakhan soon reached the *sanctum sanctorum*. It
was an alcove, separated from the rest of the temple by rails.

Coins, rice, marigolds and roses rained down on the marble
floor in front of the image. Ram Lakhan pushed through the
crowd to the rails, where he handed over a bag of rice and
lentils and a red cardboard box. One priest filled the box with
sweet *prasad*; another poured the rice and lentils on to the
marble floor, where it was promptly swept into a mound,
growing ever larger, on the side of the *sanctum sanctorum*. Ram
Lakhan stared at the modern alabaster image, the size of a
small man. Guru Gorakhnath sat cross-legged in a glass case
set high enough for devotees to get a good look at him. He
was not a god and he had no divine trappings, no extra arms
or legs, no weapons, no conch shells, no discus. But his
almond-shaped eyes were exaggerated, his face was super-
naturally smooth and his lips were bright red. He was
garlanded with marigolds and crowned with a double halo of
small yellow bulbs. The outline of his red throne was also
picked out by two strings of yellow lights.

It was not easy for Ram Lakhan to concentrate on his prayers. He was squeezed up against the rails by the pressure of the devotees behind him. One man next to him was being particularly troublesome by trying to make space to prostrate himself before Guru Gorakhnath. The priests and their acolytes kept on urging Ram Lakhan, not always too politely, to move on, but he stuck to his ground until he had spent what he believed was sufficient time, and had prayed with enough intensity, to convey his request to the *rishi*.

Ram Lakhan's wife had also been investigating the possibility of divine intervention. One of the older village midwives had told her of a Yadav lady who had suddenly produced a child after apparently being barren for nearly ten years. Ram Lakhan's wife said she would like to see her, and a meeting was arranged. When Ram Lakhan's wife entered the courtyard of the elderly lady, Sita Devi, she found her sitting alone in one corner. She asked Ram Lakhan's wife to sit beside her and said, 'I have managed to get rid of the other women because the midwife told me what you wanted to talk about, but we'd better be quick, otherwise they'll come back.'

Ram Lakhan's wife looked down at the ground and said softly, 'You know that I have been accused of being barren, as you were. The midwife told me that maybe you could say whether there was anything you did to have a child.'

'I was told by the midwife to go with another man just once or twice. She told me, "Go into the fields one night. It's probably your man's fault, not yours." But I didn't because I could not bring myself to do so, and anyhow I would have been ashamed to ask another man, although they're all such *badmashes* I am sure there would have been plenty to do the job. I wasn't that bad-looking, I can tell you.'

'So what did happen?'

'Well, I don't know that I know. I can give you only one piece of advice. If ever you hear that a wandering *sadhu* from

Rishikesh has come to that small temple of Shiva by the Ganges, go and see him.'

'Which temple?'

'You know, the small one only about three miles from here. There is an *ashram* next to it, but the temple has nothing to do with it. I still go there to pray sometimes, and if I hear that the *sadhu* has come, I'll take you to him. Now go quickly. We don't want the whole village gossiping. Everyone will be able to guess why you have come to see me.'

A week or so before Ram Lakhan was due to go to Gorakhpur the midwife told his wife that Sita Devi wanted to see her again. Apparently the *sadhu* had arrived, but Sita Devi told Ram Lakhan's wife that the ceremony was very elaborate and she would have to stay in the temple all night. She had managed to do so by telling her family she was going back to see her parents. Ram Lakhan's wife decided it would be safest if she went while her husband was in Gorakhpur. It was unlikely that any neighbours would realize she had gone and, if they did, she could always use the same excuse as Sita Devi. The boy they employed to milk and feed the cattle wouldn't think anything of her absence. He'd assume she'd gone to someone else's house to gossip.

So, late in the afternoon when Ram Lakhan had left for Gorakhpur, his wife and Sita Devi set out to bathe in the Ganges. After about an hour they arrived at a small temple on a bank high above the sacred river, in the shade of a peepul tree. Although the bank was quite high, it flooded during the monsoon, and the waters had eroded the soil, leaving the tree's thick, gnarled roots exposed like giant pythons. The temple itself was built on a brick plinth. It had just one small *shikara* tower, surrounded on three sides by a veranda. A handsome *sadhu*, looking not much older than Ram Lakhan's wife, was sitting on the veranda opposite the Ganges. With him was a middle-aged woman and another holy man wearing a white shirt and a *dhoti*. He had thick spectacles askew on his nose and an undisciplined mop of curly black hair.

As they approached the temple Sita Devi said to Ram Lakhan's wife, 'The *sadhu* in the loin-cloth – he's the one I'm talking about.'

'But he looks far too young.'

'With *sadhus* you can never tell their age.'

It was the woman who first saw Sita Devi and Ram Lakhan's wife climbing up the bank. She said to the *sadhu*, who was staring at the far bank of the Ganges, lost in contemplation, '*Babaji*, that village woman who was here the other day asking about having children – she's back. She's brought another woman with her, much younger. Maybe she's the one.'

The *sadhu* didn't turn his head but said, 'It's good.'

When the two Yadav women reached the temple veranda Sita Devi touched the *sadhu*'s feet, but he still didn't turn his head.

She said, '*Babaji*, I've brought the woman you promised to help.'

'It's good.'

The other holy man motioned the women to sit down and told them that the *sadhu* was meditating and should not be disturbed. After a short while the *sadhu* got up and, without saying a word to anyone, walked to the edge of the Ganges, took off his saffron *lungi* and walked into the river. He splashed water over himself noisily, then dipped into the water several times, submerging his whole body. When he emerged from the river he retied his *lungi*, climbed back to the temple and sat cross-legged again on his piece of sacking. He had a heart-shaped, intelligent face, which was lean but not pinched. His long, dank hair was piled on top of his head. A sparse beard straggled over his cheeks and chin, and there was no hair on his bare chest. After making himself comfortable he turned towards Sita Devi, gave her a broad grin and said, 'So you have come back and brought your friend. That's good.'

Then, lowering his voice, he went on, 'All paths to God are one. If you drive ten kilometres from here, the name of the village will be different, but it will be the same earth. There are three questions. Where are we from? Why are we like this? And where are we going? Tantra answers these questions. It's a special knowledge, and just as the torch throws out light from inside, so does the wise man who is truly initiated into the left-hand path of Tantra, who can worship with all the five elements. They include what is forbidden to ordinary people, like meat, wine and sex.

'Why have you brought this woman to me?'

Sita Devi could not return his frank, knowing gaze. With her eyes cast down, she mumbled, 'You know, *Babaji*. To do what happened to me. To get Shiva to give her a baby.'

'You have faith because Shiva gave you a baby. Do you know that the great guru Shankaracharya revived a dead snake and then went on to the funeral of a king and brought him back to life too? If that's so, why shouldn't I bring life to the womb of this woman? But it must be remembered that we are not God. We worship Shiva because we do not have his powers. We cannot stop the world spinning. We can know what man has made, and then we are stupid enough to think we have understood what God has made. If you have faith in Shiva, then only I can help you. Go now and worship the *lingam*. She will assist you,' he added, pointing at the woman who had been sitting with him.

She took Sita Devi and Ram Lakhan's wife around the corner of the veranda to the small *sanctum sanctorum* where there was a black stone that had been taken from the Ganges, nobody knew when, to be worshipped as the *lingam* of Shiva. The *sadhu*'s disciple threw herself down, prostrate, before the *lingam*, beat her head on the stone floor, repeating with mounting intensity, '*Jai bhole Shankar ki! Jai bhole Shankar ki!*' Ram Lakhan's wife and Sita Devi took marigolds and rose petals out of a cloth bag they had brought, sprinkled them on the *lingam*, placed a ten-rupee note under a coconut and sat with folded hands, waiting. Eventually the sound of '*Jai bhole Shankar ki*' got lower and lower, and the *sadhu*'s disciple rolled on to her back with her eyes staring vacantly at the ceiling of the shrine. Sita Devi and Ram Lakhan's wife went back to the *sadhu*.

'You have done the *puja* and given the *daan*?'

'Yes,' replied Sita Devi.

'Good, so you go now and leave your friend here. If you wish, you can come to collect her early tomorrow morning. Do you want someone to go with you for protection?'

'No. No one will attack an old woman like me.'

The *sadhu* chuckled and said, 'It wasn't always like that, was it?'

Sita Devi hid her face in the tail of her sari and left.

The *sadhu* then took Ram Lakhan's wife to a small room at the back of the temple. The other holy man brought in some wood, laid it in a pit in the centre of the room, dowsed it with *ghi* and set it alight. He then left. The *sadhu* sat in front of the fire opposite Ram Lakhan's wife. He recited mantras, from time to time throwing herbs into the fire. The sweet smell of the herbs and *ghi*, the low droning of the mantras, the flickering light from the fire all made Ram Lakhan's wife drowsy. The *sadhu* then poured what looked like milk into a metal glass and handed it to her, saying, 'This is Shankarji's *prasad*. Drink it.'

The milk was very sweet, just like the *thandai* served in the village on Holi. Very soon she started to feel strangely relaxed and euphoric, utterly at peace, almost removed from what was going on in the small, smoke-filled room. The *sadhu* said in a deep voice, 'You are the goddess – you are the female power, just as important as the male. If the two are not joined, there is no creation. Remember the destruction wrought by Shiva when the Goddess Sati burnt herself alive because he had not been invited by her father to the sacrifice?

Remember what Sati and Shiva created when she was reborn to life and they made love for a million years? Shiva can come to you, but you must not have fear.' He repeated, 'You must not have fear. You must not have fear,' again and again, his voice becoming softer all the while.

Then the *sadhu* produced a human skull from under the wooden platform on which he was sitting. Holding it up, he said, 'Tantrics know no fear. That's why they like to worship in cremation grounds to learn that nothing in this life is banned, and nothing in this life is to be feared. I got this skull from a cremation ground in the Himalayas, where a *sadhu* eats the flesh of the dead.'

He threw powder into the fire to produce a blinding flash of white light. The empty sockets of the skull stared at Ram Lakhan's wife. She should have been terrified – Yadav women weren't even allowed to attend cremations – but her strange sense of contentment was not in any way disturbed. She feared nothing. She could do anything.

The *sadhu* said, 'When the power of Shiva and the power of the Goddess come together I can overcome anything. Do you feel a strange power overcoming you too?'

Ram Lakhan's wife nodded.

The *sadhu* lit a cigarette from the fire and puffed on it vigorously. Then he put the cigarette in the mouth of the skull and said, 'Look. I can even make the dead come alive. I can bind spirits. Watch him smoke.'

Ram Lakhan's wife, peering through the smoke of the fire at the tip of the cigarette, saw it glow and dim, glow and dim, and was convinced that the spirit of the skull was smoking. She stared at it, fascinated. The *sadhu* came and sat beside her, looking deep into her eyes. She returned his gaze, although she would not normally have looked even at her husband so directly. Then the *sadhu* started to repeat, 'You must not have fear, you must not have fear.' She wanted to say, 'I haven't,' but somehow she couldn't speak. The *sadhu*'s words mesmerized her. The liturgy changed. The *sadhu* now repeated an invocation of Shiva and Parvati. Ram Lakhan's wife started to sway. The *sadhu* took her by the shoulders and laid her down by the fire, and she fell into a deep sleep.

Ram Lakhan's wife woke to find the *sadhu*'s woman shaking her, and saying, 'Get up, get up. You must bathe in the Ganges and then go back to your village.'

The woman helped her to stand. She felt dizzy. Her head was spinning, but the woman supported her. She picked up the cloth bag containing a spare sari which Ram Lakhan's wife had brought with her. The two walked uncertainly on to the veranda. Ram Lakhan's wife saw the *sadhu* in the same position as she had first seen him, sitting cross-legged, staring across the Ganges. The sun was just rising, and a finger of golden light shimmered on the water's surface as they tottered down the bank to the river's edge. The woman led her into the Ganges and pushed her head down. The cold water cleared her head and made her steadier on her feet, and, after changing into her dry sari, she felt able to start on the walk back to her village. The *sadhu* paid no attention to her departure. It was as though she had never been there.

By the time the next Holi came round the doctor at the local health centre had confirmed that Ram Lakhan's wife was carrying a child. Ram Lakhan made sure the whole village knew to avoid the humiliation he had suffered the year before, but he didn't know whom to thank – the medicine man or Guru Gorakhnath. His wife knew that the baby had nothing to do with Gorakhpur, but she too wasn't entirely sure whether she should thank God or man.

BLOOD FOR BLOOD

The village of Thakurdwara is situated in the *karail*, the name given to the rich and peculiarly black soil of an area of eastern Uttar Pradesh on the border with Bihar. According to tradition, 'There's only need to sow the seed. The *karail* will do the rest.'

Another tradition has it that the villagers are particularly quarrelsome because their life is so easy that they have nothing to do with their time except fight each other. The records of the local police station bear this out. The terrain is flat and treeless, and for centuries the villages have been isolated like small islands in a great black ocean. Indian politicians and journalists still describe the *karail* as 'very backward', but roads are now opening the villages to the world outside, bringing 'development' to them.

Chotu Ram knew that 'development' was not necessarily to the advantage of everyone. As he chopped the fodder for Thakur Randhir Singh's cows, he thought, 'This is not my job. At least as a potter I had self-respect. Now I'm little better than a slave of Thakur *sahib*.' Chotu Ram was a Kumhar, or potter, by caste but nowadays the farmers were cash-conscious and unwilling to spare any of their land for his caste to dig clay. What's more, clay cups and pots were today considered inferior – stainless steel, plastic and, among the wealthier, china had taken over. When the service of potters had been as essential to Thakurdwara as that of barbers or washermen, Chotu Ram's family had been reasonably well looked after. They had received grain and other gifts that at least provided their basic requirements. Now Chotu Ram had become a modern man, he'd entered the cash economy, but the wages he received barely allowed him to buy anything beyond the grain his family ate, and they certainly did not cover the emergencies that every family in the village had to face from time to time.

The Thakur's cattle ambled into the courtyard. The young boy who had been grazing them all day clicked his tongue and gave one of the stragglers a thwack across the rump with his stick. He needn't have bothered. The cows would have made their way home in their own good time. Chotu Ram put down his knife and helped the boy to tether the cattle. Then he squatted on the ground to milk the first cow. As he pulled her udders rhythmically and the milk squirted into the pail, he thought of the cause of his economic crisis. He remembered the superior smirk of the bank clerk who had told him, 'There's no government plan for us to lend you money for your sister's wedding. Government loans are for socially desirable objectives, and the government classifies wedding feasts as "wasteful expenditure".'

The government didn't realize that it wasn't just a matter of false pride for Chotu Ram to have his sister married in the style considered appropriate by his fellow Kumhars; it was essential expenditure. No one would accept her if there wasn't a wedding to be proud of.

So there had been only one alternative for Chotu Ram – the Thakur Sahib himself. The Thakur Sahib had been delighted to lend the money at 5 per cent interest a month, almost exactly twelve times more than the rate he would get in a bank savings account. The security offered was sound too – Chotu Ram's sister's gold jewellery. That was where the problem lay. The family his sister had married into were demanding that she should move to their family house, but she couldn't go without her gold.

'It will be useless to appeal to the miser's pity,' thought Chotu Ram. 'He'll never give the gold back unless I can provide some other security, and I don't have any.'

Chotu Ram considered every option. The banks were clearly ruled out. No member of his *biradari* would part with the sort of money he needed. His mother would never allow him to mortgage the small patch of land the family had been given when the government had implemented land reforms. A professional money-lender would demand security too and might charge even higher rates of interest. By the time he'd finished milking, Chotu Ram had decided he'd no alternative but to fall at the feet of the Thakur if he was to save his family from humiliation. So, after making sure that all the cattle were securely tethered, he walked out to the platform on which the Thakur sat to conduct his business and his social life.

Randhir Singh was sitting alone on his *charpoy* listening to the news on radio. He was one of the wealthiest farmers in the village, still holding all the land he had inherited, although much of it was now registered in the name of others to 'comply', as the Thakur liked to say, with the government's land reforms. He had also found ways of 'complying' with the Minimum Wages Act, which meant he was able to maximize the profits he made from the rich *karail* soil. But those profits had not been spent on improving either his or anyone else's lifestyle. In Thakurdwara, where urine was still sometimes used as an antiseptic, the villagers often said the Thakur was so mean he would refuse to piss if someone cut himself.

Thakur Randhir Singh was alone that evening because the other men of the family were over at the women's house, where the portable generator enabled them to watch television. The Thakur Sahib blamed television for subverting the old village way of life, corrupting morals and, worst of all, giving the lower castes ideas above their station. The day's news of the conflict over plans to reserve government jobs and places in colleges for the backward castes crackled from the radio – another upper-caste student had burned himself to death in protest against this. Police had opened fire on a crowd of violent backward-caste supporters of the quotas who had been blocking roads and burning buses.

'There is no end to it', the Thakur thought, turning off his radio. 'This wretched democracy and television have made people think about things outside their village. Before the eyes of villagers were turned inward, everyone knew their place and cared only about what happened here.' He raised his bushy eyebrows and sighed as he remembered how the Thakurs used to rule the village.

Randhir Singh saw Chotu Ram approaching him, rubbing clean the chopper he used for cutting up fodder on the corner of his *dhoti*.

'What does he want?' the Thakur wondered. 'In the old days everyone who was anyone used to gather here of an evening. Now I get only the poor people wanting me to use my influence with some government clerk, or in connection with some other problem, always to do with money.'

Chotu Ram folded his hands respectfully before Randhir Singh and then squatted on the ground below the platform.

'What have you come to bother me with?' the Thakur grunted.

Chotu Ram had decided to try to soften up his employer first. 'Thakur Sahib, you took such a wise decision in getting the cows in calf with that foreign bull at the government veterinary centre. The new cows are now filling the pails with milk.'

'Maybe, but I am still getting a very bad price for it.'

'Yes, these Banias in the towns, they are all thieves. Farmers like you do the hard work. They take the reward.'

Chotu Ram knew that his employer had never done a day's hard manual work, but he hoped this flattery would please him.

It didn't. The Thakur changed the subject because he didn't want anyone to hear him discussing serious matters like agricultural prices and rural economics with a man like Chotu Ram. Pointing abruptly to the chopper, he asked, 'What have you brought that with you for?'

'Ah, yes. Thakur Sahib, nowadays the man with the grinding

wheel doesn't seem to come round the village any more. Can you take this into the town to get it sharpened?'

The last rays of the evening sun were fading fast. The platform on which the Thakur was sitting was getting darker and darker. No servant had yet brought out a lamp.

Randhir Singh peered at Chotu Ram and barked, 'Is that all you've come to waste my time about? I don't believe it. Tell me what you actually want and then get going.'

Chotu Ram looked down at the ground and mumbled, 'There is something else. There's my loan.'

'Ah, I knew it would be about money. All you people think money flows from me like the Ganga. There's no end to it once you start giving.'

In spite of this unpromising beginning the potter persevered, explaining his difficulty and pleading with Randhir Singh to return his sister's gold jewellery. He pointed out that he himself was good security. He couldn't run away because he had nowhere to go. He promised to work for nothing but grain to feed his family, putting the wages he should have earned against the loan. But Randhir Singh was not impressed by that offer. He knew that Chotu Ram was effectively his slave anyhow until the loan was repaid, and with the wages he was paying and the interest he was charging, that wasn't going to happen in a hurry.

'You people,' he grumbled, 'you go and waste all your money on weddings and then you expect us to come and save you. You are all wasters and good-for-nothings. Why should I return the gold? You will just go and use it to borrow more money from someone else, and then where will I be?'

It had been a matter of great pride to Chotu Ram that he had been able to arrange a proper marriage for his sister, that the bridegroom had brought a sizeable wedding party and that the feast had been appreciated by all. He was hurt by the Thakur's scornful dismissal of that achievement. After all, the high-caste people in the village spent what was for him a fortune on their weddings: why shouldn't Kumhars at least do things in reasonable style? But he was used to swallowing insults from the Thakur and so, restraining his anger, he pleaded, 'Thakur Sahib, I have kept up with the instalments so far. I have not just paid you the interest – I have paid some of the money back too.'

'Oh, you people are getting so clever that you can calculate interest?'

Chotu Ram swallowed this insult too and replied, 'My cousin is a clerk. He worked it out.'

'How much did you say you had borrowed?'

'Five thousand rupees.'

'Don't talk rubbish to me!' barked the Thakur. 'Seven thousand. It's written on the paper which you are too ignorant to read. It's got your thumb-mark on it.'

Chotu Ram was stunned. He knew that this was untrue but he also knew he couldn't prove it. In his agitation he stood up and stammered, 'But that's all a lie, a complete lie, and you know it.'

'*Behenchod!*' shouted Randhir Singh. 'You dare to forget your place! You have the audacity to stand in front of me and accuse me of being a liar! Get out of here, *madarchod*, and tell your sister she'll have to sell herself to get the money to pay for her jewellery.'

Randhir Singh had gone too far. The blood rushed to Chotu Ram's head. The dam which had held back so much resentment, so much hatred, burst. Without realizing what he was doing, he found himself standing on the platform, shouting, '*Saale*, you think we're dogs, that we'll take any insults? I'll show you. You don't even have the shame to respect our women.'

'Get down from here!' roared Randhir Singh. 'Remember your place.'

The Thakur reached for the *lathi* lying beside him on the *charpoy* and tried to get up but Chotu Ram slashed him with the chopper and he fell back. Blood stained his white *kurta*.

Chotu Ram hacked and hacked at the Thakur's neck until his head was severed.

Then the chopper fell from the potter's hand. He stared at the body. A crowd gathered as if from nowhere. Eventually someone tugged on Chotu Ram's shirt and said, 'Run for it! Quickly! These are big people and they'll have the police after you in no time.'

That brought Chotu Ram to his senses. He leapt down from the platform on which the Thakur had been sitting, pushed his way through the crowd and ran off into the darkness. No one attempted to stop him.

The combined noise of the generator and television had been too loud for anyone inside the women's house to hear the Thakur's distant cries for help. No one in the crowd wanted to inform the family for fear of being accused of the murder, and so they all went off in different directions to find the village watchman, whose job it was to report all crime to the police. The watchman first went to the house where the Thakur Sahib's family was gathered. In his anxiety he forgot all formalities and walked straight inside. The Thakur's eldest son Chandra Kumar shouted, 'You, what are you doing, walking in here without asking?'

The watchman gabbled, 'The Thakur Sahib's dead. His throat's been cut.'

'What nonsense is this? Don't joke with me.'

The watchman rubbed the back of his neck anxiously and said, 'No, Babuji, it's absolutely true. Come with me. Come and I'll show you.'

'It'd better be,' shot back Chandra Kumar as he went out with the watchman, not appreciating what he was saying. Harbaksh, the Thakur's brother, picked up a Petromax lamp and followed him. The watchman pointed to the body lying on the *charpoy* on the platform where the Thakur Sahib always sat. The two men were stunned. They just stood for several minutes with the watchman fidgeting nervously behind them.

Then Chandra Kumar suddenly rounded on him. 'Whose work is this?' he barked.

'People say it's Chotu Ram.'

'Where is he?'

'They say he's run away into the *karail*.'

Chandra Kumar turned to his uncle and said, 'Quickly – get into the jeep. We've still got a chance to catch him.'

He rushed inside to fetch his rifle, then they climbed into the jeep and roared out of the courtyard without thinking in which direction they should go. Charging down the narrow lane straight ahead of them, they were waved down by some villagers who told them that Chotu Ram had run in the opposite direction. They reversed the Jeep and set out down a raised track across the fields. It wasn't long before the headlights picked out the figure of Chotu Ram running along the track ahead of them. He darted into the *karail*. Chandra Kumar wrenched the steering wheel and the jeep lurched off the track into the black mud, with the two men shouting 'Stop, murderer! Stop!'

If the weather had been dry, the black earth would have been baked so hard by the sun that the jeep could quickly have overtaken Chotu Ram, but this was the monsoon and the *karail* was now a quagmire. Within yards the jeep was up to its axles in mud. Chandra Kumar rammed it into four-wheel drive but to no avail. The wheels just spun wildly, throwing up showers of mud and digging the jeep ever deeper into the *karail*. Chandra Kumar fired at the fleeing figure, but Chotu Ram didn't even look back. He was soon beyond the range of the rifle and the jeep's lights.

When the two men returned home, their white *kurtas* and pyjama trousers spattered with mud, they found Randhir Singh's widow, Vaidehi, sitting cross-legged on the *charpoy*, cradling her husband's headless body in her lap. She was silent, staring out into the night, while women squatting on the ground in front of her wailed and beat their chests.

Throughout the thirteen days of mourning that followed, the Thakur's widow was never seen to weep. She was withdrawn, talking to no one, taking her part mechanically in the complicated Hindu death rites. Some of these rituals Vaidehi refused to observe, without explaining her reasons – she didn't break her bangles, and she kept the *bindi* on her brow that had marked her as a married woman.

After the official period of mourning was over, Vaidehi summoned her son and her brother-in-law to the inner courtyard of the family house. She was sitting on a wooden bed wearing a spotless white sari, the dress of a widow. Bangles still covered her wrists and there was a red *bindi* on her forehead. The two men touched her feet and then stood before her with their heads bowed. She asked just one question. 'Are you going to fulfil your duty?'

Both men replied, 'Yes.'

Then for the first time Vaidehi broke down. For nearly two weeks she had been sustained by the need to observe all the funeral rites in a seemly manner, but now there was nothing left. The realization that she was on her own, that her husband was dead, finally struck her. Vaidehi had never known passion or love. She had only ever hoped that her husband would be dutiful, if not kind at least not cruel, and above all that he would protect her and her family's honour. Randhir Singh had cared for all her needs, had never beaten her and had certainly maintained her prestige among Thakur women. Now he'd gone, leaving her a lonely and vulnerable widow, but, what was worse, his death had been so demeaning. 'How could a man who'd done so much to defend our honor die so dishonourably?' she sobbed.

Her son Chandra Kumar knelt beside his mother and embraced her, saying, 'You've been so brave, Mother. Weep now, weep. It will comfort you.'

'Could there be a worse death? To be cut down in his own home by the son of a low Kumhar. What could be more shameful?'

'We'll show what a Thakur's revenge means, Mother,' said her son, looking up at his uncle. 'We promise you blood for blood. That Kumhar will die a dog's death, we promise you.'

Vaidehi's shoulders shook, and she stammered, 'I will not break my bangles, I will not wash off my *bindi*, until his throat's slit and the ground is drenched in his blood. I will not. I tell you by the mother's milk I fed you, it's your duty. There must be blood for blood.'

'Mother, nine months you kept me in your womb. Just give me nine months and I will take revenge for my father's death, I promise you,' her son replied.

A few days later Chandra Kumar and his uncle Harbaksh went to see the head of their *biradari*. He inevitably approved of their intention to preserve the honour of Thakurs by taking revenge but warned them to plan the murder well. 'You must have a lawyer,' he said.

'But if we plan the murder well, we'll not need a lawyer,' said Harbaksh. 'The police won't question us.'

'Of course they will, fool. You'll be the prime suspects. That's why you need a lawyer now. They know all about murders, and how they are committed, so that murderers have a case which makes fools of the police. A lawyer will tell you how to have him killed.'

'You mean we get a lawyer to plan the murder for us?' asked Chandra Kumar.

'Yes, that's exactly what I mean. Go to Ghazipur and try to see Om Prakash. He's the best man − expensive but the best.'

The next market day the two Thakurs drove to the courts in the district headquarters, Ghazipur. They expected to find Om Prakash among all the other lawyers milling around, touting for business. But the man they were looking for was no common *vakil*; he had what he liked to call chambers, and the two Thakurs were directed to a building behind the premises of a well-known grain merchant.

They walked into the merchant's *godown*, where they found an ancient clerk sitting on the floor surrounded by sacks piled up to the ceiling, peering through wire-framed spectacles as he made entries laboriously in a vast ledger. When Chandra Kumar asked for the lawyer the clerk didn't look up but simply pointed to a door at the back of the *godown*, which opened on to an alley. It took only one step to cross that narrow, dark alley and the two men were in the entrance of another building. On the wall were boards advertising the names of the tenants. One read 'Om Prakash, LL.B., Advocate, Second Floor'. They climbed up narrow, dark and dingy stairs and made their way into the lawyer's office after first satisfying an unshaved, burly man with a gun slung over his shoulder that they were genuine clients.

Om Prakash was quite tall but elderly, with thin, rounded shoulders. He looked over the spectacles on the end of his long nose when the two men entered and told rather than invited them to sit down. When they had explained their problem the lawyer said, 'You have done well to come to see me first. It's always better to plan such work so that you can be sure you will have a good case. But there is one thing I must make clear. I don't give advice to people who, after the event, go to another, cheaper lawyer, as one or two people have tried. They ended up in jail because I have many contacts everywhere.'

The two men assured him that they were not double-crossers, and the lawyer then went on to repeat the *sarpanch*'s warning that they were bound to be the prime suspects. 'Of course, you must not do this work yourselves,' he said. 'That will make the police case difficult from the start, as it's much harder to prove conspiracy than murder. You must have a foolproof alibi.'

'What's the best alibi?' Harbaksh asked anxiously.

'To be in police custody. And the best time to commit murder is harvest-time. So many scores are settled then that the police never have time to follow up investigations. And if, say, an absconder is killed at night, with no witnesses, there is little chance that a proper case could be made.'

'But how do we find Chotu Ram?'

'Does he have any land?'

'Yes, one small field,' replied Harbaksh.

'Then he's likely to come back to the village to see no one else harvests it.'

The lawyer agreed to find a gang who would commit the murder and took a considerable advance from his new clients.

The most immediate problem that the two Thakurs faced was to find out when their father's murderer would return to the village. They couldn't be seen hanging around the huts of the *basti* where Chotu Ram's family lived, and so they chose Kalua, the younger of the two family servants, to act as their spy. He was much sharper than normal servants and for that reason was not entirely trusted by the family, but then, as Chandra Kumar said, they needed a cunning man for this job – a faithful old retainer would be no use. Kalua told his employers that he would need a regular supply of wheat, rice, vegetables, *ghi* and milk if he was to ingratiate himself with the murderer's mother and become her confidant.

The servant set off for Chotu Ram's *basti* with enthusiasm. His new role gave him an interest to relieve the monotony of his life. It allowed him to steal freely from the kitchen, and he had the cunning to realize there might eventually even be opportunities for blackmail.

Chotu Ram's mother was surprised and suspicious when Kalua arrived outside the door of her broken-down hut with some milk and *ghi*, but he soon put her at ease, saying, 'I've stolen these from the Thakurs' kitchen. I want to help you because I hated that fly-sucking miser Randhir Singh and I admire Chotu's courage in killing him. You know, there are a lot of other people who sympathize with you.'

Chotu Ram's mother was far too hard-pressed to question this unexpected bounty. She was a widow, and now that her son had run away, she had to provide for his wife and three children, as well as her own daughter, whose in-laws refused to have anything to do with her after the murder. To support all of them she had only one small plot of land, and so she was happy to accept the gifts Kalua brought as the answer to her almost incessant prayers. Folding her hands and looking up to the sky, she said, 'It is the grace of Lord Ram.' Then she put her hands on the young man's head and blessed him. 'Live long, son, live long. You understand my sorrow. You are my son too – my home is your home. Whenever you want to, you may come here.'

Kalua bowed his head and said, 'My own parents have passed away. What more could I want than your blessings?'

Almost every evening Kalua would come to listen to Chotu Ram's mother's woes like a dutiful son. Crouching over her clay stove, with the smoke from the dried *brinjal* plants she used as kindling stinging her eyes and making her cough, she would speak to Kalua of the drudgery of her life. 'I had never thought my fate would be so bad,' she told him, 'but I was sent into this family, and it's a woman's fate to put up with what she's given. Now my husband is dead, my son is as good as dead, and look at this house. What do we have? A few pots and some broken *charpoys.* We are Kumhars and yet we don't even have the means to repair the clay tiles on the roof. If we sleep inside, we have no protection from the rain, and now there's no man in the house we don't dare to sleep out in the yard even when the sky's clear.'

Chotu Ram's mother was also very fond of speaking about her sister. She'd married a man who had stayed on at school and had become a college clerk. 'Who would think, to look at us now, that we are real sisters? My brother-in-law has earned well and bought land. Now he's a member of the *panchayat* and respected in his village. That's why I want to keep my grandchildren at school,' she would say, pointing at the wooden slates hanging from a nail by the door.

Kalua would often ask whether Chotu Ram's mother had heard anything from him, and for many months the reply was always no. But then in April, the month of the wheat harvest, just as the lawyer had expected, she told him that she'd heard from another family of Kumhars whose son was pulling a cycle rickshaw in the town of Buxar.

Apparently on the night of the murder Chotu Ram had hidden in the long grass on the banks of the Ganges, and he had crossed the river the next day into Bihar, where the writ of the Uttar Pradesh police did not run. He had made his way to the town of Buxar but, fearing it was too small and too close to the border for safety, he'd gone on to the state capital, Patna. There he'd even managed to save some money pulling a rickshaw, but he had not been able to send anything to his family because the postmark on a money order would have given his whereabouts away. Now Chotu Ram had returned to Buxar to plan how he could visit his village briefly, hand over some money and find out what had happened to his land. He intended to cross the Ganges two nights after the festival of Ramnamvi in one of the small wooden boats moored on the banks. Boatmen were willing to paddle their craft across the river at any hour of the day or night and never asked any questions about their passengers or the cargo.

Kalua advised caution. 'Don't make a big *tamasha* out of this, whatever you do. Just sit quietly. If news gets out that you are expecting him back, it will reach Randhir Singh's family, and they will see that the police arrange an ambush. They will probably kill your son, saying that he opened fire on them first, rather than go to all the trouble of bringing him to trial.'

When Kalua reported to Chandra Kumar and Harbaksh that their man was planning to return, they went to see the lawyer again. He arranged for them to meet some criminals from Bihar the next day in a toddy shop in Ghazipur.

The Thakurs were not drinking men and, even if they had been, they would never have gone to a toddy shop, where the riff-raff of the town hung out. They knew the shop was behind the sheds of the timber merchants, but they were too embarrassed to ask where, so they wandered past piles of logs and planks for some time before chancing on an open space surrounded by palmyra palms. The Thakurs saw small groups of drinkers, some sitting on *charpoys*, some on single bricks. Boys brought the toddy from large clay flasks standing under the shelter of a tattered thatch roof propped up by bamboos. The ground was littered with broken *kulhars*, the small clay cups the customers drank from, and leaf plates and stained newspapers on which the roast gram, green chillies or mutton snacks that went with the toddy were served.

Chandra Kumar and Harbaksh Singh stood uncomfortably on the edge of the toddy shop until the Bihari criminals recognized them and called them over. The head of the gang had sent three men to take revenge on behalf of the Thakurs. They had coloured cotton cloths tied loosely round their heads. They wore capacious *kurtas*, under which weapons could easily be hidden, and pyjamas that were more practical than flowing *dhotis* if they found themselves obliged to run for it. The Biharis poured toddy into two *kulhars* and offered them to Chandra Kumar and Harbaksh, but they refused. One of the Biharis said, 'Come on, toddy won't do you any harm. It's not adulterated like all that *desi* and foreign wine you get at the *thekas*. The tappers shin up these palm trees twice a day to bring it down fresh.'

But the Thakurs were adamant – a fact that did not go unnoticed by a group of drinkers squatting nearby. 'Come to a toddy shop and not have a drink? What do they think they've come to? *Aarti* at a temple?' said one drinker scornfully. Another laughed, 'It's more like going to a whorehouse to sing hymns.' But a third said, 'Wait a bit. I know those two. One's the son of that Thakur whose head was cut off last year. I think the other is his uncle. There was a real uproar about it but even the Thakurs' rupees couldn't get the police off their backsides to catch the man, although everyone knows who it was. Many of the villagers saw him.'

Chandra Kumar and Harbaksh overheard this and urged the three criminals to move somewhere else for fear that others would recognize them too, but they refused. The man who appeared to be their leader said, 'Ignore these people. This is the sort of place we like to talk business. If you want to get involved in this sort of game, you must accept the way we play it.'

The criminals claimed that this was a particularly dangerous assignment because they might have to wait all night for their victim and might easily be seen by other villagers. Because there was nowhere to hide a vehicle near the village, they would have to escape on foot. A shot might alert the village and so they would have to use a knife, which meant dangerously close contact with the victim. They normally worked in towns, where they could fire at their victims from a safe distance and get away on a scooter. The Biharis therefore demanded danger money in addition to the agreed fee. They also wanted someone to show them where to lay an ambush and to stay with them to identify Chotu Ram. The negotiations were protracted, especially the haggling over the price, but when the Thakurs realized that the supply of toddy had run out and their group was left alone amidst the debris of the day's drinking and the sulphurous smell of toddy, they were alarmed and settled everything quickly, handing over another substantial advance.

On the way back to the village Harbaksh began to have second thoughts. After all, murder was murder. Randhir Singh had been his elder brother and a very domineering one too. Why should he care so much about his killing? Why should he risk his life or face a sentence in jail? He turned to his nephew and said, 'I don't like this. Those men are *goondas*, cent per cent, and we have entrusted our lives to them. It's as dangerous as playing with snakes. We must call it off and think of something else.'

'Keep your eyes on the road or we'll skid into the *karail*,' snarled Chandra Kumar. 'You're like a snake with a muskrat in its mouth – you can't swallow those *goondas* and you can't let go of them either. How can we even try to call it off? In any case, where will we find them? Do you want to go asking all the whores of Ghazipur where they are?'

'All right,' replied Harbaksh, 'But you just remember he was my brother . . . It's all right for you, he was your father, you have a duty. I . . .'

Chandra Kumar cut his uncle short. 'You remember you made a commitment to my mother. I will come for you wherever you are if you even think of going back on that.'

'All right, all right, but I still think this is madness. I don't know how we ever came to think those Bihari *goondas* could be trusted.'

The lights of the jeep caused a small group of blackbuck to scatter in panic. 'If only I had my gun,' said Chandra Kumar.

'It's not shooting blackbuck you've got to worry about,' muttered Harbaksh angrily and then drove on in silence until he turned into the courtyard of the family home.

The next morning Chandra Kumar went to his mother, who was sitting on her wooden bed, still wearing a white sari, her bangles and her *bindi*. He bowed down, touched her feet and told her, 'I am going to Ghazipur. By the time I'm back our honour will have been restored.'

Chandra Kumar then called his uncle, who made one last effort to protest. But when his nephew reminded him that there was no way he could stop the murder now, he reluctantly climbed into the jeep and the two men drove off.

When they reached Ghazipur they parked the jeep and strolled around the market trying to look busy. They argued about the wholesale price of potatoes with a trader weighing a sack on cantilever scales suspended from a bamboo tripod. They watched a *nalban* nailing thin metal shoes on the hooves of a white bullock that lay on its side on the ground, its four legs trussed. They bought pumpkins as big as the head of a horse, spiky green jakfruits, chilli seedlings and black plugs of tobacco. Then, realizing that they could not leave their shopping in the open jeep, they went to the street of the grain merchants, where a long line of bullock carts was unloading. Finding a man from Thakurdwara, they paid him ten rupees to take their purchases and deliver them home. They spent a long time sitting in the office of the commission agent, chatting to him and other farmers. Providing an endless supply of tea and joining in interminable conversations was all part of the agent's sales campaign to persuade farmers that they would get a better price from him than they would in the grain market.

At last darkness fell and the two men made their way to the shack where *desi* liquor was sold. Chandra Kumar went up to the metal grill protecting the proprietor and demanded six pouches. The proprietor asked, 'What do you want to do? Drown yourself in the stuff?'

Harbaksh, who was standing nervously a few feet away, so that he couldn't be seen in the dim light from the shop, pulled his nephew back and whispered, 'I told you so. We are drawing attention to ourselves by buying so much.'

'Shut up, you fool,' snarled Chandra Kumar. 'That's just what we want to do.'

He then collected the six sealed plastic pouches of *desi* liquor and led his uncle back to the jeep. They drove out of town and stopped by the first field of sugar cane they came across. Pushing far enough into the cane to be hidden from the road, they drenched themselves in the strong-smelling *desi* liquor, then returned to the jeep and drove back to Ghazipur. Climbing out of the jeep, they lurched down the street, imitating a couple of drunks. No one paid much attention to them until they reached the police station. There they stopped and shouted abuse at everyone who came by. The police on guard outside the station ignored this charade; drunks were not of much interest to them. Desperate to provoke a reaction, Chandra Kumar eventually went up to one of the constables and said, slurring his words, 'You *behenchods*, you haven't the courage to fight a couple of drunks. You couldn't protect your mother from rape, you bastards.'

That did the trick. One of the constables swung his ancient ·303 rifle at the Thakur, knocking him down. Another blew shrill blasts on his whistle. Police poured out of the station, gave Chandra Kumar a few more whacks with their *lathis* for good measure and dragged him into the station. Harbaksh was spotted trying to sneak away. A policeman thwacked him across the shins with his *lathi*, felling him with one blow, and then sat on his chest until another colleague came over, snapped a pair of handcuffs on his wrists and led him ignomini-ously into the police station, saying, 'This one smells like a liquor factory.'

Inside the police station the inspector on duty was not impressed by the complaint of the constable who had been insulted. 'Don't give me that one,' he said. 'It's the oldest excuse in the book. If you want to arrest two drunks to show your power, do so, but don't bother me with charging them for insulting a police officer. Throw them in the lock-up, and we'll let them out tomorrow. I don't want to be bothered with a petty case like this.'

The two men were led away, with Chandra Kumar shout-ing, 'Register my case, register my case, I demand it. It's my right, my right.' He kept on yelling until the sub-inspector could stand the racket no longer. Pushing back his chair, he strode across the hall to the lock-up. The flustered constable on duty fumbled with the lock on the cell door but eventually managed to open it. The officer strode up to Chandra Kumar and hit him across the face three times, shouting, 'That'll shut your mouth, you drunken loafer.' Chandra Kumar reeled but remained on his feet. Suddenly the sub-inspector stopped and stared at Chandra Kumar, then, turning to the constable, he said, 'This is an odd business. If this bastard was really drunk, one slap would have knocked him over, but I have slapped him and slapped him and he's still standing. Bring him to my desk.'

Standing before the desk, Chandra Kumar kept up his pretence, swaying from side to side, as the officer bawled at him, 'Just make a little more noise and I'll bury a bamboo up your arse. Who do you think you are, squealing like a stuck pig, shouting to have your arrest recorded? Are you proud of being drunk, you *chutiya*? Do you want everyone to know about it?'

'It's my right to have my case recorded,' mumbled Chandra Kumar.

'Your right? Wait till the women of your house find out that the whole town knows you were running around like a mad bull.'

'I want my case entered in the record.'

The officer was exasperated. He knew there was something wrong, but he couldn't for the life of him think why this man wanted to be charged with drunkenness.

'If I register your case, the charge will be very serious. I won't just charge you with drunkenness: I'll throw the book at you. I'll charge you and your friend with assaulting a police officer.'

'Register what you want.'

The sub-inspector gave up, called for the station diary and took down the details of both Chandra Kumar and his uncle.

Just before it got dark that evening the Biharis reached the bus stop where the track to Thakurdwara joined the main road. Kalua was there to meet them. As they walked the last four miles to the village, the Biharis' tempers got worse and worse. They were used to the comforts of working in towns and cursed their leader, who'd sent them to settle this trivial country murder. They also cursed the Thakurs, who didn't have the courage to do their own dirty work. Kalua joined in cursing the Thakurs enthusiastically and took part with even more enthusiasm in swigging from the plastic pouches of *desi* liquor the Biharis had brought to help them through this tedious assignment.

Kalua was not a hardened drinker and by the time they reached the threshing floors on the outskirts of the village he was not his usual cautious, canny self. Pointing the beam of his torch at one of the piles of wheat stacked up waiting for the threshing machines he said, 'This'll do. I'm going to lie down here and wait for the bastard.' Before long he was fast asleep.

This was not the best place to lay an ambush because there were several ways through the piles of wheat, and Chotu Ram could easily get past his assassins without their ever knowing it. The chances of success were further diminished when, one after the other, the Biharis also fell asleep. Their only tactical advantage was that they were under a broad mahua tree that shaded them from the moonlight.

That was perhaps why, in the early hours of the morning, one of the Biharis was woken by someone tripping over his legs. He let out a yell. 'Who's the *behenchod* who's kicked me in the ribs?'

The man who had fallen attempted to pick himself up, but the Bihari caught him by the ankles. By this time everyone was awake, and shouting, forgetting their fears of waking the village. The man managed to break free and was just getting to his feet when he was pulled down by another Bihari. He started shouting, 'Save me! Save me!' but even if he'd been heard, no one would have dared to venture out from the village at that time of night. He struggled and managed to throw the Bihari off, got up and ran. One of the Biharis pulled out a knife and hurled it at him. He fell again, blood oozing from his back. The Biharis pounced on him, turned him over and shone a torch in his face.

One said, 'Call that *chutiya* Kalua to find out whether this is the man.'

Another shut him up abruptly, 'You're the *chutiya*. We've no time to waste. I'll kill the bastard anyhow, whoever he is, and run for it.'

Saying that, he yanked the man's head back and slit his throat. The Biharis then lumbered off into the night, shouting at Kalua, who was cowering behind one of the stacks of wheat, 'Don't know whether that's your man or not, but it's the only one you will get.' Kalua went over to the body, looked down at the face and saw that the Biharis had got their man. He ran from the scene, wanting to make sure that he was back in his hut before dawn woke the village.

The Biharis now had no guide, so they staggered into the night. After a mile or so the dawn broke, and the heat of the April sun soon dried out what little moisture the crude liquor had left in their bodies. They had nothing to relieve their thirst except the remains of the *desi* liquor, so they strayed off the track to a clump of trees, where they sat down to drink. It wasn't long before the liquor sent them to sleep again.

In Thakurdwara villagers who found the body on their way to the fields to perform their morning offices told the watchman about the murder. He decided to report it immediately to the police station so that he wouldn't have to walk through the midday heat. On his way he passed the three Biharis, still fast asleep. He recognized them as the murderers by their blood-stained clothes, but he didn't stop to investigate further. He hurried on to the police station.

The watchman found the officer in charge of the police station sitting under a neem tree, dressed in a flowing *dhoti*, rubbing a pinch of chewing tobacco between his palms and belching contentedly after a substantial breakfast. The Thanedar Sahib reacted with less than enthusiasm to the watchman's information that one Chotu Ram, a Kumhar of the village Thakurdwara, had been murdered last night. '*Arre*, so many people are getting murdered at this time, fights over the crop, fights over women, blood for blood, everything happens at this time of year. What's the hurry about one more killing?'

The watchman, anxious to ingratiate himself with the man who could make his life a misery, said eagerly, 'Sahib, this is a very easy case. You only have to arrest Thakur Randhir Singh's son. Chotu Ram murdered his father. It's clear this is revenge. I can take you to the men who actually did the murder too. They're quite near here, asleep under a tree. I saw them with blood on their shirts as I was coming to the *thana*.'

The *thanedar* sat up. He was suffering from a new, keen superintendent of police who took statistics of crimes solved seriously, and here was a chance to gain credit for solving two. Maybe it was worthwhile taking some action. 'What do you think, Digpal?' he asked one of his colleagues who was sitting beside him.

'Sounds like easy work to me, *sahib*. Why don't I take a force with this watchman to guide us and arrest the murderers? We can go for the Thakur later.'

The *thanedar* agreed and the force set out. They found the Biharis still asleep and had handcuffs on them before there was any chance of resistance.

This was not the first time the Biharis had seen the inside of a police station. They knew what they might expect. Maybe they would be ordered to be 'chickens', which would mean squatting on their haunches holding their ears for hours on end, or maybe they would be made to stand on one leg with their arms stretched out – as 'aeroplanes'. But to their surprise the *thanedar* who faced them across the desk smiled pleasantly, told his colleague Digpal to undo their handcuffs, called for chairs and invited the prisoners to sit down. Then, leaning back in his chair, with his thumbs tucked under the brown leather belt of the immaculate uniform he was now wearing, he asked them, 'Have you had a good night?'

The Biharis didn't know how to reply. The group of policemen who had gathered to watch the interrogation muttered among themselves, 'What's happening? This is very strange. Why is the bastard in such a good mood today?'

The officer went on, 'I can still smell the *desi* on you. I know what it feels like after filling your belly with that stuff. I'm fond of a good drink too, but as a *thanedar* I can afford whisky and other Indian-made foreign liquors. They aren't so bad the next morning. You must be very thirsty. You must be as dry as the Tahr desert.'

The Biharis looked at each other and shrugged their shoulders as though they thought the *thanedar* was out of his mind, but they did not see why this should not be to their advantage. One of them said, 'Yes, *sahib*, some water would cool my head.'

'Why just water? Have tea too,' replied the *thanedar* and shouted at the policemen standing around him, 'Bring water, bring tea, at once.' The Biharis gulped down several glasses and then poured tea from their cups into saucers to cool it. Feeling more relaxed now, one of them said, 'Thanedar Sahib, there's no need for any *zulum*. You've caught us with blood on our clothes. We'll confess because there's no way we can get off.'

The officer held up his hands and, with a look of shock, as if the last thing he would think of doing was torturing prisoners, said, '*Arre*, how could you think that I would break the law and extract evidence by using force? How could you imagine I would do such a thing? You speak like Biharis. Perhaps you don't know that in Uttar Pradesh we police would never do such a thing.'

The Biharis were dumbfounded. They knew this to be quite untrue, but they were not going to argue.

The officer went on, 'In Uttar Pradesh the police are here to help the public, but perhaps you haven't read our advertisements in the newspapers.'

This was too much for the Biharis. One of them burst out, 'Thanedar Sahib, just because we're illiterate doesn't mean we're sons of owls. We know perfectly well what the police are like. There's no difference between Bihar and UP.'

'Calm down. Why should I make fun of you? You also know that the police help those who help them, and I need your help.'

The *thanedar* was not interested in common criminals. He wanted to get the Thakur, and these men could help him. The government of Uttar Pradesh was in the hands of a backward-caste party, and he knew that bringing the upper-caste Thakurs to book would go down well with his superiors. It might even lead to a transfer from this rural and unprofitable police station to a lucrative post in a town, perhaps even a town near his own home on the other side of the vast state. All he needed was for the murderers to implicate Chandra Kumar.

When the Biharis understood what the *thanedar* was about they offered not just Chandra Kumar but his uncle too. They promised to give evidence that both men were present when the murder was committed. In return the police officer agreed that he would persuade the magistrate to grant them bail, which in most cases was as good as being set free because of the length of time taken by investigations and trials.

Chandra Kumar and Harbaksh, who had returned to Thakurdwara after being released on bail from Ghazipur, were rearrested the next day on a murder charge. They were not so lucky as the Biharis. The police argued that men of their influence would certainly be able to 'tamper' with the witnesses to the murder, and the *munsif* magistrate remanded them to judicial custody in Ghazipur jail, where they were locked up behind twenty-foot-high yellow walls. Their fellow prisoners, most of whom were, like them, on remand, assured them that life was not too bad. The food wasn't exactly home cooking, but visitors were allowed every day and could bring supplies to supplement their diet. Visitors were not permitted to bring cigarettes, liquor or drugs, but this was to prevent them from spoiling the market of the warders, who provided anything at a price.

All this was no comfort to the two Thakurs facing the humiliation of living, sleeping and eating with people they would usually barely deign to talk to. When they eventually managed to free themselves from their helpful but inquisitive new companions they went to the far end of the barracks to review their position. Harbaksh said angrily to Chandra Kumar, 'I thought that bastard lawyer you paid so much money to was going to look after us.'

'Who says he won't?' replied Chandra Kumar without too much conviction.

'Strange way to look after us. First of all we are arrested for being drunk when we are sober, and then when we're released on bail, we are immediately arrested again for committing murder, which we didn't.'

'Om Prakash didn't advise us to be arrested for being drunk.'

'No, that was your nonsense.'

'You contributed nothing to the whole scheme, except trying to get out of it.'

'I wish I had.'

This was too much for Chandra Kumar. Shaking his fists in his uncle's face, he shouted, 'What sort of brother are you? My father did everything for you and you can't even defend his honour.'

Harbaksh grabbed his nephew by his *kurta* collar and shouted back, 'What sort of brother am I? What sort was he when he swindled me out of my share of our father's property?'

'So my father was a thief, was he?' shouted Chandra Kumar, dropping his fist and hooking his uncle a vicious blow under the chin. Harbaksh staggered back, his jaw sagging in pain. Chandra Kumar went after him, hitting out wildly. The other prisoners surrounded the fighters, shouting encouragement, whistling, catcalling and yelling obscenities. Chandra

Kumar came on, his fists flailing, but Harbaksh side-stepped and his opponent charged past, crashing into a bunk. Harbaksh leapt on him, his hands round his throat. Chandra Kumar jabbed his knee into his uncle's groin and he fell back, clutching himself in agony. The spectators roared louder and louder, urging the two men to fight to the end. There was so much noise they didn't hear the warders coming until they felt the numbing blows of *lathis* on the back of their necks. The crowd fell away and the warders dragged the two Thakurs off to solitary confinement, blood drooling from Harbaksh's mouth and angry red marks on Chandra Kumar's neck.

The next morning a black, snub-nosed car, a Hindustan Ambassador, drew up outside Ghazipur jail. The driver and a burly security guard got out and went over to the prison gate to negotiate entry. An elderly man sitting in the back of the car peered anxiously around. When the driver came back and opened the back door the passenger got out hurriedly and scurried to the prison gates, his head forward, darting glances to left and right like a mongoose. Om Prakash had made many enemies in his long career as a criminal lawyer and had survived more than one attempt on his life.

Although the lawyer was well known to the jail authorities, even he had to have the palm of his hand stamped before he was allowed through the second pair of gates that led to the spacious compound in which the prison barracks were set. Om Prakash walked swiftly past a patch of stubble of recently harvested wheat, down an avenue flanked by neem, anvala and gulmohar trees and beds of bright-red hibiscus. He passed prisoners sitting under a banyan tree talking to their visitors, and made his way to the shed where lawyers were allowed to meet their clients. Inside he found his clients sitting with two warders standing behind them.

Om Prakash said peremptorily, 'You people, go. You know that according to the jail manual you are not allowed to hear a conversation between a lawyer and his clients.'

One of the warders replied, 'Vakil Sahib, we're here for your protection. These two are violent. They fought like dogs and the superintendent had to have them put into solitary confinement.'

'What's the meaning of this?' Om Prakash asked, looking sharply at the Thakurs. The two looked down at the ground shamefacedly and said nothing. 'What's the meaning?' repeated the lawyer.

Harbaksh mumbled, 'He attacked me.'

Chandra Kumar said, 'He insulted my father.'

'Fools,' said the lawyer and, turning on his heels, walked towards the senior warder supervising the shed.

Om Prakash was particularly anxious not to be overheard because he didn't want even a rumour about his strategy in this case to get out for fear it might reach the prosecution, so he discreetly slipped the warder a note of sufficient value for the guards to be called off and then returned to his clients.

Sitting down in front of the two Thakurs, he took out a pair of spectacles, polished them with great care, holding them up to the light from time to time to make sure they were absolutely clean, and then perched them precariously on the end of his nose. Next he produced a file from his briefcase, untied the faded white tape binding it with great deliberation and laid it open on the bench. Then, peering over the top of his glasses, he read with the utmost solemnity, 'Thakur Chandra Kumar Singh, son of Thakur Randhir Singh, and Thakur Harbaksh Singh, son of Thakur Ajay Narayan Singh, both of village Thakurdwara, District Ghazipur, you have been charged under section 302 of the Indian Penal Code with murder, read with section 34, which states: "When a criminal act is done by several persons, in furtherance of the common intention of all, each of such persons is liable for that act in the same manner as if it were done by him alone".'

The lawyer looked up at his clients to make sure that the gravity of his words was going home, polished his glasses

again and then went on with the solemnity of a judge condemn-
ing a prisoner, 'The sentence for murder is hanging or life
imprisonment. Hanging is still prescribed in India in some
cases, and . . .'

Harbaksh blurted out, 'But it was you who told us to do it.
You hired the Biharis and now you say we're going to be
hanged.'

Om Prakash closed the file, looked at Harbaksh severely
and said, 'If you don't trust me, I will leave your case.'

'No, no, Vakil *sahib*,' interjected Chandra Kumar hurriedly.
'Of course I trust you. Don't listen to him. But explain how
you are going to get us out of here.'

'I'm not.'

'What did you say?'

'I'm not — at least not for the moment. If you remain under
arrest, your case has to be tried as a matter of urgency, and
that is to your advantage. If you get out on bail, the court is
under no obligation to hear the case quickly, you will probably
give away the most important secret, which is your alibi, and
you could find yourself remaining at the mercy of the police
and the courts for years and years.'

'So that's why you didn't persuade the magistrate to grant
us bail,' suggested Chandra Kumar.

'Yes.'

'Well, you might have told us,' grumbled Harbaksh.

The prospect of remaining in Ghazipur jail was not attractive, but Chandra Kumar reckoned he had no alternative
other than to trust the lawyer, who had such a reputation for
craftiness. Doubtless this was just one of his tricks to deceive
the police and the prosecution, and it would be better to put
up with a few months' inconvenience to free himself from this
case for good. So he accepted the lawyer's strategy, leaving
his uncle with no choice but to agree too. The consultation
ended when the warder shouted, 'Outside-*wallahs* out, inside-
wallahs in!' Om Prakash walked back down the path leading
to the gates where he would have to show the stamp on his

palm to prove that he was an outside-*wallah*. The two Thakurs made their way back to the barracks, hoping that the lawyer's largesse had been generous enough to end their solitary confinement.

Om Prakash was as good as his word. In a remarkably short time the two Thakurs found themselves being hustled into a police van with all the other remand prisoners from Ghazipur jail who were due to appear in court that day. As the driver wrenched the steering wheel, and the lopsided vehicle lurched off the road into the court compound, Chandra Kumar peered through the rusty window bars and saw familiar faces from his own village among the black-coated lawyers, litigants and relatives hurrying towards the court. He nudged his uncle and said, 'Look, there are some of our village people here to see us.'

'I expect the entire village will turn out,' Harbaksh replied glumly. 'You've made a real spectacle of us.'

Inside the characterless new court building that the government had built to cope with the boom in litigation, Harbaksh found his worst fears confirmed. Almost the whole of Thakurdwara seemed to be crowded into Mr Justice Saxena's court to watch the trial. Those with any experience of courts, and there were plenty of them, knew they would hear very little. The proceedings would for the most part be conducted as conversations between the judge and the lawyers standing in front of his desk, but at least the villagers would see how the Thakurs looked, whether they were still so haughty after spending months in the company of common prisoners.

Om Prakash had arranged things so that the case was heard by a judge who would suit his strategy. Mr Justice Saxena was known not just for his honesty but also for his aversion to being bullied by the police, and so it came as no surprise that the prosecutor soon found himself in trouble. The Uttar Pradesh police had persuaded the three Biharis to become witnesses for the prosecution, but Om Prakash was cleverer than the police. Knowing that the murderers had gone back to Bihar after they were released, he sent money to the gang leader and instructed him to bribe the police of that state. As the police in Bihar seldom cooperated with the police in Uttar Pradesh, who were bringing the case, the gang leader had no difficulty in persuading them to turn a blind eye to the disappearance of the murderers. So when Justice Saxena asked the prosecution lawyer impatiently, 'Where are your witnesses?' he could only reply, 'Your honour, the police can't trace them.'

'You mean to say that you have let the men against whom you have direct evidence – that their clothes were stained with blood – get away and have brought before me two men against whom there is no such evidence?'

'But they are the murderers, your honour,' the prosecutor said eagerly. 'They planned and paid for it. They had the motive: revenge. They are the culprits.'

'That may be your view, but it will certainly not be mine unless you come up with some witnesses.'

The prosecutor turned to the police team behind him and held an earnest consultation. Those standing at the front of the court could hear the prosecutor saying in desperation, 'Not *him* – surely we can do better than that.' But the police could not, so one Ram Prakash was called and gave evidence that he'd been drunk and had fallen into one of the stacks of corn outside Thakurdwara but had been woken up by Chotu Ram shouting for help and had witnessed the whole murder. The Thakurs had been there, had identified the victim and had given orders that he should be killed.

The judge leaned back in his chair and sighed. 'Mr Prosecutor, I know – we all know – that the witnesses you bring before the court have been paid to give evidence, but why do you have the same ones time and time again? Wasn't it only last week that I saw this man in connection with a completely different case?'

'But, your honour, there was no one else available today,'

blurted out a police sub-inspector who was a member of the team that had briefed the prosecutor.

The audience, which had so far been dutifully solemn, burst into laughter and excited chatter. The prosecutor held his head in his hands. Om Prakash smiled with superior satisfaction. The judge eventually restored order by threatening to have the court cleared and asked the sub-inspector sarcastically, 'No one else available? No one from your list of known *badmashes* anxious to earn a few rupees for committing perjury? Ghazipur must have become very prosperous and law-abiding all of a sudden, Inspector *sahib*.'

The sub-inspector was about to defend himself but the prosecutor silenced him and attempted to repair the damage by doing everything but falling at the feet of the judge to demonstrate his contrition. Mr Justice Saxena was unimpressed. 'It's the government, your client, that you should apologize to,' he said. 'The whole system of justice depends on public confidence. You, in front of the members of the public crowded into this court, have demonstrated how much you care about their confidence. You've made a joke of justice.'

The judge looked down at his notes. He despaired. He knew that the government would take no action against the policeman. He couldn't be too harsh on him either, remembering the case of Justice Mullick. He had described the police as 'organized *dacoits*' but had suffered the humiliation of having his judgment overturned by the Supreme Court. As for charging the witness with perjury, that would be like punishing the servant for a theft by his employer, and anyhow he couldn't remember when the last case of perjury had been brought.

After what seemed to everyone in the court, particularly the policeman and the witness, like an eternity, Mr Justice Saxena looked up again and said wearily, 'Call your next witness.' There wasn't one.

The prosecution case was now in tatters, but Om Prakash was not leaving anything to chance. When he was asked to call his witnesses he produced the duty officer of the Ghazipur

THE HEART OF INDIA

police station who had arrested the two Thakurs for drunken-ness. After eliciting all the details of the first information report and the station diary for the night of the murder, Om Prakash turned, pointed dramatically to the two accused and said, 'So you see, your honour, these two innocent men could not have been anywhere near the place of the murder. The police case is a tissue of lies, a fraudulent fabrication, a maliciously motivated action, a deliberate distortion . . .'

Om Prakash was getting carried away by his own oratory. The judge pulled him up short. 'All right, all right,' he said. 'That's enough. You have made your point. This is Ghazipur, not the Supreme Court of India. Does the prosecutor wish to question this witness?'

'No, your honour.'

When the court reconvened to hear the lawyers' arguments, Om Prakash thought the outcome of the case was a foregone conclusion, but to his amazement the prosecutor asked to call another witness.

'Call another witness? What for?' the judge asked. 'You've had your opportunity. If you want to call witnesses now, you will first have to convince me of the need.'

'We have a witness who heard the two accused admit that they were going to murder the victim. The witness is of an unimpeachable character.'

'That'll be something,' the judge remarked drily.

'Your honour. I'm sure you will agree that this is no paid witness. This is not someone who has any motive to give evidence for the prosecution – rather the opposite, in fact.'

'I can't wait to hear him. Who is this remarkable witness?'

'I want to call Vaidehi Singh, the mother of one of the accused and the sister-in-law of the other.'

'What?' exclaimed the judge in amazement.

Om Prakash protested. 'Your honour, there can be no question of calling a relative of the accused. She cannot be asked to testify against her own son. It's preposterous that you should even consider such a thing.'

'I should be obliged if you would allow me to decide what can and cannot happen in this court,' retorted the judge sharply.

But Om Prakash did not take the hint. 'This is absurd,' he said, throwing his hands in the air in a gesture of disbelief. 'How can a lawyer represent his client if a case is to be conducted like this? The prosecution had no credible witnesses − you said as much − and now, in their desperation, they ask to call the accused's mother, and you even consider allowing her to appear.'

'Shri Om Prakash, I will not be addressed like that in my own court. I never said that I would allow her to be called, but now I shall, and you had better mind your conduct.'

So it was agreed that Vaidehi Singh could be produced in court, and a new date was set for her appearance.

When that day came Vaidehi stood proudly in the witness box, still wearing the white sari of a widow but no bangles and no red *bindi*. The villagers, who were, as one said, 'packed into the courtroom like chickens in a cage going to the bazaar', stared at her in silence.

Om Prakash was at a loss to understand the prosecutor's strategy, but he had made it absolutely clear to Vaidehi that lying in court was an accepted practice, especially when it came to saving members of the family. The prosecutor began his questioning. Gravely and sympathetically, he led her to recount each detail of her husband's death. Her anger was controlled but apparent in the way she spoke of being told of the murder by a family servant and of being taken out to see his headless body.

It was a most violent death, a criminal act against an innocent man, a disgrace to your noble family,' said the prosecutor.

'Yes,' replied Vaidehi. 'You are absolutely right to say that.'

The prosecutor's attitude changed. Gone was all pretence of sympathy. With a sneer he continued, 'And your fine family has so little respect for the tradition of Thakurs that you say your son did nothing to take revenge for his father's death.'

'Objection!' boomed Om Prakash, but the widow ignored him. She was so incensed by this insult to her family that she forgot all the advice she had been given. 'How dare you claim I ever said that?' she asked the prosecuting lawyer. 'Who gave you the right to insult the memory of my husband, asking all these impertinent questions and then suggesting that I would insult my son?'

'Objection!' roared Om Prakash again. 'The witness can't be asked to implicate her son in a crime.'

But Vaidehi paid no attention. Her pride had been hurt, and there was no controlling her temper now. 'Of course my son and my brother-in-law arranged for the killing of that disloyal criminal,' she went on. 'I made them take an oath to do so. I will not allow you to insult us any more.'

'Your witness,' said the prosecutor, turning to Om Prakash, but for once the famous lawyer was silent.

The judge looked up from his notes and asked in surprise, 'No questions from the defence?'

Om Prakash still did not reply.

'The court is adjourned,' said the judge.

When the court reconvened Om Prakash argued that Vaidehi's mind had been disturbed by the murder of her husband, that her evidence was in any case only hearsay, as she was not present at the time of the murder, and that it was highly irregular to allow her to be called as a witness against members of her own family. He quoted many precedents at great length and made many telling points. The judge listened intently, and the prosecution lawyer's spirits fell. But at the end of his summing-up of the two sides of the argument the judge said, 'I have come to the conclusion that the defence argument rests on questioning my decision to allow Vaidehi Devi to appear in the witness box. I stand by that decision. Her testimony is damning. I find Chandra Kumar Singh

Thakur and Harbaksh Singh Thakur guilty of conspiracy to murder Shri Chotu Ram and sentence them to imprisonment for life.'

Om Prakash, his reputation in tatters, shouted, 'This is a mischievous, perverse, deliberately distorted judgment. I will appeal to the High Court, and I will most certainly win.'

'Meanwhile your clients will go back to jail, and I will see that you are punished for contempt of court,' replied the judge.

THE *IKKA-WALLAH*'S LAMENT

Mohammad Islam lay on his *ikka* outside Chunar station, half asleep. His horse was asleep in the shafts. The *ikka*, a particularly uncomfortable form of pony trap, had waited all morning in vain for some passengers. Mohammad Islam had returned home at midday to give himself and the horse a rest during the time when the sun was at its hottest and was now back, hoping to pick up some passengers from the early-evening train. *Ikkas* did not boast any form of seating. They were just flat, wooden platforms set on top of a chassis that supported two large, old-fashioned spoked wheels and two shafts for the horse that drew them. The only concession to comfort was a shade in the middle of the platform, supported by four bamboo poles, which passengers could cling to.

Nobody, least of all Mohammad Islam, knew the year of his birth. He did know that he had been born in Chunar, where the Ganges takes a right-angled turn towards Benares, less than 20 miles away. He was old enough to remember the days before Independence, which, he would invariably tell his passengers, were much better than the present times. His bald head was covered with a cloth. His outsized black glasses had slipped down his nose. There was sweat on the shaved lip above the white beard trimmed in the Muslim fashion. His yellowing *kurta* was certainly not freshly laundered that day. His blue tartan *lungi* was pulled up above his ankles, revealing his bare feet.

The *ikka-wallahs'* business had declined severely since the roads in Chunar had been tarmacked some ten years before.

With the roads had come rival forms of transport. There were scooter rickshaws which, although designed for only two passengers, usually took eight or nine, just as many as an *ikka*. There were bigger three-wheelers called tempos. There didn't seem to be any limit to the number of people who could be crowded into them. Cycle rickshaws had also made an appearance. The railway, which had been the main source of Mohammad Islam's business, had been challenged too. Buses and jeeps could now deliver their passengers direct to the Muslim shrine on the banks of the Ganges and up the hill to the fort built high above the river dominating that strategic bend. The railway had provided a need for intermediary transport like *ikkas*. Now the *ikka-wallahs* could compete only by charging half the fare the scooter rickshaws demanded or by carrying goods, and then customers always insisted you took a heavier load than any horse could reasonably be asked to pull.

Mohammad Islam often cursed the motor engine. He had seen the best days of transport when there were trains for longer distances and horses for short runs. In those days there hadn't been all this senseless moving around the place. He himself had never been further west than Allahabad, about 75 miles away, and Dehri-on-Sone, not much more distant to the east. Although he was in the transport business himself, he had not felt the need to go beyond the bus stop on the main road the other side of the Chunar railway crossing for many years now.

As he dozed, Mohammad Islam also considered how motorized transport had ruined Chunar. It wasn't just the black, poisonous smoke that the scooter rickshaws belched into the nostrils of his horse. In his younger days Chunar had been a cluster of villages set in a jungle. Now, because there was so much movement and it was so easy to get around, it had spread into a small town. The population had increased too. Then there had been only one bazaar around the *tehsildar*'s court and Lower Lines, a little further down the road, where the Anglo-Indians and some other Christians had lived. Even around a place as important as the railway station there hadn't been any shops. There had been very little cultivation apart from some orchards. Now all the trees had been cut down, and Chunar was one long bazaar. All the roads were lined with ugly concrete boxes housing shops, and they couldn't cope with the modern demand to be forever spending, although only God knew where people got the money from. As he left the station he always had to manoeuvre his *ikka* through the trolleys of vegetable sellers and other hawkers, as if the road wasn't narrow enough already. There were teashops on every corner, where people wasted their time gossiping. Mohammad Islam didn't approve of drinking tea. It was a new-fangled habit. Very few people drank it when he was young.

All this was progress, Mohammad Islam had been told – what all those politicians always talked about as 'development'. But it had made his life harder. All right, the old paths had been potholed and bumpy, but an *ikka* driver who knew his road well took pride in negotiating those hazards. The trees he had loved had provided shade and the delight of watching the seasons change as he drove along the rutted paths. The new red leaves of the mahua trees gradually turning green, the pale-green mango flowers falling to the ground and the tiny seed cases growing into succulent fruit, the saal trees shedding their broad leaves which, when dried, made such useful plates. Now the tarmacked roads threw the heat of the sun back in his face. The blue plastic bags that had replaced more natural wrapping for shopping survived summer, winter and spring too, littering the roadside and the hill leading up to the fort. The piles of garbage seemed to grow bigger and bigger, whatever the season.

Mohammad Islam's horse stirred in the shafts, tried to switch the flies with its tail, and took a step forward, jolting his driver from his somnolent reminiscences. Mohammad Islam made soothing sucking noises to quieten the horse and patted him on the haunches. Laloo was really nothing more than a pony, but Mohammad Islam could not bring himself to acknowledge that. In the old days he had always had a big horse, but now they were very expensive and cost a lot to feed, so no one had the courage to keep them. Anyhow the *ikka-wallah* acknowledged that he'd got used to a small horse and was even rather fond of Laloo, so called because he was *lal*, or reddish-brown. The horse had seen him through ten years and could well be good for another ten. Laloo was reasonably good-tempered and affectionate too, especially when Mohammad Islam was grooming him after a hard day's work.

After Laloo settled down again Mohammad Islam stretched, yawned and turned to the *ikka-wallah* next to him, saying, '*Arre bhai*, it looks like another day when I'm not going to have any passengers. I don't know where I'll get my own food from, let alone the horse's.'

The other driver was a Hindu, younger than Mohammad Islam. He said, '*Miyan*, you have to compete for passengers these days. There is some work to be had, but you won't get it by sleeping on your *ikka*.'

'Work? What do you mean? A few years ago there were one hundred and fifty *ikkas* here and there was plenty for us to do. Now business is so bad that my sons have got out of the trade and are weaving rugs. There are only about fifteen *ikka-wallahs* left, and most of us are lined up here, just waiting. That doesn't fill a man's stomach.'

'That's because you're waiting for the train. We go where the passengers are likely to be, and you should do that instead of spending all day in the station yard. You should move where the passengers are, and if you can't find any, you can go to the bus stand across the railway line. There are usually packages marked for the Chunar bazaar being unloaded there.'

'I have been at the railway station all my life, and anyhow I don't think it's an *ikka* driver's job to carry goods.'

Mohammad Islam lay back on the sacking that covered the platform of his *ikka*, closed his eyes again and thought of the passengers he had carried. Nowadays it was only the poor who used *ikkas* because they couldn't afford the scooter rickshaw fare. It hadn't always been like that. He had been a favourite of Surinder Pratap Singh, the *zamindar* of the village just across the Ganges. Whenever he arrived at the station on the mail train from Calcutta, he would come over to the *ikka* stand and shout, 'Mohammad Islam, we've got to go to the *ghat*!' Mohammad Islam would then take him down to the banks of the Ganges where the boats crossed to his side of the river. The *ghat* business had been remunerative, but now there was a pontoon bridge across the river all year except during the monsoon months. The toll was too expensive to make it economic for *ikkas* to ply across the bridge.

He remembered that Surinder Pratap Singh had always been known as a very strict man. He looked terrifying with his big moustache, his hair cut like an army man, his loud voice and the stick he always carried. More than once he had slapped a man in the station yard just for staring at him. But Mohammad Islam knew that he was really a man of butter. He always gave a full rupee for the fare to the *ghat*, although normal passengers paid only two annas. Mind you, he wouldn't let anyone else on the *ikka* except the servant who had travelled to Calcutta with him. Mohammad Islam had also heard in the bazaar that every day the *zamindar* held a *darbar*, or court at which any villager could come and ask for help.

Surinder Pratap Singh was a great lover of horses and hunting. He used to say to the *ikka-wallah*, 'Your horse looks as if he is in need of a good drink.'

Mohammad Islam would reply, '*Sarkar*, as a good Muslim, I don't have anything to do with drink.'

He would bellow with laughter and say, 'I'm not suggesting that you have a drink. But your horse isn't a Muslim, so why shouldn't he? After a hard day's work, and especially after *ikka* racing, I give my horses some whisky or rum in sherbet or milk. You know my record at the races, so it can't do them any harm.'

That was a time when Mohammad Islam did sometimes cross the Ganges, when there were *ikka* races down the road leading from Surinder Pratap Singh's village to Benares. Even the big horse he had kept in those days had been no match for the magnificent animals belonging to racing men like Surinder Pratap Singh. Their *ikkas* were also especially built to race. They were very light and had rubber rims around the outside of the wheels. They even had bearings, so that the wheels turned freely and didn't wobble like those of an ordinary *ikka*. There was a lot of betting, but Mohammad Islam never remembered being tempted by that. It was stupid to risk hard-earned money, which had not been easy to come by then any more than it was now, besides which betting was forbidden by the Quran. He went just because he loved to see the magnificent horses gallop and the brightly painted *ikkas* bounce perilously along the road. Now if you tried to hold an *ikka* race down that road there would be blood everywhere. The *ikkas* and their horses would be massacred by those young fools who drive buses and refuse to move over for anyone.

Thinking of Surinder Pratap Singh, the *ikka-wallah* recalled the day when a young man had galloped into the station yard shouting, 'Mohammad Islam, where is he? Where is he?' When he made himself known the rider said, 'Come quickly! Sarkar's *ikka* has fallen over the bank. It's lost one wheel, and he has to get to a shoot in a hurry. He sent me to bring you.' Mohammad Islam dispatched one of the boys who used to hang around the *ikka* stand, waiting for any odd jobs, to tell his family he would not be back that night, and set off.

What a sight met him when he turned the corner just before the track leading up to the fort branched off. The smart family *ikka* was on its side, halfway down the bank. One wheel had spun into the fields below; the shafts were pointing to the sky; the food, the pots and pans and the bedding that Surinder Pratap Singh had packed for the shoot were spread all over the bank. Miraculously no one appeared to have been hurt. The horse was calmly grazing, but Sarkar was jumping up and down, waving his stick and bellowing like a bull plagued by a swarm of bees. His tormentors were a crowd who had gathered to witness his discomfiture. He would charge them from time to time, his moustache bristling and sweat pouring down his face, bawling, 'Don't you dare to stare at a man of my position! Don't you dare stare!' The crowd was nimble enough to avoid his flailing stick, and when he retreated to defend his *ikka* they simply regrouped and stood watching him in silence. They did not quite have the courage to laugh at a *zamindar*, but staring was just as effective. Shortly after Mohammad Islam arrived they were driven away by a party sent from the police station by the *thanedar* in charge, who had received news of Surinder Pratap Singh's embarrassment. Even in those days the police were always on the side of the big men.

Eventually they had picked up all the supplies, tied the net carrying fodder under Mohammad Islam's *ikka* and set off, after Surinder Pratap Singh had sworn at his driver once more for driving into a pothole so fast that he had knocked out the pin that held the *ikka* wheel in place. He ordered the driver to make sure the shameful sight was cleared away long before the shooting party returned.

How smoothly Mohammad Islam's *ikka* sped towards the camp in the forest. The sound of the wheels as they spun along was beautiful, *karoor kuroor, churoor muroor, machar muchoor* – what rhythmic music. The Forest Department maintained the tracks, and they had very little traffic on them, so there were far fewer hazards than on his usual runs, and it seemed to take no time at all to reach the pool where the other *zamindars* had already set up camp.

Mohammad Islam knew nothing of shooting, but then he wasn't expected to. All he had to do was look after his horse and *ikka* and make sure they were ready to return to Chunar the next day. The *zamindars* set off on foot in the late afternoon to take up position on a platform erected in a tree above a buffalo calf which had been killed by a tiger. The *ikka* driver remembered the water bubbling, *qul, qul, qul*, through the hollow centres of the mahua flowers as they dropped into the pool. As evening fell he had watched the succession of animals which, undeterred by the camp, came to drink water – small, nervous, spotted deer, blackbuck with magnificent horns, muddy wild boar with tushes protruding from their pointed snouts. He even saw a bear shamble down to the edge of the tank and take water.

The next morning the *zamindars* came back empty-handed and not speaking to each other. Neither would accept that he had fired that unfortunately not fatal first shot that had frightened the tiger away. Mohammad Islam recalled how disappointed he had been. He had hoped that maybe he would bring back a dead tiger to Chunar on his *ikka*. That really would have been something to talk about on the station stand.

He dropped Surinder Pratap Singh at the *ghat* where a group from his family were waiting to make sure that he got back without his dignity being further impaired. The *zamindar* paid him handsomely and said if ever he was in difficulty, Mohammad Islam should cross the river to seek help from him.

Of course, life had not been easy in the days of the *zamindars*. The small Muslim community of *ikka* drivers had lived in huts in the bazaar. Each year during the monsoon they had to pick up everything they could and go to the nearby Muslim shrine to seek refuge from the floods. When the water level receded they returned to rebuild their huts. Now the government had provided them with small plots on a hill above the shrine, well away from the floods. They had been given no help with building their huts, but at least they weren't flooded each year.

The year of the hunt the floods had been so severe that there was virtually nothing left of Mohammad Islam's hut. He remembered the *zamindar*'s offer of help and decided to see where it would get him. The river was still high the day he chose to cross, and flowing fast. There had been a wind too with waves on the normally placid Ganges. Mohammad Islam had admired the way the boatman, using just two crude oars, had managed to avoid being blown into the whirlpool just off the *ghat* and pulled his heavy wooden craft to the other side in the face of a strong head wind.

He'd found Surinder Pratap Singh's village much better laid out than Chunar bazaar. There were even underground drains, and the paths were paved with brick. The villagers had been very helpful and taken him to the *zamindar*. As they passed one substantial two-storied house built on a twelve-feet-high plinth to protect it from the floods, a villager had told him the ladies of Sarkar's family lived there in *purdah*. The door posts were made out of sandstone, and above the door, which was firmly locked, was carved an image of the Hindu elephant god Ganesh. The villagers had said only Surinder Pratap Singh himself had the key to that door. Even the pillars at the well, which supported the rope and pulley for the bucket, were of beautifully carved stone.

Mohammad Islam had come across the *zamindar* sitting on a veranda with village men squatting on the ground in front of him. This was the court he had heard about. Standing against the back wall of the veranda was the cycle that Sarkar had brought back from his last trip to Calcutta. He remembered how difficult it had been to tie it to the back of the *ikka*. Sarkar had been very proud of it, saying it was only the third in the whole district. Now everyone seemed to have a cycle, which just made the life of an *ikka* driver even more difficult.

Mohammad Islam had said, 'Salaam, Sarkar,' and the *zamindar* had asked, 'Everything well?' When he had explained that he was in some difficulty the *zamindar* had asked him to sit down. Then he had been given some tobacco to chew.

It was top-quality *zarda* from Mainpuri, not the cheap stuff available in Chunar bazaar. When the villagers had been given their orders, and their complaints had been heard, Mohammad Islam had explained about his hut being washed away. Surinder Pratap Singh had called over a clerk and ordered him to write. 'Wood and thatching straw needed to rebuild one hut to be sent to Chunar bazaar for *ikka-wallah* Mohammad Islam. I don't suppose there is any shortage of mud for the walls, is there, after the floods?'

Mohammad Islam was aroused from his dreaming again, this time by a blast on the horn of an electric locomotive pulling into the station. He remembered the way new horses used to rear in their shafts, terrified by the roaring, the hissing and the smoke of the old steam engines. His luck had at last turned. A family of five came over to him and asked to be taken to the bus stand on the main road. A fare was negotiated, and they climbed aboard.

After negotiating the scrum outside the station, Mohammad Islam whirled the string which passed for a whip, clicked his tongue and said, 'Chalo, get on.' When this didn't produce any acceleration Laloo received a sharp tap or two from the stick to which the string was attached. This prompted him to break into a desultory trot. Mohammad Islam's passengers seemed comparatively prosperous, so he asked the man of the family why he hadn't taken a scooter rickshaw. He replied, 'Those young scooter rickshaw drivers are so shameless. You always have to argue about the fare and then they become rude, and I don't want my wife and children to hear their language. They promise they won't take any more passengers and then they do and that means everyone is squeezed up against each other, and that's not proper for my wife either. We could see that you were a reliable old man who would stick to what he had agreed.'

'Yes, there are very few of our sort left now. Before you came I was just thinking of the old days and the sort of passengers we used to carry. How we were always busy.

Come to Chunar in five years and I don't expect you will see a single *ikka*.'

The *ikka* pulled up at the level-crossing gates to allow the Brahmaputra Mail to pass. A scooter rickshaw, bulging with passengers, forced its way into the queue in front of Mohammad Islam. The driver shouted at him, 'Make way, old man. Your donkey carts are just a nuisance, blocking the road. Why can't you realize that your time is over?' Mohammad Islam turned to his passengers and remarked, 'Just like you said.'

After dropping the family at the bazaar which had sprung up on both sides of the main road from Benares to Mirzapur, Mohammad Islam waited for return passengers. All facilities for long-distance truck drivers and bus passengers were available, including even an English wine and beer shop, but that did not make it a pleasant place to halt for a meal or to shop for Chunar's famous pottery because, unfortunately, few drivers bothered to pull off the main road when they stopped, so there was an almost continuous traffic jam. The noise of drivers senselessly sitting on their horns was deafening. This was a place Mohammad Islam hated, a hell filled with dark black, poisonous, suffocating smoke.

After half an hour or so the *ikka-wallah* saw the sun setting dimly through the thick, black haze and decided he could stand it no longer. He turned his empty *ikka* back down the main road and went off at a brisk trot, the bells on the harness jingling. 'Laloo always knows when he's going home,' Mohammad Islam thought. They were out of the bazaar, and into the short stretch of open country before the road to Chunar turned off to the right, when he saw a jeep taxi approaching him, attempting to overtake a bus. The bus driver, who was without the gift of a mirror and probably couldn't hear the jeep's horn above the roaring of his own engine, was careering down the middle of the road. The jeep was bucketing along the rutted path beside the tarmacked road, coming straight for the *ikka*. Mohammad Islam wrenched Laloo's head to the left. A wheel of the *ikka* slipped over the bank, skewing the shafts into the path of the on-coming Jeep. It swerved to avoid the *ikka*, clipped Laloo's head, narrowly avoided colliding with the bus and continued its mad race, the driver wholly unrepentant, the passengers afraid that any remonstrance would only provoke him to even more outrageous feats of what he regarded as daring.

Mohammad Islam was not hurt, but he took one look at Laloo, who had fallen between the shafts, and could see he would never pull an *ikka* again. He unstrapped the collar from the shafts and freed Laloo's body from them, but he didn't bother to remove the cheap harness which consisted mostly of rope, only taking away a lucky charm hidden by the plastic flowers which adorned the bridle. Then, after rubbing Laloo's forehead for the last time, he crossed the road and set off through the fields to Chunar and home. He'd been a hard-working horse, Mohammad Islam thought, but what could he do for him now? He might as well leave him for the vultures, who would gorge themselves until only the skeleton was left and they were so bloated that they couldn't fly. There was no point in going to the police. It would be him they would charge with dangerous driving, and they wouldn't let him go until he paid a bribe. The days of the *ikka* were nearly over, and so were his, so why not accept that this was a sign from Allah. Let his sons look after him now. They wove carpets, which was a good business. Why shouldn't he spend the days he had left with his grandchildren? By the grace of Allah, he would pass away in peace far from that hellish motor engine which had ruined his livelihood and so nearly caused him to die a violent death.

GIRLFRIENDS

Ram Prasad Vishwakarma, manager of the village school in Narayanpur, had no children. Perhaps that was why he outdid the rest of the village in his zeal for interfering in the affairs of other families. That was quite some achievement. In the case of Suryakant Dwivedi the manager felt his zeal was fully justified. After all, Dwivediji was the Principal of the school, and if all was not well with his family, all would not be well with his care of the children. Only a man who kept a traditional and disciplined household could hope to prevent the schoolchildren from being led astray by all the modern pressures threatening the ordered structure of Narayanpur's life.

The Manager Sahib had few qualms about the Principal until he learned that he had allowed his only daughter to go to Benares Hindu University to study for her B.Ed. It had been bad enough when she had gone to the women's degree college in the nearby small town of Mohlanganj, but at least there she had come home every evening. In Benares she was staying in a hostel, and goodness knows what bad habits she might learn there. That was surely why it was his duty to talk to Dwivediji.

He found the Principal sitting on a wooden chair outside his house, listening to the radio. The house was a long, ramshackle building, a traditional village home built of mud. The tiled roof swelled and dipped ominously, but then it had done so for many years without quite collapsing. There was a stack of straw outside the door, cow pats were laid out to dry in the courtyard and the producers of that essential fuel sat on the ground peacefully ruminating. The manager was reassured by the fact that the principal had not built himself one of those new concrete boxes which some of the more prosperous villagers, who wanted to show how modern they were, now lived in. He was further reassured to see that the principal was wearing a white *kurta* and a neat *dhoti*, not the shirt and trousers which so many of his staff now wore.

'Ram Ram, Dwivediji,' the manager said, as he approached the principal.

'Ram Ram,' replied the principal. 'Come, sit down. Listen to the news.' He then turned his head and shouted, '*Arre*, boy, bring a chair quickly for the Manager Sahib!'

'You don't sit on a *charpoy* now?'

'No, I prefer a chair. It gives some support to my old back.'

A ragged young boy, who was not one of Dwivediji's pupils because he was too busy being his servant, appeared with another chair and the manager sat down.

'What's the news then?' he asked.

'Well, I suppose it's good news. The government has won that vote of confidence. It's not much of a government, as corrupt as the rest of them, but at least that means we are not going to have another wretched election. What with politicians changing parties like we change our clothes, and governments collapsing like walls of sand, I can't even count how many times we have had our peace disturbed by all the commotion and noise of an election.'

'Yes, and what's worse is the expense. After all it's we villagers who have to pay in the end for all the money the politicians spend on getting elected.'

'And on losing too.'

The manager laughed. 'Yes, that costs too.' Then, thinking it was time to end the formalities and get down to business, he pulled on his white moustache, moved his chair up, leaned forward and said, 'Well, Dwivediji, have you done as I suggested? Have you written to her and told her you have arranged her marriage and she must come back?'

'Bring some tea,' shouted the principal. No matter how much he might resent this intrusion into his family's affairs, the rules of hospitality must be observed.

Suryakant Dwivedi was a widower. His wife had died giving birth to her first child, Madhu. Although his had been an arranged marriage, he had quickly come to love his fair-skinned, beautiful young wife, and at first he resented the baby girl who had brought about her death. How much better it would have been if the baby had died and his wife had lived, perhaps even to produce a son.

As the years went by and the baby, cared for by the Principal's mother, grew into a young girl with the promise of a beauty which would rival his wife's, the Principal learned to love her too — so much so that he found it very hard to resist her demands. That's not to say that Madhu was particularly demanding. She was a respectful daughter who returned his love, but she did have one obsession. She was determined to be educated and to follow in his footsteps as a teacher. That was why he had reluctantly agreed that she should go to Benares Hindu University, which was the best possible chance she could get of starting a successful career.

The conversation between the principal and the manager returned to the iniquities of politics and politicians, as village conversations tend to do, until the boy returned with a tray of tea and biscuits. Vishwakarma noisily slurped his tea, replaced the chipped cup in the saucer, patted his belly and then leaned forward again. This time he was determined to come to the point.

'So, Dwivediji, as I was saying, I hope that you have written to your daughter. From what I read in the paper it's clear that BHU is not a suitable place for a respectable girl.'

Dwivediji was a fastidious man, in so far as that was possible on the small salary he was paid and the surplus produced by his few acres of land. Vishwakarma had far more land, some of which he had given to the village to build the school, but no one could call the manager fastidious. His *kurta* was crumpled, his *dhoti* had not been washed too recently, the pocket of his shabby waistcoat was torn and the strip of cotton cloth tied loosely round his head was sweat-stained. The Principal wondered whether he really did have to discuss his beloved daughter with such a man as this, but in the end he decided that he did. After all, Vishwakarma had given the land for the school. This, all the evidence went to suggest, had given him the right to retain the powerful position of manager in perpetuity.

'Well, yes, manager *sahib*, I do agree I was not happy about allowing Madhu to go to Benares, but the local degree college does not have a course for B.Ed. and she really does want to become a teacher.'

'That's so. But do you have to allow her to do what she wants? You have the right to tell her she must get married. All these women working, they are just increasing the chaos we see around us. If they accepted the old traditions, then there would be order in our society. After all, everyone now says one of our biggest problems is unemployment, so why should women take men's jobs?'

The headmaster was not entirely in disagreement with these sentiments but in his case there were advantages in having a working daughter.

'I take your point,' he replied, 'but my pension will not support me in old age, you know that. If I have to sell what little land I have for a dowry, where will I be? A well-educated girl who can earn her own living does not cost so much to get married. She is a dowry in herself.'

Eventually a compromise was reached. The headmaster refused to order his daughter to come home, but he did promise to write to Madhu saying he had arranged her marriage, and telling her that the wedding would take place immediately after she ended her one-year course. It was not strictly true that a marriage had been arranged, but Suryakant Dwivedi did not think a beautiful BHU-trained teacher would be a drag on the market, in spite of the fact that village girls were usually married much earlier.

There was only room for three beds in the room Madhu shared in BHU's New Hostel, but that had not prevented the university authorities from declaring it what the girls called a 'four-seater'. Madhu was lying on one of the beds, reading a psychology textbook, when Tripti, one of her room-mates, burst in shouting, 'Letter, letter, somebody loves you. Open it. Let's see who it's from.'

Madhu recognized the carefully formed handwriting and said, 'Don't be so silly. It's from my father.'

'Open it then. There must be something interesting in it.'

Madhu could never quite understand why Tripti took so much interest in her. Nor could she understand how a girl from such a sophisticated background often behaved so childishly. She did not know how long it took to outgrow a convent-school education. Tripti's father was a businessman who lived in Calcutta, and she had been sent to boarding school in the hill station of Darjeeling. She was reading chemistry because she believed that a modern girl ought to read science. She had a strong face, dominated by a large nose – one of those commanding rather than beautiful Indian faces. With her height, her short hair and the jeans she was wearing she looked distinctly masculine as she bent over the slender, sari-clad Madhu, trying to read her letter. That wasn't easy because it was written in Hindi, a language that had not been encouraged by the nuns in Darjeeling.

'What does it say? I can read the word *shadi*. Is your father marrying again?'

'No, don't be stupid,' said Madhu with an embarrassed giggle. 'He would never do that. He has arranged a marriage for me.'

'Who to?'

'How should I know? I may not even see the boy until the wedding day.'

'Oh, for heaven's sake,' Tripti said angrily, 'you are not going to fall for that. After being at BHU you must realize that there is no need to have a boy found for you. The way the students look at you here, you could pick any one of them.'

'I loathe the way they ogle girls. I hate their crude remarks. It makes me feel filthy too. I know my father will find me a decent boy, and that's all I want. You and I are different. You can cope with boys. I don't even want to.'

Tripti had never seen the mild Madhu so upset. 'Has someone been Eve-teasing you?' she asked anxiously.

'If you mean whistles, cat-calls and stupid remarks like "Hello, darling, hello, sexy" – yes.'

'That is Eve-teasing. So is bottom-pinching and touching breasts.'

'Well, you may think I'm a simple country girl, but at least I have never let a boy get near enough to me to do that.'

'Not even in a crowded bus?'

'No, not even in a crowded bus. Not on a railway station. I'm sure you have. You encourage boys with your jeans, your short hair and your blouse half-open.'

Tripti didn't hesitate to wear jeans in Calcutta, but in BHU she never wore them outside the hostel. That would have been courting disaster in an atmosphere which was still so traditional. She had, however, started meeting one of the chemistry postgraduate students. It was all very innocent – cups of coffee together in the cafés in Lanka bazaar just outside the main gate of the campus, soft drinks sitting on the benches in front of the white marble temple in the middle of the campus, even occasionally holding hands under the table in the library. As yet she didn't even know whether she wanted more. She did know the dangers of going as far as she had. Some girls in the hostel had already asked her who the boy was. She had replied, 'My brother.' Nobody believed that old alibi, and so if she didn't break off the relationship, there was a risk of being reported to the warden. That would mean a letter to her parents, who for all their outward appearance of tolerance were as determined their daughter should make a suitable match as Madhu's father was.

Tripti was hurt by Madhu's unusual outburst against her. She needed Madhu's friendship. She found her self-containment comforting after her brash convent-school friends who behaved as though they knew so much about the world – but, in fact, knew so little. With Madhu she did not have to pretend to cleverness or courage she did not have. There was no need to create any impression. She just had to be herself and Madhu would respond with generosity. So to end their first row quickly, she sat down beside Madhu, put one arm round her shoulder and said, 'Madhu, I'm sorry. It was very stupid of me. We are very different, that's why I am so fond of you. I had no business to tease you about your father's letter. I know how much you love him. Please don't think I'm crude and vulgar, and that I chase boys. I wear jeans just to annoy the warden and because I do honestly find them comfortable. I promise I'll come to your wedding, whoever you marry.'

Madhu took hold of Tripti's other hand, smiled and said, 'Of course I'm fond of you. I depend on you. You know that I wouldn't have survived in this place if we had not become friends. I often wish I had never left my father and home, and it's only you who stop me running straight back there, so please don't be upset. I should be more thick-skinned.'

As the term went on Madhu did indeed become more resilient. So much so that one late afternoon in October she found herself with Tripti and two boys sitting on the slopes of a hillock on the top of which stood a small, white-washed stone pavilion. They were part of the crowd which had gathered to watch the Ram Lila, the enactment of the Hindu epic staged by the Maharaja of Benares every year.

For some time now Tripti had been under pressure from her boyfriend, Vijay, to be a little more adventurous, but how could she avoid being caught and reported to her parents? It was Madhu who, by accident, put an idea into her head. Madhu had been brought up on tales from the Ramayan. In the university she had heard of the famous Ram Lila of the Maharaja of Benares. She only had to cross the Ganges to join the crowds watching the story of Ram's sacrifice of his kingdom, the kidnapping of his wife by Ravan, the demon-king of Lanka, and her rescue. But she couldn't get there because she was locked up in the hostel every evening. There was one way out. Madhu had an aunt in Benares who was registered with the university authorities as her local guardian. She could take a pass from the warden to spend the night there, but she could not go to the Ram Lila on her own.

Madhu hadn't thought that Tripti, who missed no opportunity to debunk religion, would want to go the Ram Lila with her, but when she mentioned it, her friend replied enthusiastically, 'I would love to go. I will get a pass to stay with your local guardian too.'

So it had been arranged, and Tripti had little difficulty in persuading Madhu that it was necessary to take her boyfriend and his classmate Anand with them for protection.

This was the twentieth day of the month-long Ram Lila. The audience and the cast were waiting for the arrival of the Maharaja. Two lines of young boys dressed in cotton pajama trousers with torn and faded shirts – some green, some orange and some red – lined the pathway up to the pavilion. They carried wooden maces and their monkey masks were slung over their shoulders. The boys were the army of the god-king Ram. They were being controlled by a lean man of about fifty wearing a spotless *dhoti* and *kurta* with a sash of office over one shoulder. A neatly bound, flat-topped turban covered his head, and his brow was marked with the horizontal lines of a devotee of Shiva.

'Who's he?' Anand asked a member of the Raja's personal security force armed with an ancient sabre, who was sitting on the ground because he was so far beyond the age of military service that he couldn't stand for long.

'That's a Vyas. See that book he's holding? All the words and actions of the whole Ram Lila are written in it. He's responsible for seeing that the actors turn up in the right place at the right time. It's not easy work. The Ram Lila goes on for a month and moves over a wide area and the Maharaja insists that everything must be just right.'

The leading members of the cast sat on top of the hillock in front of the pavilion. There were the two young boys who played the god-king Ram and his brother Lakshman. Their faces sparkled with the pink, blue and green sequins spread in floral patterns over their cheeks and across their brows. On their heads were tall, gold-wire-and-sequin-embroidered crowns – the wire dull with age. They carried bows and quivers of arrows. Beside the royal brothers was their faithful lieutenant, the Monkey God, Hanuman. He was played by a well-known wrestler with two days' growth of stubble, a springy tail jutting out jauntily from his back and his monkey mask also slung over his shoulder.

At the bottom of the hillock was a circle of men wearing brightly coloured turbans. They were the Ramayanis who sang the words of the Ramayan in between the characters' dialogues.

A woman sitting behind Madhu nudged her in the back and said, 'Look, look, he's coming.' Madhu turned her head and saw a procession approaching.

Anand whispered to Vijay, 'And I thought the days of the maharajas were over.'

So they were, officially, but Kashi Naresh, or the Lord of Benares, was accompanied by all the panoply of royalty. His coach, pulled by two grey horses, was flanked by mounted troopers carrying lances, and he was shaded by a pink silk parasol embroidered with gold. He wore the small white cap of a nobleman, and there was a string of gems around his neck. Behind the buggy came his son and guests on five elephants, those most royal of animals. The prince wore pearls around his neck. A great shout of 'Hara, Hara Mahadev!', the greeting for Shiva, went up. The faithful believe that the Maharaja represents Shiva at the Ram Lila.

When the coach stopped the monkeys hurriedly pulled on their masks and the Vyas turned to face the audience. He stretched out his arm and shouted, '*Chup raho! Savdhan!* Be quiet! Beware!' There was instant silence. Then Ram stood up and announced to his army in a clear, sing-song voice designed to carry to the very back of the crowd, without benefit of microphone or any other new-fangled aid, 'Now we must make ready to leave.' The Vyas prodded the monkey soldiers in the back and in a stage whisper ordered, 'Salute him, all of you!' The boys lifted their metal monkey masks from their mouths and roared an enthusiastic salute. Then the Ramayanis began to sing the words of the epic to the clashing of small cymbals. They were led by an old priest with a refined face, a neat white moustache and the red-and-white V of Vishnu on his forehead.

The Maharaja climbed out of his coach and mounted an elephant. Hanuman picked up Ram and put him on his shoulders. The other leading members of Ram's entourage followed the Monkey God, and everyone, including the audience, moved from the hill symbolizing the monkey kingdom towards the temple symbolizing Rameshwaram. It was the port on the southern tip of India from where the monkeys were to build a bridge across the narrow straits to the island of Lanka, so that the army could cross to rescue Ram's wife Sita.

As they walked to the small temple the audience talked excitedly among themselves. An old man warned Tripti, 'Be careful of the Prince's elephant: it's said to be unpredictable.'

A village woman said to Madhu, 'I wouldn't miss this Ram Lila for anything. It's a long way from my village. I bring all my children in a tractor trailer. We get so jolted about that my bones ache by the time I get here, but I have to come for at least four days each year.' As they approached

Rameshwaram the village woman pointed out a 1927 Mercedes parked by the temple and said, 'That's the Maharaja's car.'

The Maharaja remained on his elephant to watch the next stages of the epic unfold. The demon king Ravan made an impressive entrance, dressed in white and red, a sword held upright in his hand. Five blue wooden arms with silver hands were strapped to each shoulder. His face was covered by a wide, black cloth mask embroidered with gold. Five loops of gold, representing five tongues, hung from the bottom of the mask. The mouth was covered by a ferocious black moustache. This year the man playing Ravan had some difficulty with this cumbersome contraption. Madhu heard a saffron-clad holy man say to Vijay, 'It's not surprising he's got problems. He's not the real Ravan. The man who normally plays this part has had to go away to attend his uncle's funeral.'

The action was interrupted to allow the Maharaja to perform his evening *puja*.

'We'll treat you,' Vijay told the two girls. 'What would you like? Tea, sweets or *paan*?'

The four students made their way past handcarts heaped with mounds of green betel leaves to one of the many tea stalls which had sprung up on the edge of the open field where this part of the Ramayan was performed.

'Four special teas,' Anand ordered. Vijay paid and then handed steaming clay cups of tea to the girls.

'So you'll be leaders from Benares, then?' asked an elderly farmer. 'And I suppose these girls will be from the university.'

Anand laughed. He and Vijay were both in *kurta*-pyjamas, the uniform of political leaders. 'It's strange but true,' he said. 'You can tell immediately we're from the town just by looking at us. Perhaps if we wore *dhotis* it wouldn't be so obvious. And, yes, you're right, our companions are from BHU.'

'Then maybe you don't know that much about this Ram Lila,' the farmer went on, insisting on relating the miracles performed by Tulsi Das, who had written this version of the

Ramayan sitting on the banks of the Ganges. Apparently the poet had himself been rescued by an army of monkeys when he was imprisoned by the emperor for refusing to reveal the source of his miraculous powers.

Thousands of people had gathered to watch the final scene for that evening, the building of the bridge to Lanka. Madhu had never been in such a big crowd before, but she was not frightened. This was a happy crowd.

'I really like this,' she told Tripti. 'It makes me feel I'm back in my village watching the Ram Lila there. I know this is much grander but it's still like you're really part of the whole thing. And Ram and Lakshman are so good. You feel so much love for them.'

A tired Ram sat on the ground, took off his crown and loosened the marigold garlands around his neck. The police were having some difficulty in keeping a way open through the crowd for Ram to make his final entrance, but for once they refrained from using their *lathis* and contented themselves with shouting, 'Make way! God is going to run through here!'

The crowd was now gathered around a small, dried-up pond which represented the straits between India and Lanka. The Ramayanis resumed their singing, the yellow light from the sweet-smelling flames of their linseed-oil torches reflecting on their faces and making their bright-coloured turbans glow.

The Vyas ordered the monkey army to bridge the straits. They scampered off into the darkness and raced back carrying branches and flimsy imitation rocks made of painted paper stretched over bamboo frames. Unfortunately the boys had run the wrong way round the temple. The Vyas headed them off and sent them round the back of the temple. They returned roaring as they ran past the four students and tossed their branches towards the pond. Some missed their target. One landed on Anand who laughed and stood up to throw it into the pond. The bridge was apparently built, but then suddenly two lost monkeys charged out from behind the temple. Much to the delight of the crowd, they ran past the

the pond and had to be brought back to add their little contributions to the bridge.

The audience rose to its feet to witness the final scene of the evening's performance. Madhu said, 'This is the most beautiful part of all.'

The gods and their faithful servants were standing in a tableau on the temple plinth, being showered with flower petals, while the Vyas worshipped them, a lamp in one hand and a bell in the other. Bells also rang from inside the temple, and from behind her Madhu heard the trumpeting of a conch. It was past ten o'clock. There was no electricity – the Maharaja wouldn't allow that – so the scene was illuminated by hissing Petromax lights. Suddenly a firework flared up. The gods were bathed in bright pink light, and a deafening cry came from the crowd, '*Bol! Raja Ram Chander ki Jai!* Say, victory to Raja Ram Chander!'

Madhu was transfixed, but Tripti pulled her by the sleeve and said, 'Let's get away quickly before the crowd starts moving.'

The four students picked their way through the throng of worshippers and started to walk back towards the Ganges. Tripti and her boyfriend went ahead. Madhu saw that they were holding hands and talking animatedly, but she did not know what to say to Anand, who was walking beside her. She was worried that he too might try to hold her hand. But the young student made no move towards her and no effort to break the silence.

Eventually Madhu said shyly, 'I thought that was absolutely beautiful. I am very grateful to you for accompanying me.'

Anand replied, 'I must say I was impressed. As a socialist I don't believe in Maharajas, but I must say this Ram Lila is very moving. I suppose it means even more to you because you believe in Ram.'

Madhu had never talked to a boy before about religion or politics (in fact, she had always tried to avoid talking to boys about anything), but she found herself being drawn into this conversation. 'I believe in Ram. After all, it was this epic which kept Hinduism alive when the Muslims ruled over us.'

'Yes, that's true. You probably don't know, but India's greatest socialist leader, Ram Manohar Lohia, loved the Ram Lila because to him it symbolized something which was essentially Indian. He fought against Nehru because he thought he was a brown Englishman. One of those people who think it's superior to have been educated abroad. One of those people who in their heart of hearts still think Englishmen and Americans are better than Indians.'

The couple continued to talk about politics and religion until they reached the banks of the Ganges. They crossed the river on a crowded ferry and crammed into a scooter rickshaw on the other side. The boys got out just before they reached Madhu's aunt's house because she would be waiting up. Madhu asked, 'Where will you go?'

Anand laughed. 'Oh, with boys it's not like it is with girls at the university. We are not locked in like you are. We have ways of getting in at all times of the night.'

Madhu and Tripti were sitting together on a wooden bench in the mess of New Hostel. The fingers of Tripti's right hand were mashing a watery *daal* and an even more watery vegetable curry into the rice in the middle of her *thali*. She said angrily, 'This is meant to be mixed vegetables but as usual it's nothing but potato. Wait until the student elections really start – I will make mashed potato out of the catering contractor. I'll see that he gets thrown out.'

Madhu, who had been no more successful in finding anything but potato in her curry, said, 'Of course, Vijay is the socialist candidate for president of the Students' Union. I suppose you'll be campaigning for him.'

'Yes, and I've got news for you. You must remember Anand, I'm sure. You obviously liked him because afterwards you said you had been surprised how easy it had been to talk to him. Well he's the agent for Vijay, and he wants you to help in the campaign.'

Madhu was shocked. 'No, Tripti, I can't do that. It's all very well for you girls who have been educated in English medium – you can do that sort of thing. You know very well that we *Hindi-walis* don't do that.'

'What are you talking about? What have elections got to do with language? Anyhow in BHU the whole campaign is in Hindi. No one would win in a place like this if they just spoke in English.'

'You know that's not what I mean,' replied Madhu firmly. 'I am proud that you are my friend, but I'm still a *Hindi-wali*. I'm not smart like you. We are not taught in Hindi-medium schools to be confident and aggressive like you are. We are quite happy to be quiet. Anyhow, my father would be very upset if he heard that I had got involved in politics. It would also be considered shameful in the village, and that would make his position very difficult.'

Because she was unsure of herself Madhu had come to depend increasingly on Tripti, and eventually she did allow herself to be persuaded to meet the two boys again, although she still insisted she would not take part in the campaign.

They met the next afternoon by the hostel gates and sat in the shade of an old banyan tree by a small shrine built against its gnarled trunk. There were other boys and girls talking to each other, some leaning on cycles or scooters, some walking up and down the path. Elections brought a remarkable change in the atmosphere at BHU. Much that caused malicious rumour in normal times passed for election campaigning. Vijay was explaining to Madhu that she would not have to canvass outside the girls' hostels.

'Personal canvassing counts for a lot,' he said. 'That's what we would want you to do. You can do it with Tripti. It's always much better when two go together.'

Seeing that she was still far from persuaded, Anand said, 'You seemed to be very interested in our party and in our leader Ram Manohar Lohia once. We want to show those Hindu fundamentalists in the BJP that to be a good Indian you don't need to hate Muslims and go around the place pulling down their mosques. Surely you, with your feelings for Ram and Ram Lilas, want to do that?'

Madhu looked down at the ground and said, 'I did get a book out of the library about Lohia after meeting you, and I liked many of his ideas, but I really can't go putting myself forward in the way you want. I really am sorry. But if Tripti thinks it will be of some help, I will go with her, although I won't try to persuade anyone.'

Tripti embraced her friend and laughed, saying, 'I knew you would. Don't worry about what to do – just having you with me will be such a help. It will especially impress your *Hindi-walis.*'

Madhu found, much to her surprise, that she enjoyed going around with Tripti and meeting other students. Very few of them knew much about politics or even read a newspaper regularly, but those who had been educated through Hindi were interested to hear about Lohia who had been such a great champion of that language and deadly opposed to English. In spite of her original reservations it wasn't long before Madhu was taking the lead in preaching the Lohia gospel. Obviously it came much better from her than from Tripti. Madhu also found herself looking forward to the daily meetings the two girls held with Anand under the banyan tree. She saw him looking at her with new interest as Tripti praised her powers of persuasion. She realized that she wanted to please Anand.

Madhu and Tripti managed to persuade two hundred girls to join them for the last socialist election rally. They came out of the gates of the Women's College and marched up the broad avenue lined with mango trees towards the Students' Union. Tripti led the procession, shouting, *'Chatra neta kaisa ho, kaisa ho?'* Madhu marched at the side of the procession making sure the girls responded, *'Vijay Sharma jaisa ho, jaisa ho!'* At the Students' Union they turned around and marched back past the university buildings, all painted cream outlined in ochre, to the main gate. As they marched they converged with other processions.

Lanka, the bazaar outside the main gate where the rally was to be held, was plastered with election posters. Banners stretched across the small roundabout dominated by the statue of the founder of the university. If spending money was going to win this election, the Hindu party, the BJP, would be the clear winner. Their saffron posters and banners far outnumbered all the other parties'. But a good crowd had gathered to hear the socialists.

Anand was one of the speakers who addressed the crowd before the candidate himself. He wasn't a man who automatically commanded attention – he was too small for that – but he was a very good speaker who had a knack of involving his audiences. He wore the uniform of a student politician in Benares – *khadi kurta* and pyjama trousers – but his hair was neatly cut, and he was clean-shaven. That gave him an appealing air of innocence compared with most other student leaders, who emphasized their manhood by sporting five-day-old stubble or by growing a moustache.

Anand shouted in a voice hoarse from too much speaking, 'Do you want the Students' Union to belong to the government, to the politicians or to us?'

The students roared, 'To us! To us!'

'Who has provided all the motorcycles, scooters and even jeeps the Congress students have been driving around the campus?'

Back came the reply: 'The government! The government!'

'Where do all these saffron posters and banners you see around you come from?'

'The BJP party funds!'

'Have you seen us in cars or scooters?'

'No, on bicycles!'

'That's because the socialists belong to the people, and in this election you are the people!'

A young man shot up from the audience and started shouting, 'Socialist Party Zindabad, Zindabad, Zindabad!'

As the crowd took up the refrain, Madhu felt a strange sense not so much of pride as of belonging. After all, she was a part of Anand's team. She was close to him. She had never consciously felt lonely during her life, except during the first weeks at BHU before Tripti befriended her, but she had felt apart, on her own.

Much to the surprise of the political pundits among the students who had predicted a close-run race between the BJP and the Congress, Vijay was elected president of the BHU Students' Union. This was in part because the votes of the two dominant higher castes, the Brahmins and the Thakurs, had split between BJP and Congress and partly because many students voted for the candidate, not the party. They had not been impressed by the wanton extravagance of the two main parties' candidates, nor had they been cowed by the thinly veiled threats of their henchmen. They had been impressed by the simplicity of the socialists' campaign and the sincerity of their candidate.

During the weeks that followed the elections the leading members of the socialist party met regularly to discuss the students' grievances. Most of the grievances were mundane – bad food, overcrowded hostels, the price of books, lazy lecturers and many others. Tripti took Madhu with her to these meetings. Drinking coffee afterwards she often found herself talking to Anand. One day he said to her, 'I must see you on your own just for a short time. Can we meet at the Ease Sweet House in Lanka at lunchtime tomorrow?'

Madhu found herself agreeing before she had time to wonder whether she was being wise.

Coming out of the bright sunshine into the darkness of the Ease Sweet House, Madhu panicked. She couldn't see Anand anywhere. She had never been in a place like this on her own before. She couldn't wait for him in the restaurant because boys would mistake her for one of those fast girls. She turned to go but as she opened the door she felt a tap on her shoulder and Anand said, 'Where are you going?' Madhu turned sharply and, out of a sense of relief, took both his hands in hers. They walked back to the corner where Anand had been sitting.

After the waiter had brought them two Pepsis and a plate of *pakoras* Anand said, 'I must talk to you about Vijay and Tripti.'

'Why?'

'Well, you know that he's her boyfriend.'

'Yes, but what has that got to do with us?'

'Do you mind that she is his girlfriend? Do you see anything wrong in it?'

'It's all right for her. She's had that sort of education. She comes from that sort of family. She can cope with it.'

'But if it's not wrong for them, why should it be wrong for us?'

Madhu rubbed her hands together nervously, looked away from Anand and said, 'Because I am not that sort of girl, and I don't come from that sort of background.'

That night was stiflingly hot. The girls had, as usual, locked their door, so their room held the heat like an oven. The fan, which might have made the heat just bearable, was not working because of an electricity cut. Madhu was lying on her back, thinking about her conversation with Anand. Tripti sighed impatiently, sat bolt upright and said, 'My sheet is bathed in sweat. I can't lie here any longer. Let's get out of this furnace and go up to the roof. At least we will get a little breeze there.'

There were several other groups of girls on the roof talking among themselves. Madhu and Tripti went to one corner and sat on the parapet. Madhu looked down at the courtyard below and said, 'Tripti, do you mind if I ask you something about Vijay?'

She spoke so quietly that Tripti barely heard her. 'What did you say about Vijay?' she asked.

Madhu asked, 'What exactly does it mean that Vijay is your boyfriend?'

'Well, it means that we are in love. That we see each other as often as possible and that we go as far as possible.'

'You mean you kiss each other?'

'Yes, of course, on the very rare occasions when there is no one around to see us. What do you think we do? Just hold hands and stare stupidly into each other's eyes? Really, Madhu, sometimes your naïveté is just too much.'

Tripti tossed her head and turned her back. Madhu got up and walked slowly away. Tripti called out. 'Where are you going? Come back. I'm sorry. I wasn't really angry.'

When Madhu returned Tripti asked, 'Why do you want to know about Vijay and me? This is the first time you have ever asked that sort of question. Do tell me. I won't be annoyed, I promise.'

Madhu replied in little more than a whisper, 'Anand has asked me to be his girlfriend.'

Tripti leapt up, hugged Madhu and yelped, 'Madhu, that's great! It's really wonderful!'

Madhu said anxiously, 'Shush! Do be quiet. Everyone will hear you. I don't want a whole lot of stories about me spread around the university.'

Tripti sat down again, close to Madhu, to hear the story of the meeting in Lanka that morning. Needless to say, she encouraged her friend to go ahead. 'You don't have to do anything unless you want to. Just agree to see him as often as you can. After all, you do like him, don't you?'

'Yes, I like him. It worries me. I like him too much. I do find myself thinking about him more than I should, and if I agree to see him, that will get worse.'

'You mean *better*, don't you? At least I do, and I ought to know.'

'I mean worse because it will become harder and harder to forget him, and, of course, I will have to do that when I leave after my exams. I must go back to my village, and then I'll get married. Supposing I'm still thinking about Anand after my wedding – how will I learn to love my husband? And my father says that is the only way to live a happy life.'

The discussion continued until it started to get light, but in the end Tripti once again overcame Madhu's reluctance and persuaded her to see Anand from time to time.

By the time the exams came Madhu was in love. She couldn't get Anand out of her mind. She recognized that, but she also recognized the futility of her love. In a few days she would be back in her village, and there would certainly be no place for Anand in her life after that. But Tripti did not agree. She was determined to persuade her friend that there was a way out.

On the last Sunday morning that the two girls were to spend in the hostel there was a more than reasonable *pulao*, cottage-cheese balls, curd and salad on the menu for lunch in the hostel mess. There was a sweet too. But Madhu did not enjoy this remarkably good meal, and she couldn't understand why Tripti was so excited. After all, she too was going home and would be leaving Vijay for good because her smart parents certainly wouldn't let her see a student leader who, they would think, was far below their social class. His indifferent English alone would bar him from the sort of Calcutta parties that Tripti had described.

As they left the mess Madhu said, 'Tripti, I'm surprised. I really thought that you would be sad, like I am. You know that this is the end of your love affair, don't you?'

Tripti laughed and said, 'No. I have decided that my life is my own. I don't care what my parents or anyone else says. To hell with them and their petty-minded snobbery. I'm getting married.'

Madhu gasped. Tripti pulled her by the hand and started running towards the gate, saying, 'Come on. We'll go for a walk on the *ghats* and I'll tell you everything.'

The two girls climbed out of a cycle rickshaw and followed a sign pointing down a narrow alley which read 'Electric crematorium: 50 rupees per dead body'. After passing the ugly new crematorium they came out on to Harishchandra Ghat. A group of men were arguing angrily with the Doms, who supervise traditional cremations, about the price of performing their relative's last rites. Their women squatted on the ground, watching indifferently, as though they had nothing to do with the row. The body, draped with a gaudy shroud and covered with marigold garlands, lay neglected on a stretcher at the bottom of the steps lapped by the Ganges. Nearby two Doms were poking a funeral pyre with bamboo sticks.

Tripti caught Madhu's arm and pulled her away, saying, 'Come away. It was very stupid of me to bring you here when I want to talk about beginning our lives, not ending them. Let's walk towards Assi. There are no cremations on the *ghats* in that direction.'

As they walked along the banks of the Ganges, Tripti explained that she and Vijay had decided to go to Lucknow, the state capital, to have a court marriage. They didn't want to go to the courts in Benares because Vijay had too many relatives there. Then she would just tell her parents it was too late for them to do anything. She might not even go back to Calcutta. She might just write to them. Vijay had been promised a career in the socialist party, and that would mean an exciting life. He had decided to stay on in Benares and was confident that, with his political clout, he could find her a job too. Her task now was to persuade Madhu to do the same.

'Do you really think that you can just go home and forget Anand?' she asked.

'No, of course I don't. I love him. But you just don't understand what happens in a community like ours. If a couple even have an affair, they are summoned before the whole village. The Pradhan abuses them and tells them that they have disgraced the village and they'd better separate or it'll be the worse for them. If there is a love marriage, it's considered no better than an affair. They won't let it last. I couldn't do that to my father, and that's why I have to end this now and hope it stays a secret between us.'

'But, Madhu, you've changed. I have seen you changing. You can't go back and submit to living the life of a meek cow. You will never learn to love your husband after Anand, whatever your father says about happy arranged marriages. Anyhow I don't believe in that. Your husband will probably treat you like a chattel after a year or so. He'll use you to breed children and look after his house.'

Madhu was far too infatuated with Anand to imagine she could forget him, but nor could she imagine breaking her father's heart and bringing disgrace on him in his old age. Tripti had an answer to that. She knew that Madhu was worried about what would happen to her father after she married and went to live with her husband's family. She said, 'You know if you have a traditional marriage your mother-in-law won't allow your father to live in her house. She won't even let you visit him very often because she'll say you belong to her family now. If you marry Anand you can come and live in Benares near us, and bring your father with you. Anand has shown that he can get on in politics and you can find a job as a teacher.'

It took more than that walk on the *ghats* to persuade Madhu, but once she had seen there was a way out, a way out which meant keeping Anand and still looking after her father, returning to the village did not seem quite so inevitable. She realized that she had changed. She would, she had to admit, find it very hard to live under all the constraints of village life now. She did acknowledge that by following Tripti she had lived a far more adventurous life than she could ever have dreamed of. Tripti would stay with her if she took this next step. She had promised that they would all four go to Lucknow to get married together and had even suggested that they could all live in Benares.

The final decision was never quite taken. Even when the

four boarded the express to Lucknow, Madhu thought to herself, 'I can always catch a train back home when I get there. Even if we do get married, I can run away, and somehow my father will find a way to put it all right.' She still wanted to go home, but she also wanted to stay with Anand. She was drifting, unable to make up her mind, carried along by events. It was Tripti who made sure she kept drifting in Anand's direction.

When the four students came out of Lucknow station they stood hesitantly, surrounded by an ever-growing crowd of touts offering hotel rooms. Then Vijay saw an eight-storied building across the road with a large blue-and-white sign on top – Varma Hotel. Pushing his way through the touts, he said, 'We are going to Varma's. You people get lost.'

Madhu's spirits sank as they entered the narrow alley leading to the hotel entrance. Two policemen sprawling on benches outside one of the makeshift cafés which lined both sides of the alley stared at them insolently. They didn't need to speak – their looks said it all. From another café a young man dressed in a tight-fitting, grubby suit shouted out, 'Hi, sexy! Where are you going?'

There was worse to come inside the hotel. There were pictures of Hindu gods above the reception desk. A red bulb gave an air of seedy sanctity to a ferocious Durga riding her tiger. There was a poster of two hands holding roses under which was written 'Welcome'. But there was also a list of rules for guests which was anything but welcoming. One of the rules was 'Two days' rent in advance'. A toothless, surly clerk grunted, 'Eighty rupees with a common bathroom. One hundred and ten with your own.' Vijay asked for one with a bathroom for the boys and one for the girls and paid for both. The clerk said, 'You don't have to make a fool out of me. We don't care who you sleep with here. We wouldn't do much business if we did.' Then, after counting the advance twice, he handed them two keys.

The rooms were built around a well, not unlike a prison.

The walls were grimy, and the bathrooms proved to be far from clean. The filth of the place made Madhu even more depressed. An arranged marriage might not be romantic, but at least it wasn't sordid. This whole episode suddenly seemed to her just that. But still she did not resist.

That night the two girls slept in the same room, and the next morning all four got up in time for the opening of the courts. Vijay had found out that court marriages could be completed in one day, but lawyers had a propensity for dragging matters out.

The lawyers sat outside the court, some under open-sided shelters with asbestos sheets as roofing, some under the sun. There seemed to be advocates everywhere, with their starched tabs and black coats. Apparently it did not matter what colour shirt a lawyer wore under his tabs, or what was the colour of his trousers, or indeed of his shoes. All that mattered was those tabs and that black coat. Lines of typists clanked away on ancient Remingtons, a café and a *paan* stall both did brisk business. There were shops selling the stamp paper without which nothing can be concluded in an Indian court. There was even a small temple under a tree.

Half the state of Uttar Pradesh seemed to be litigants, but a foxy-faced young lawyer with a neat black moustache and oily black hair smarmed over his forehead picked out the students from among the crowds milling around the advocates' desks. He came over and said, 'You will be wanting to be married.' Vijay was too surprised to ask how they had been spotted, so he meekly followed the man to a table where sat the lawyer's senior, his clerk and his *munshi*. The lawyer asked Vijay his name and then to whom he wanted to get married. A document was drawn up stating, 'I Vijay Sharma am marrying Tripti Banerjee.' It went on through a long rigmarole which neither the bride nor the groom had any hope of understanding.

When the forms for both couples were completed (of course on stamp paper) the junior took them to the 'Ten-minute

Photographer'. This was instant development by hand. After taking each picture the photographer put his hand inside a black cloth sleeve attached to the cumbersome camera, fiddled around inside like some magician, pulled out a small square of photographic paper and dropped it into a bucket of water. When the photos had dried the lawyer took the students back to his senior. From there they had to go to a notary public's stall. He certified their signatures. After that, for some reason, they were taken to the land registry, not to a marriage officer, to file the details of the marriages. Then came the final reckoning. The lawyer eventually settled for four hundred rupees each marriage, with, of course, stamp paper extra.

The two couples had breached almost every canon of matrimonial law. They had declared their intention to marry, not the fact that they had married. They had been married in one day when time should have been allowed for objections to be raised. They had registered the wedding with the Land Registrar because he was permitted to accept any document. Nevertheless the students were now married in their own eyes, even if not in the eyes of the law.

The four celebrated with a vegetarian dinner at Chowdhury's restaurant in the main street of Lucknow, and then the girls insisted on a late show at the Capitol Cinema. It was as though they were delaying the final encounter, nervous of its outcome.

When they eventually returned to the hotel the girls separated and locked themselves into their rooms with the men they believed were now their husbands. Madhu sat beside Anand on the edge of the bed. He looked down at the grey sheets and the torn pillow cases. 'This is hardly a romantic place to make love for the first time, is it? The windows are broken, the bathroom smells and the walls are so thin I can hear the man next door snoring.' Madhu did not reply. 'We are going to make love, aren't we?' Anand too was very nervous and this made him abrupt. 'If you're feeling shy, go and get undressed in the bathroom.'

Madhu came out of the bathroom, wearing her petticoat and sari blouse, to find Anand lying on his back in his underpants and vest. She lay down on her back and stared at the fan blades slowly turning above her. Anand took her hand, squeezed it. Madhu didn't move. So Anand leant over and started to undo the hooks of her blouse. Madhu moved away and sat up. 'Put off the lights first,' she said.

Anand had never seen a naked woman. Although for months now he had been imagining what Madhu's body and the breasts which swelled under her blouse would look like, he restrained himself and switched off the lights. He could hear voices from the neighbouring rooms and, beyond them, the roar of trucks driving in convoy down the main road. He waited a few seconds and then pulled Madhu down and lay on top of her. He kissed her face and her neck, and then put his mouth on hers. Madhu kept her lips tightly closed. She somehow could not bring herself to allow his tongue to enter her mouth. She was hot, oppressed by his weight and the dampness of his sweat, and frightened. Anand rolled off her, lay on his back and asked angrily, 'Why don't you let me kiss you?'

'I will, I'm sure I will, but don't hurry me.'

Anand leant over her and started to kiss her mouth again, but her lips did not open. She felt him trying to lift her petticoat but she pushed his hand away. She kept her legs closed. Then Anand lay on top of her and she could feel the hardness of his erection through his underpants as he rubbed himself against her. His embrace became tighter and tighter until Madhu felt she would suffocate. Then suddenly his whole body stiffened, he groaned and rolled to one side, turning his back to her. After some time Madhu realized he was asleep. She turned on her side and began to sob.

The next morning Tripti and Vijay went back to Benares. Vijay had arranged a room for them in the house of a socialist member of the State Assembly. Madhu knew that she could not respond to Anand, or even accept the marriage, until she had gone back to her village and persuaded her father that it was better to acknowledge what had happened, even though she knew how difficult that would be. But when she suggested that they should go to her village Anand exploded. 'I'm not going to be dragged back to your village. I know what you want. You want me to live the life of some country yokel. I have got a good career ahead of me in politics, and I don't intend to give it up for anyone, least of all some man who could never get beyond being a village schoolmaster.'

Eventually they agreed to spend one more night in their hotel and decide what to do the next morning. That night was no more successful than the first, but the next morning Madhu was surprised to find Anand willing to catch a train back to her village. They walked across the street to the station where they found that an express making its weekly run across northern India from Jammu, the winter capital of Kashmir, to Guwahati in Assam was due in Lucknow that afternoon and would get them to Deoria that night. They had to travel in the unreserved second-class section of the train, which was, as usual, grossly overcrowded. Anand forced his way through the narrow door, pushing past the passengers who were trying to get out of the train at Lucknow, and managed to grab two places which had just been vacated. It was a hot and embarrassing journey, with inquisitive passengers wanting to know why a leader and his wife were not travelling at least second-class, air-conditioned. At Gorakhpur Anand stood up and said impatiently, 'I can't bear this any longer. I have got to stretch my legs. You stay here and keep the seats.'

The twenty-minute halt seemed interminable to Madhu, confined in the crowded compartment, trying to protect Anand's seat and fend off the vendors of tea, stale snacks and magazines who attempted to force their wares on her through the open window. The beggars were even more persistent. Eventually she heard the guard's shrill whistle, a long blast from the engine's horn and the train moved slowly out.

There was no sign of Anand, but she thought he must be pushing his way towards the compartment. The train gathered speed but there was still no Anand. She hoped that perhaps he had been at the wrong end of the platform when the train had left and had jumped into another compartment. She couldn't get up and look for him without losing the seats; she couldn't pull the communication cord because that would mean facing the guard. She would just have to catch up with him at Deoria. But when she got out at that station there was no sign of him. She watched the crowd on the platform thin as the train pulled out again, but there was no sign of Anand. She picked up the small suitcase, which was all she had travelled with, and walked from one end of the platform to the other, but he was nowhere to be seen. Her last hope was the station superintendent. She went to his office and asked whether anyone had been inquiring about her. He was a kindly old man, but he couldn't help beyond suggesting that she got a jeep taxi or a scooter rickshaw to her village as soon as possible because it was getting late, and nowadays there were highway robbers everywhere.

Fortunately she found a jeep going in her direction which was still waiting for one more passenger to fill it up. She got down at the cart track which led from the main road to her village and walked the last half-mile home.

She had decided that she wouldn't say anything until she heard from Anand, or he turned up in the village, but as the weeks went by her father became more and more insistent. He had identified a suitable husband for her, the son of another schoolmaster who, like Madhu, had graduated in Education and had managed to get himself a job near his home. The caste was right and so was the horoscope, the dowry was reasonable and the family were said to be good people. All was as it should be except that Madhu would insist on delaying. If he didn't land the fish soon, it would jump out of his net, but what could he do?

The weeks turned into months and nothing was heard of Anand. Madhu didn't write to Tripti to find out what had happened – she was too ashamed. Eventually she started to think it might be possible to put the whole incident behind her. Those two nights in Lucknow hadn't deepened her love for Anand, and now that she was getting used to village life again she was surprised how little she thought of him. She had found out from a lawyer that the kind of marriage certificate she had was not worth the paper it was written on. She wasn't pregnant – in fact, she was still a virgin – so that was no barrier to marriage. The only difficulty was those two nights. If her in-laws ever learned about them, they would throw her out of the house. But why should they? If she had been recognized by anyone in Lucknow, it would have been all around her village by now. So Madhu eventually agreed to the arranged marriage, and it was, as her father had always told her it would be, a happy arrangement. Her husband allowed his beautiful wife to adjust gradually to married life. His mother treated her like a daughter, not a daughter-in-law. She learned to enjoy her husband's embraces and, to the delight of all his family, produced a son. Madhu may not have been deeply in love but she was contented.

Then one day she received a postcard from her father asking her to come and see him urgently. Her mother-in-law was generous in the visits she allowed Madhu to pay to her father, so she had no difficulty in getting away. When she reached the village she found her father sitting with other members of staff outside the school building. Most unusually his chin was covered with grey stubble, and his *kurta* was creased. He greeted her and then asked a colleague to teach his next class so that he could take her home. This too was most unusual. Dwivedji was generally most punctilious about his teaching.

As they walked home Madhu asked her father what the matter was, but he refused to be drawn. There were some chairs in the yard, but her father insisted that they went into the hot, stuffy house. Then, without even offering her a glass of water, he said, 'The day before yesterday an unpleasant young man came here to ask after you. He said he was your friend at BHU and needed your help urgently. What sort of friends did you have? I didn't like the look of that young man at all. Anyhow, why should a man be your friend? I can't believe that you had friends who were men. He left this letter for you.'

Madhu didn't reply. She opened the letter and read, 'My dear wife, I have come to hear that you have made another home. You should have waited for me. It's against the law to have two husbands. I have been in trouble and need money. Unless you meet me in Benares with your wedding jewellery, I will have to tell your father about us. Please write to me at the above address and tell me when we can meet. I am sure you don't want me to come to your new home. Yours affectionately, Anand.'

Madhu couldn't look her father in the eye. She stuffed the letter into the blouse of her *sari* and stared at the ground.

Her father said gently, 'Daughter, there is something wrong. Please tell me. I will try to understand and help. I cannot believe you would do anything bad, but there is some trouble and you must let me know.'

But Madhu couldn't tell her father. It would break his heart, disgrace him in the village and end her marriage. She had to sort this out herself. She bent down to touch his feet and said, 'Father, I can't explain now. All I can say is that this man is a liar and a thief, and no friend of mine. He has a habit of spreading ugly rumours, but I will not let him harm you. I must go back to my in-laws now.'

Then she left without giving her father a chance to say any more.

The only person who could help was Tripti. Madhu had not been in contact with her, but she remembered the address of the friend she and Vijay had gone to stay with. Hoping that he would forward a letter, she wrote explaining everything. Back came a letter full of affection and sympathy. According to Tripti, Anand hadn't been seen at the university and had been avoiding Vijay ever since the marriage. Now she understood why and was confident that he could be 'fixed'. All Madhu needed to do was to write to Anand agreeing to meet him by the Electric Crematorium on a certain date and at a certain time and to let her know well in advance when the appointment was.

On the day that Madhu had agreed to meet him Anand waited for her, leaning against one of the concrete stilts on which the crematorium stood. He noticed one or two police-men standing around, but that didn't worry him. It was normal in Benares. He was confident that Madhu was far too naïve to trick him. She would come and the jewellery would be his. Suddenly he saw Vijay walking up from the *ghats*. That was a little inconvenient. He turned away, but Vijay had seen him and hurried over.

'Anand, where did you disappear?' he asked. 'I haven't seen you since we were married. How's Madhu?'

'Oh, she's fine. We've had trouble with finding jobs and we didn't want to bother you. It was a matter of pride too. I hear that you are doing well in politics.'

'You've come to meet Madhu now, haven't you? I'll wait. I would really like to see her again.'

Anand's face fell. 'How did you know I'm meeting her?'

'Because she told me, you *saale* blackmailer.' With this, Vijay shouted to the police, 'This is him! Get him!'

Anand reacted faster than the constables, sprinting over the dried mud-covered steps of the *ghats*, through a knot of young boys playing marbles, and pushing past a wedding party come to garland the Ganges. The steps were uneven and steep. He tripped and fell heavily, giving the policemen time to catch up. They grabbed him just as he was coming to his feet and dragged him to a jeep parked near by. When they reached the police station he was taken straight to a cell and locked behind iron bars.

The officer in charge of the police station told Anand, 'Don't worry. We know how to take care of *badmashes* like him. This arrest may not be strictly legal, but we are always glad to oblige a leader.'

'How long will you keep him?'

'Oh, we don't need to keep him very long. But we will show him something. He won't come to give you trouble again.'

The police officer was as good as his word.

THE *GOONDAS* OF GOPINAGAR

On returning from his office Vishnu Swarup Saxena, Chief
Engineer of the Gopinagar Division of Indian Railways, told
his wife they could not have their usual tea and *samosas*
together because he had some important business to discuss.
As he sat awaiting sentence in the sitting room of his spacious
bungalow in the Railway Officers' Colony, he thought, 'I
can't for the life of me understand how I allowed myself to
be out-manoeuvred at the meeting this morning. After all
these years of experience I've been trapped at last. I had
promised that contract to Makhan Lal Gupta's gang. Now I
can't deliver, and everyone knows what that means: *khatam* –
finish.'

The disaster had taken place in the red-brick office of the
Divisional Headquarters, whose grandeur still reflected the
days when the British regarded railway architecture as a
symbol of the might of the Raj. Gopinagar had been a sleepy
division, but it had been shaken out of its lethargy by the
government's announcement that the line to Varanasi was to
be converted to broad-gauge so that through trains could run
from Delhi to the holy city along both banks of the Ganges.
That had produced lots of juicy contracts and tempting
bribes for railway officials. There were more than a hundred
kilometres of track to be relaid, bridges to be widened, stations
to be rebuilt, sidings to be lengthened and signals to be
repositioned.

Saxena had started off that morning's meeting by pro-
posing that, as usual, a lucrative contract to provide earth for

embankments should go to Gupta. He was surprised and not at all pleased when his junior colleague said, 'I don't see why we should give all these contracts to Gupta's nominees. This broad gauging has changed things in Gopinagar. Other Mafia men were prepared to let Gupta corner the railway market, but now they are not. I have been approached by one of Jang Bahadur's men and warned that he too wants a share of the railway work. What's more, he is offering us a bigger cut than Guptaji has ever given us.'

Saxena was surprised that his junior should have the temerity to contradict him and said angrily, 'I'm the one who decides the contracts. You are lucky that I give you a share of the payoff – and don't forget that I was dealing with these contracts when you were a child. Don't you remember what happened to the last railway officer who annoyed Gupta. He got a bullet through the head.'

The other two railway officials at the meeting were accountants. One of them, a thin man with venality written all over his mean narrow face, said, 'Saxena Sahib, there's no need to get upset. What has been said is true. We must also consider the alternatives. If one offer is better than the other from our point of view, why should we necessarily reject it?'

'And get our heads shot off too?'

'We must not be too dramatic. After all, even a man like Gupta is going to be reluctant to kill another railway officer so soon. Then there is another problem. I come from the headquarters in Delhi, and people there are beginning to talk about the undue influence of Gupta. We don't want the press to get hold of that story, do we?'

Saxena saw this for the threat it was – the threat to leak damaging stories to the national press. After that there might even be questions in Parliament. He would not be dismissed, but at the very least he would be transferred to a far less lucrative post, and he might even be suspended.

The junior engineer spoke up again. 'Talking of being shot through the head, I'm the one who has been threatened by

Jang Bahadur, not you. Looking at the way the Mafia war is going on in Gopinagar, I'm not at all sure that I, or indeed you, can rely on the protection of Gupta. His men are taking a beating.'

Eventually Saxena, finding himself outnumbered three to one and threatened with the press, gave in. At the time he comforted himself with the thought that this was only one contract. It could be seen as a sort of experiment, and the higher commission he would earn would come in very handy. He didn't have that many years left before retirement, so he needed to make the most of his remaining opportunities. There was his house, which was still not completed, and he had three daughters to get married.

By the time Saxena arrived home he had come to realize there was no escape for him. He would have to tell Gupta what had happened.

When Gupta's man came, he walked through the door without ringing, sat down without being asked and, without even greeting him, asked bluntly, 'Everything all right? Sethji wants to know.' Gupta was a Bania and his men always referred to him respectfully as Sethji.

Saxena looked down at his left hand, which was nervously caressing his right arm, and said nothing.

'What's the matter?' Gupta's man asked. 'Explain.'

Without looking up Saxena said, 'Well, actually, this time it's like this. It's not so easy. There are some things which need to be put right.'

'You mean you want a bigger commission?' Gupta's man asked threateningly. 'I wouldn't play that game if I were you. Sethji does not like people who try to twist his arm.'

Saxena's head jerked up, 'Oh, no, that's not the problem. No, no, it's nothing like that. Sethji is very generous. I assure you, I give my assurance, please accept it. I have the highest respect for Sethji and am very, very grateful to him for his generosity. How could a small man like me even think of twisting such a powerful and respected man's arm, as you say? Please let me just explain personally to Sethji and I am sure he can put it right.'

'He doesn't usually like to discuss such matters. After he has given orders he expects to hear that they have been obeyed. But you are an important person, so I don't think I can act for Sethji in this case. What I will do is go back now and someone will come again tomorrow evening to let you know what Sethji has said.'

The next evening Gupta's man returned and ordered Saxena to get into the car parked in his porch, saying simply, 'Sethji has agreed to see you.' The two men sat in silence until the car drew up at the iron gates of Gupta's compound. An armed guard looked through a barred window in the high wall. Seeing the car's number plate, he pulled the heavy gates back slowly. A man broke away from one of the many small groups standing around in the yard, came to the car and said, 'Engineer Sahib, Guptaji will see you shortly. Come with me to wait for him.'

The waiting room was full of supplicants seeking a few moments of Guptaji's time, as are the outer offices of all important people in India. After a wait long enough to ensure that Saxena was fully aware that the man he was going to meet was very important and very busy, the engineer was shown into Gupta's room. The Mafia leader stood up, folded his hands and said, '*Namaste*, Engineer Sahib. How very kind of you to spare the time for me. I know how busy you railway officials are. Please sit down. Sit down.'

Guptaji's politeness was legendary. Outside his immediate circle he had never been known to raise his voice. He was very careful about his appearance too. His close-cropped white hair, large moustache, immaculately pressed *kurta*, waist-coat and *dhoti* were all designed to give the impression that he was just another farmer who had gone into public life. But when his mouth smiled his small, deep-set, cold eyes did not.

After the usual politenesses had been concluded and glasses

of milk served, Gupta said in a soft, nasal voice, 'My man tells me that there has been some trouble about the work he discussed with you. Perhaps you can explain, and we will see what is best to be done.'

Saxena sat forward on his seat, twisted his hands nervously and said, 'Sethji, you know I have always obliged you. I have the highest respect for you, and I was once again confident that I would be able to show that respect in the matter of the embankment contract, but then this happened and what could I do?'

'What happened?'

'Well, I'm sorry — I don't like to say this to you, but it happened like this. The other engineer, he said you were no longer the only person in Gopinagar. Of course, I didn't agree, but he said it had become a war between your men and Jang Bahadur's Thakurs and it looked as though the Thakurs were winning. Lots of your people were being killed.'

'What did he mean by that?'

'He said that Jang Bahadur had demanded this contract and he felt it was safer to give it to him. The accountants accepted. Of course, one of them came from the audit department and doesn't live here. He's in Delhi, so he was not worried about the local consequences. He was just worried about the size of his share, and Jang Bahadur had offered more.'

'*Accha.* I see.'

'Sethji, you must do something,' the engineer blurted out. 'We were all very happy when you were on your own. This war which is going on now is very bad for us. No one knows which way to turn. You must teach Jang Bahadur a lesson that all Gopinagar will understand.'

Gupta replied, 'You can leave that to me. You go now. You have nothing to fear because you have been loyal, and next time there will be no difficulty in doing as I ask, I can assure you of that.'

Saxena rose hurriedly, bent to touch the Mafia leader's feet and left the room a much relieved man.

Jang Bahadur Singh was celebrating his victory in Sunny's Restaurant with his close colleagues, drinking Royal Challenge, one of the most expensive Indian whiskies, and eating plate after plate of *pakoras*. Jang Bahadur was a complete contrast to his rival. The Bania was tall and had a commanding presence; the short Jang Bahadur certainly did not. Gupta was a remote autocrat, who ruled his subordinates by fear. Jang Bahadur was a man who liked to be loved. He was only happy when surrounded by admiring friends. Gupta demanded to be known as Sethji, the traditional term of respect for a prosperous Bania. Jang Bahadur was always called Bhai Sahib, or brother. Gupta, for all his wealth, lived an austere life. Jang Bahadur was flamboyant. That day he wore white leather shoes and a smartly cut safari suit whose half unbuttoned jacket revealed the gold chain around his neck. An expensive watch hung loosely from his wrist, and there were rings on several of his fingers. His black curly hair flowed over his ears and his collar.

'*Arre*, Bhai Sahib,' one of his friends said, 'we have got Sethji on the run now. He never believed we could get into the railway business. We'll run him out of town soon if we go on like this.'

Another colleague added enthusiastically, 'We Thakurs are Rajputs, the ruling caste. Who ever heard of a Bania raja? They were always the sly bastards buttering up the rajas and sucking the blood of the poor, but Sethji thinks he can lord it over Gopinagar. Now we are showing him something, the *chutiya*.'

Jang Bahadur slapped him on the back, laughed and said, 'Yes, we Thakurs have been the rulers, but somehow or other we are always quarreling amongst ourselves. That's why the Muslims were able to pick us off one by one, and now we are under the thumb of the Brahmin Nehru family. We are so busy not allowing anyone to do anything against our honour that we waste our energy in fighting. Look at us today. We have to have Ram Sevak here with us to give us political protection because we can't do politics ourselves.'

Ram Sevak was a man in his mid-forties who had entered politics as a student leader. He had started out with socialist ideals but was now a member of the State Assembly, or MLA, belonging to a faction which had broken away from the Congress Party. He had changed parties several times, backing the leader who served his personal interests best at the moment, whatever may have been the leader's professed political persuasion. Ram Sevak was a political operator nimble enough to have influence with the government whichever party was in power. That was what made him invaluable to Bhai Sahib and gave him the right to say exactly what he felt without any fear.

'What do you mean "can't do politics", Bhai Sahib?' Ram Sevak asked. 'Our difficulty is that you Mafia all think you are better politicians than we are. When I first joined politics we used to employ the Mafia to give us protection. Now you see what's happening. You Mafia are pushing us out and becoming politicians yourselves. Look at Sethji. Everyone knows that he is the biggest Mafia boss in eastern Uttar Pradesh, but at the same time he's a respected Congress leader. Whenever the Chief Minister sees him in the Assembly he bows so low he almost touches his feet. The way things are going I wouldn't be surprised if he becomes Chief Minister himself one day.'

One of Jang Bahadur's friends laughed, 'Why not you for Chief Minister, Bhai Sahib? Who's Gupta, *madarchod*? He's nothing but a clerk. All he does is find out what tenders are coming up and pass on the details to the contractors. He has no support among the poor, only among the big people who are terrified of him. He stays in his compound like a rat in his hole. You go around the town openly. You are a hero to the poor. You have real support among them.'

Jang Bahadur smiled, turned to Ram Sevak and said,

'Don't worry, my friend. If I choose to become Chief Minister, I'll make you Minister for Public Works and Irrigation so that you can see that Sethji does not get any contracts from the two most lucrative departments. For the moment you stay where you are and I'll stay here in Gopinagar. I'm having a great time twisting that rat's tail and I want to hear him squeal. You can stay in Lucknow. I need you there to do my work and grease the politicians and bureaucrats, you *chamcha*.'

'That's just what I've got to do right now. I don't want to break up the celebration, but I'll have to go because I have a train to catch.'

'*Accha*, I'll drive you to the station, then we can discuss who you have to creep to on the way.'

The two men roared with laughter, got up and walked out of Sunny's restaurant, accompanied by an ex-serviceman carrying a sten gun, who towered over them. They sauntered towards a white car, Jang Bahadur telling the politician to make sure the whole of Lucknow knew of Sethji's discomfiture, when suddenly there was a burst of fire from the opposite side of the street. All three fell to the ground. Blood was oozing through Jang Bahadur's trousers. He had been hit in the shin, but he didn't feel any pain. He lay absolutely still, knowing that he had to give the impression that he was dead, otherwise his attackers would fire on him again. Then he saw two men, barely bothering to hide their guns, climb into a cycle rickshaw and ride slowly away. Both the Mafia gangs of Gopinagar committed their murders in daylight to demonstrate their contempt for the police.

Jang Bahadur's friends rushed out of the restaurant, laid him on his back and tied a handkerchief around his shin in an attempt to staunch the flow of blood. His panic subsided. He no longer had to be alert, to protect himself – he was in good hands. But now that his mind was no longer distracted by tension he felt the pain. It was so overpowering that he couldn't prevent himself from sobbing. He heard one of his friends say, 'Don't worry about the other two. They're gone. Get Bhai Sahib to the car and take him to hospital quickly before he bleeds to death.'

After Jang Bahadur was discharged from hospital with a slight limp, he returned to his village to convalesce and rethink his strategy. There he was still a big man and could massage his pride by interfering in the affairs of the school named after him, sorting out various local disputes and threatening corrupt local officials. But Jang Bahadur was not given the opportunity to lord it over the village.

The morning after he arrived he was summoned to see his father who was perched on a high wooden chair in the open space outside the family home. The old man sat bolt-upright, his small legs barely reaching the ground. His face was set in a permanent frown. The seventy-year-old irascible and erratic former stationmaster was the one person Jang Bahadur feared.

As the Mafia leader bent to touch his father's feet, the old man shouted, '*Behenchod!* Who else's feet have you been touching? You have disgraced our name by running home like this.'

He threw a half-smoked *bidi* to the ground, lit another one, drew the smoke deep into his lungs and then went on, 'I had been telling everyone that you were a big man, but now you're like some village cur bolting with your tail between your legs because another dog has snarled at you. Look at this house. What am I going to tell the other villagers? I have been boasting about the concrete rooms you have built on this side of the courtyard but now they will come and laugh at me because the other side of the house is collapsing, the roof has fallen in and the mud walls are crumbling away. Now you tell me. Where am I going to get the money to build that in concrete too? And I'll tell *you*, it would have been better if you had never got these big ideas into your head.'

'Father, give me a chance to speak. Give me time to think.'

'Think – rubbish. I have always taught you that there's only one rule which counts – the man who holds the *lathi* owns the buffalo. That's the rule every time.'

'You are always so angry. You don't understand city life. Fights there are not like fights in the village where the man with the biggest stick always wins. In the city you need to use your head, to think, and that's what I have come here to do.'

'Don't give me all that nonsense about the difference between cities and villages. Go back and pick up your *lathi* again, and don't come back here until you've got enough money to make the whole of this village in concrete. It's a matter of honour. We Thakurs never allow anyone to loot our honour.'

'Of course I'm going back, but I need a little time here.'

'What about my honour? How can I face the council members? They are already sniggering behind my back about you running away from that Gupta. They are saying, "He boasted about his son: now we will put him in his place again, the upstart."'

'Tell them I will fix Gupta.'

The old man sneered. 'You expect them to believe that? The older people here remember that Bania bastard as a boy. Don't forget, he drank from the same river as you did. Now he is their MLA and you're the fool who thought he could take him on. Get out of here and don't come back until you have restored my honour.'

Jang Bahadur had learned from his childhood that there was no end to his father's anger, and so he left the village that very day, more determined than ever to take revenge. Killing Gupta was out of the question. Killing one of his lieutenants would be inadequate. It had to be a blow to the Bania's own honour. Gupta was proud of his place in public life, the respect he was shown by politicians, officials, police officers, academics – anyone, in fact, who was afraid of the influence he wielded over the government. The source of his influence was the gun and it had taken him into the State Assembly.

Jang Bahadur decided the way to get at him was to destroy his public life, and he knew the very man to do it, the neighbouring MLA, Ishwar Dutt Tiwari. He was also a politician, but a politician of a very different sort. The source of his influence was his honesty.

Jang Bahadur felt it would be best to wait for the start of the State Assembly session and then go to Lucknow when Ishwar Dutt would certainly be in the state capital. Trying to find him in his constituency, where he was forever on the move, might lead to rumours that the MLA was now relying on Mafia support. If those rumours were to reach Ishwar Dutt's ears, as they surely would, he would not even consider Jang Bahadur's scheme.

So it happened that early one morning, before the crowd of supplicants that every MLA attracts had gathered, Jang Bahadur knocked on the door of Ishwar Dutt's flat. The MLA opened the door himself. When he saw the Mafia leader he stepped back, and half-hid behind the door.

'You have come for me,' he said, calmly. 'I thought it was Makhan Lal Gupta who was after me, not you.'

Jang Bahadur folded his hands, bowed his head and said, 'Tiwariji, how could I ever do you harm? I respect you greatly. But you are right. Sethji is out to get you, and I have come to warn you.'

'I am not going to fall into a trap. I'm not going to use one Mafia to protect me from another. If you really want to help me, go away before anyone sees you standing here. That would embarrass me greatly.'

'I have not come to offer my help, but to seek yours.'

'What do you mean? Are you suggesting I should help a Mafia? Have you gone mad?'

'No, I'm not mad. Let me in and I will explain everything.'

Ishwar Dutt stepped back to let the Mafia leader walk through the front door. It led straight into the small living room of the poky little flat in a dingy block built by the government for legislators. There was a low wooden bed in one corner covered with a white sheet. The two men sat cross-legged on it.

Jang Bahadur knew that honest men could still be vain and so he appealed to the MLA. 'Makhan Lal Gupta has shot an MLA, Ram Sevak. He was a friend of mine too. No one is doing anything about it. If Sethji can shoot even an MLA and get away with it, it's a disgrace to the Assembly. I knew that you were the only man with the courage to speak against this. That's why I am here.'

Ishwar Dutt asked, 'Why should I attack one Mafia leader to help another?'

'You can call me and Guptaji Mafia, but actually we are not the same at all. I have only taken to the rifle to protect the honour of my friends and associates. When they are not threatened I will put it down again. I don't make capital out of killing people. I have not become an MLA by killing – in fact, I don't want anything to do with politics. I have never raped, robbed or kidnapped anyone. I admit I'm not Mahatma Gandhi. If someone is killed, I kill, but there has to be an honourable reason for killing.'

'So why not kill again? Isn't Ram Sevak's murder an honourable reason?'

'Gupta doesn't regard losing one of his men as a disgrace, and that's what is needed. Gupta needs to be put to shame. Surely you admit he has become too big? He virtually runs the whole of eastern Uttar Pradesh.'

Ishwar Dutt was a politician who believed that the tactics Mahatma Gandhi had used against the British were the most effective way of fighting the rulers who had followed the Raj. He believed the Mahatma had shown that ultimate power lay with the leader who could convince the people that he was a moral and honest man. Ishwar Dutt knew that in his own case it was the respect he had earned by his honesty and hard work which enabled him to hold on to his seat as an Independent, defeating all the money and all the guns at the disposal of the major political parties. Ishwar Dutt had also learned the power of symbolism from the Mahatma. He didn't go quite so far as wearing a loin-cloth to identify himself with the poor, but he did live an ostentatiously simple life. He had also invented a symbolic form of protest based on Gandhian non-violence. He called it '*Ingit Karo*' or 'Point the Finger'. But he realized that his successes so far had been limited. His victims had been comparatively minor figures. He had never tackled anyone approaching the stature of Gupta.

As though he was reading the MLA's thoughts Jang Bahadur said, 'Perhaps Sethji has already got too big for you. I don't believe he has, but you had better act quickly. You know that he is trying to undermine you too? My men tell me that he is trying to win over the Pradhans in the villages loyal to you by bribes and threats. If you lose your Pradhans, who will see that the villagers vote for you?'

'Why should he be interested in my constituency?'

'A man like Gupta is never satisfied. He wants his son to win your constituency in the next election.'

This was certainly an added reason for taking action against Gupta, but the problem for Ishwar Dutt was – what action?

He dismissed Jang Bahadur with far more civility than he had greeted him and then sat to think.

He realized that he couldn't tackle Gupta on his own. This time he would need the help of political parties. The Congress Party was obviously out. Gupta's influence there was impregnable. The opposition might be a possibility. The Congress had been in power in Uttar Pradesh for two years, and the opposition was united in only one aim – to get rid of the government. If the Congress survived its full term, it could use the loaves and fishes of office to divide and demoralize the opposition further.

The opposition knew that its only hope was the sort of people's movement which had swept the Congress out of power in more than one state before, and once reduced Indira Gandhi to such a state of panic that she proclaimed a national emergency. Those movements needed an issue to focus on, and a leader. Ishwar Dutt understood that Gupta symbolized two of the issues which agitated people most – lawlessness and corruption. At the same time, he thought, I symbolize honesty and non-violence. Maybe I could be the leader.

The eight peacocks which embellished the great white dome of the State Assembly looked down on an unusually full chamber whenever Ishwar Dutt spoke, as he had a habit of raising embarrassing scandals which interested the members not involved just as much as those who were. This time even the Chief Minister, who was not known for his zeal in attending the house, was in his seat because he knew that Gupta was to be attacked, and he didn't want to run the risk of annoying the Mafia leader, who had political connections in Delhi as well as Lucknow. All Congress Chief Ministers ruled at the pleasure of what was known as the party High Command, a euphemism for the Prime Minister.

Ishwar Dutt started his speech by drawing the house's attention to the murder of Ram Sevak, who had been a member himself. He then went on to talk of the growing list of murders in Gopinagar. He maintained the number had now reached seventy-five. He blamed the lawlessness on 'a war between two Mafia gangs' and called for a complete overhaul of the system of awarding government contracts, claiming that it was the root cause of the violence. Up to that stage the house heard Ishwar Dutt in silence, but then he went on to say that the violence was spreading to the countryside, and he named Gupta's constituency. This enraged the Congress benches. Angry members leapt up, waving their fists and shouting, 'Sit down and shut up! You can't insult members of this house!' The speaker hammered the top of his desk with his gravel and shouted into the microphone, 'Order! Order! No member can make allegations against another honourable member.'

The Congress members, seeing that the speaker was support- ing their attempts to protect Gupta, allowed Ishwar Dutt to continue. 'I'm not accusing anyone by name,' he said. 'It seems to me that the Congress members are accusing their own colleague.'

The opposition roared with laughter. Some MLAs banged their desks, and others rose to their feet and shouted at the speaker, 'Honourable sir! Honourable sir! We demand an adjournment motion!'

Chaos then took over from Ishwar Dutt. The speaker tried to make himself heard above the shouting but no one was interested in what he had to say. The leader of the opposition, knowing that the speaker would never allow a motion censuring the government, waited until the storm had reached its full velocity and then turned and signalled to the MLAs sitting behind him. They all trooped into the well below the platform on which the speaker was sitting, shaking their fists at him and shouting, 'Adjournment motion! Adjournment motion! Discuss the murder of Ram Sevak!'

White-uniformed security officers formed a line in front of the speaker. One of them rashly tried to push an MLA back, but fortunately he was restrained by a colleague before a full-scale fight broke out. The confrontation continued until the speaker yelled, 'The house will adjourn for twenty minutes.'

The MLAs walked out, chattering excitedly. After two more such confrontations the speaker adjourned the house for the day and called the Congress Party and the opposition leaders to his office. There a compromise was eventually agreed whereby a magistrate, not the judge whom the opposition had been demanding, would inquire into the murder of Ram Sevak.

The Chief Minister was forced to concede an inquiry because otherwise he would have had to face continuous disruption of the Assembly's proceedings, making it impossible to get the government's business through. The longer the row went on, the more unwelcome publicity there would have been about the murder. Although Gupta was not unduly worried about the inquiry itself, believing that with his influence he could drag it out until everyone had forgotten who Ram Sevak was, he had been deeply embarrassed by Ishwar Dutt's speech and the ensuing commotion in the Assembly. He felt that his failure to prevent the inquiry might also weaken his position in his home town by giving the impression that his writ did not run as strongly in Lucknow and Delhi as he had made out.

The next day MLAs stood in small groups in the wood-panelled Central Hall of the Assembly, where Uttar Pradesh political gossip originates and is exchanged, discussing the likely impact of the government's climb-down. Ishwar Dutt and the leader of the opposition were standing alone in one corner. The Independent member was speaking excitedly.

'Don't you see that we can now turn a demand for the arrest of Gupta into the symbol of a movement? It could be just as big as the agitation in Gujarat which launched the movement led by Jayaprakash Narayan, and you know where that eventually led – the fall of Indira Gandhi and the formation of the first non-Congress government in Delhi. We can make Gupta a symbol of the corruption and violence that people hate and, what is even better, blame it all on the government because Gupta is a Congress MLA.'

The opposition leader needed some convincing. He replied, 'That would be a very big decision. If we announced a movement and then it petered out, we would be in an even weaker position than we are now. Organizing strikes, sit-ins, road and rail blocks, processions, rallies and all the rest of it, not just here in Lucknow but throughout this vast state – that would take some doing. Then who would lead it? There are five recognized opposition parties. Mine is far the biggest, and I have the support of the farming castes. The timing is right for me too because the wheat harvest is almost over and there's not much work in the fields now until the monsoon. But none of the other parties are going to accept me.'

'I will lead the movement,' said Ishwar Dutt. 'No one can object to that. I don't have any ambition to be Chief Minister, so in a way I will be like Gandhi or JP – I will provide the moral leadership from outside. That will strengthen the symbolism of the movement, especially if I offer to resign my seat in the Assembly the day the government concedes our demand or falls. That will impress people because they think we politicians are interested only in holding on to our seats.'

'Like Gandhi and JP? Who do you think you are? I wouldn't talk like that if you want to get our support. But still you may have something. Let me speak to the other leaders.'

The leader of the opposition found the other parties surprisingly receptive, but they insisted that Ishwar Dutt should first test the water by launching a protest movement of his own. If it picked up momentum, they would join it.

When Ishwar Dutt returned to his village to plan the movement he found his Pradhan a worried man. He had received several letters warning him that the MLA had annoyed some very influential people and that anyone who continued to support him would pay a heavy price. The heads of other village councils had told him they'd been receiving similar letters. The son of one had been beaten up in the bazaar of the local town, and the police had refused to register a case. A wheat field of another had been mysteriously set on fire one night. The village watchman claimed he had seen no one. There was a growing atmosphere of fear in the constituency.

Ishwar Dutt went to complain to the Superintendent of Police. The Superintendent's neatly pressed khaki uniform and the smart leather-bound cane lying on his desk did not go with his owlish face and thick spectacles. The uniform and the trappings of office could not hide the fact that the Superintendent was not by nature a policeman, that he would have preferred a more thoughtful profession. He had joined the police only because he had not got enough marks in the highly competitive entrance exam for the élite services of the government to join any organization better suited to his temperament. Although only in his early thirties, he was already thoroughly disillusioned by the consistent political interference in his work. He did not react very sympathetically to Ishwar Dutt.

'You have brought this on yourself by that speech you made in the Assembly,' he said. 'You knew Gupta would never let you get away with that speech. The trouble with you honest people is that you can't see the reality of the situation.'

'You mean that in the India of today the honest are the fools and the corrupt the wise?'

'You said that: I didn't. But you know as well as I do that the police can do nothing to help you. My men are more afraid of the Mafia than the law when the Mafia have the politicians on their side. Anyhow I can't take any action unless we get political clearance.'

'Supposing there's a murder?'

'We'll have to register a case then, but you know nothing will happen.'

There was a murder. The Pradhan of Ishwar Dutt's own village was shot. A case was registered, but it bore no relation to reality. The Pradhan had been sitting with some of his friends discussing the threat from Gupta when two young men rode into the village on a motorcycle. The pillion rider had a crude locally made gun across his lap. They were seen by many villagers as they bumped down the cart track leading to the Pradhan's house. They were seen by his friends as they opened fire. But the police registered a case of suicide.

This was the opportunity Ishwar Dutt had been waiting for. Gupta's responsibility for the murder was not carried by the newspapers, but that didn't prevent the rumour from spreading rapidly throughout the state. The murder was also seen as a deliberate insult to Ishwar Dutt. Now he had to react, and his first step was to be seen to be doing just that. He sent a letter reminding the Superintendent of Police that he had been told there might be a murder but had taken no action and warning him that unless a murder case was opened within fifteen days, political workers would squat outside his official residence until action was taken. They would hang up banners describing him as a lackey of *goondas* and shout slogans in a similar vein.

The Superintendent was trapped. On the one hand he knew he could not change the First Information Report to an allegation of murder without getting sanction from his seniors, and Gupta's influence would ensure that was not forthcoming. On the other hand he had heard many reports of the humiliation the victims of Tiwari's campaigns suffered. He took the only way out he knew – he applied for sick leave and left the district.

Ishwar Dutt saw this as an opportunity to persuade his followers that they had to take the risk of challenging Gupta directly. As a peaceful sit-in was not going to work, they would have to use another Gandhian method of protest which might – a *padyatra*, or march from village to village, in Gupta's constituency. That would be dangerous but would certainly embarrass the Mafia leader deeply and could well be the beginning of the movement that the opposition leaders had promised to support.

Padyatras always start with a rally, so Ishwar Dutt called a public meeting in the only town of any consequence in Gupta's constituency.

The centre of town was almost empty on the day the meeting was held. The shopkeepers had closed their shutters for fear that Gupta's men would attack Ishwar Dutt's followers. The handcarts piled high with vegetables and fruit which normally lined the roadside were nowhere to be seen. The cycle-rickshaw pullers had moved to another part of town. Even the junior magistrate deputed to observe the meeting on behalf of the government stayed at home. The Superintendent of Police had, of course, already disappeared. The only police officer to appear for the meeting was a lowly sub-inspector, accompanied by a *havildar* and ten constables. They stood well away from Ishwar Dutt's two hundred or so political workers who had gathered in the dusty square just off the main road which ran through the town.

Ishwar Dutt's workers had agreed to the march in part because they were inspired by his honesty and integrity and in part because they had a vested interest in his continuing success. His campaigns against corrupt officials had been so effective that in his constituency much of the government money was actually spent on development work because the bureaucrats did not dare to fill their own pockets. Ishwar Dutt rewarded his workers by seeing that roads were made, schools were built, wells were dug and electricity was supplied to their villages.

He did not need a microphone to make himself heard by so small a crowd, which was a good thing as no one had been willing to hire him one.

'Brothers, we have been fighting against corrupt officials,' he shouted. 'Now we have to fight against the source of all corruption, the Mafia and their *goondas* who have made the bureaucracy and the politicians their slaves. They have shown that they fear us, otherwise Gupta would not have killed Surinder Lal Singh, the Pradhan of my village. That was a threat to all of us, but it's a threat that will not deflect us from the road Mahatma Gandhi showed us. We do not believe in blood for blood, we believe in non-violence.

'Now is our hour of trial. Now is the time to show that non-violence works. If we let that gangster Makhan Lal Gupta get away with this murder, he will finish us and our families. We have had great successes: we will have more. We have marched a long way down the road Mahatma Gandhi showed us. We can and we will march further.'

Knowing that an appeal to self-interest would help too, Ishwar Dutt explained that a victory for Gupta would mean no jobs, no development grants, maybe even no ration cards for them. But he ended his speech with a rallying, 'Mahatma Gandhi *ki jai*!' – 'Victory to Mahatma Gandhi!'

Back came the response, 'Mahatma Gandhi *ki jai*!'

'*Goondon hatao! Desh bachao!*' — 'Drive out the *goondas*! Save the nation!'

'*Goondon hatao! Desh bachao!*'

Satisfied by the enthusiastic response to his slogans, Ishwar Dutt climbed down from his makeshift platform and started walking along the main road. His small army followed, shouting slogans. The police who were meant to accompany them stayed behind in the centre of the town.

The first stop was to be the village of Imlipar. There the villagers were at first astounded to hear someone speak out openly against Gupta. They muttered among themselves, uncertain whether it was safe to stay or whether it wouldn't be wise to leave. They saw their Pradhan, Gupta's man, watching with a small group of his supporters a little distance away from the meeting. When he made no effort to disrupt the meeting or to argue with Tiwari the villagers decided to stay. At the end of his speech Tiwari went over to the Pradhan and said in a voice that all the villagers who had gathered could hear, 'We are not like your Sethji. We don't kill our enemies, otherwise you too might be dead. We believe in honesty and the right to live in peace and without fear. The people are coming to us. You can see that in my constituency, and you will see it here. If you don't mend your ways, you will have no chance of winning in the next Panchayat elections.' The Pradhan could find no reply, so Tiwari turned to the villagers who had watched their elder's humiliation and said, 'We need volunteers from every village. Are there any who will join our march?'

Such a public display of revolt was too much for all but a handful of young men, so Ishwar Dutt's ranks did not exactly swell when he marched out of the village, but he did have a few new recruits.

News of the village leader's humiliation spread through Gupta's constituency like wildfire. More recruits were added everywhere the march went. Jang Bahadur sent some of his men to swell the ranks and rub salt in Gupta's wounds by publicly siding with the movement against him, but they were told they were not required. No Pradhan had the courage to resist the marchers. Everywhere they went the revolution grew and so did the enthusiasm of the revolutionaries. Then Gupta struck back.

One evening Ishwar Dutt and his supporters were walking down a remote mud road, when they saw a cloud of dust approaching and heard the throb of diesel engines. Three jeeps pulled up just in time to avoid running them down, and a group of about twenty young men jumped out, armed with rifles and shotguns. They fired in the air and shouted, 'Run for it, dogs, run! What do you think, you bastards? That you can talk back to Sethji?'

The leader ordered his men to fire another salvo in the air, and then shouted, 'If you don't run, the next round will be fired at you!'

There was still no movement. The leader walked slowly over to Ishwar Dutt and stopped directly in front of him, insolently staring him in the face. Ishwar Dutt was quite still. After a few moments the young man slowly and deliberately took out a revolver, pressed it against Ishwar Dutt's chest and said, 'Tell them to run or I will kill you.'

Ishwar Dutt replied, 'You don't have the courage to kill me.'

The young man stood his ground but he was visibly taken aback by the Gandhian's response. His orders had not included shooting him. Feeling the pressure on his chest relax slightly, Ishwar Dutt threw up his arm, sweeping the revolver from the gang leader's hand. 'You are the ones who are going to run,' he said sternly. 'Get going now, and tell Gupta that he's not dealing with the cowards he normally deals with.'

The leader stood, humiliated, confused, at a loss. The other members of the gang, seeing him collapse, lost their nerve too and started to drift back to the jeeps. Realizing that he was no longer in command of the situation the leader suddenly bowed down and said, 'Panditji, I touch your feet. Forgive me.'

Then, without allowing time for an answer, he ran back to his jeep and drove off with the sound of '*Mahatma Gandhi ki jai!*' ringing in his ears.

Gupta was sitting in his office with two of his closest advisors when the gang leader returned. When he admitted his failure, one of the advisors said, 'Sethji, there's only one answer. Kill Ishwar Dutt.'

'Why do I surround myself with such fools!' an exasperated Gupta exploded. 'You are all fools. You can only think of killing anyone who crosses your path. I am going to make such a dreadful example of Ishwar Dutt that no one will ever dare challenge me again, not even that *madarchod* Jang Bahadur. And to do that I need the bastard alive to remind everyone what happens to Makhan Lal Gupta's enemies.'

A few nights later Ishwar Dutt's son, Ramesh, was sitting on the veranda of the family house, a concrete building on the edge of the village, when some neighbours came up and suggested he should go with them to see the *nautanki*, a play being performed by a party of travelling actors who had arrived in the village. Ramesh had married a year before, but his wife was away on a brief visit to her parents. As his father was on his march, and there was no other member of the family in the house, he decided to go to see the play.

There was a new moon, and the glow from the stars in the clear sky barely penetrated the mango grove through which the men were walking to the play. They could hear the beat of the drums and raucous singing from the centre of the village where it was already under way. Suddenly a man, his face masked with a black handkerchief, stepped out from behind a clump of bamboo and blocked the path. As if at a signal, the neighbours stepped off the path and disappeared into the darkness. Ramesh turned and ran, but the man dived for his legs and pulled him down. Ramesh struggled and nearly got away, but his assailant managed to hold on to his ankles. It was an uneven battle. Ramesh was small and had never been in a fight before. His attacker was a dismissed constable, and the police had trained him well. Eventually he managed to pin Ramesh to the ground. He sat on the young man's chest, put both hands round his neck and squeezed tighter and tighter until his victim was no longer breathing.

The next morning at dawn an elderly villager making his way down the track to perform his ablutions saw Ramesh's body hanging from the branch of a mango tree. It was suspended by the turban cloth he had been wearing over his shoulders.

Gupta appeared to have miscalculated again. When Ishwar Dutt returned to his village for the cremation of his son, his brothers were amazed by his apparent calm. They thought he would be distraught with grief, but all he said was 'No one can bring him back. Now we have to see that Makhan Lal Gupta, who committed this murder, is brought to justice by the people. Theirs is the only court which works.' He refused to register a case with the police or make any attempt to discover who had murdered Ramesh. He knew who was behind the murder, and he knew that meant the police would not take any action. He left for Lucknow, as soon as the the funeral rites were over, to meet the leaders of the opposition parties. This, he felt certain, was the opportunity they had been waiting for.

The opposition leaders received him with an unseemly enthusiasm, given that his son had just been brutally murdered. They recognized this as the moment to launch their movement and promised that they would use all their resources to bring villagers from every corner of the state to Lucknow for a mammoth rally. Pity for Ishwar Dutt would hightlight corruption. Its symbol was to be the issue they had already decided on – Makhan Lal Gupta. He would be made to appear the embodiment of all the corruption, the threats, and the politically inspired violence that villagers had come to hate. The rally would demand Gupta's arrest. The leaders were confident that the Chief Minister would not accept that demand because, if he did, he would lose face – one of the worst fates that can overtake a politician. Then the opposition parties could march through cities, have strikes and sit-ins, block roads and railways until the government was brought to its knees. If, by chance, they could force the Chief Minister to accept their demand, that would be even better. He would be seen to be on the run. All they would have to do would be to keep up the chase.

The rush started the day before the rally. Trains arriving in Lucknow were packed with villagers from all over the state. Special parking arrangements had to be made on the outskirts of the city for the buses and trucks which poured in from the countryside and the other towns of Uttar Pradesh filled with slogan-shouting, flag-waving opposition supporters. Long processions wound their way through the streets of the capital, blocking the traffic and causing the shopkeepers to close their shutters in panic. The marchers carried banners and shouted, 'Hang Gupta the murderer! Dismiss this government of murderers!' By the time the rally really got under way there must have been 200,000 people in the park in the middle of the city, and more were still arriving.

The crowd became increasingly restless and rowdy as speaker after speaker attacked the government for harbouring murderers, for looting the public and for failing to protect the lives and property of honest citizens. The Chief Minister was sitting in his office, just two miles from the rally, getting minute-by-minute reports. Many of the speakers did not share Ishwar Dutt's non-violent convictions, and the Chief Minister was told that some of them were openly calling on the crowd to burn down the secretariat if the government did not act immediately. These calls were greeted with angry roars from the crowd.

The Director General of Police was by the Chief Minister's side. When he was asked whether there was any way of dispersing the rally he replied, 'Not without bloodshed.'

'What shall I do?' asked the Chief Minister.

'There's only one thing you can do. Announce the arrest of Gupta immediately.'

'But I must get clearance from the High Command in Delhi before I do that. Gupta is a very influential man.'

'If you wait for that, the streets of the city will be running with blood. I can't even pretend that I'll be able to control the situation. The army will have to be called out, and that will be the end of you.'

The Chief Minister calculated that he might be able to pacify the High Command because he was needed. He was the only person who could hold the fractious Uttar Pradesh Congress together and prevent an outbreak of that plague 'dissidence' which was damaging the party in so many other states. Anyhow if the High Command did take umbrage at his exceeding his authority, it wouldn't necessarily be the end for all time to come. Politics within the Congress Party were an ever-changing kaleidoscope. It was more than likely that he would be needed again. On the other hand the electorate would never forgive him if he presided over a massacre in the capital. The Chief Secretary was summoned and told to order the Commissioner of Gopinagar to arrest Gupta and report back as soon as the Mafia leader was safely in custody.

At the rally the Inspector General of Police in charge of security received an urgent wireless message ordering him to tell the speakers on the platform about the arrest and to plead with them to ask their supporters to exercise restraint. He climbed the stairs to the dais and whispered to Ishwar Dutt, 'Tiwariji, Sethji has been arrested. Please inform the crowd immediately and ask them to disperse peacefully. You are known as a man of peace. You don't want to have innocent blood on your hands.'

Ishwar Dutt agreed. He made his way to the battery of microphones and told the politician castigating the government to move aside. He took charge and his voice rang out over the vast crowd.

'Brothers and sisters. I have just been informed by the

Inspector General of Police that we have won a great victory. Seth Makhan Lal Gupta has been arrested in Gopinagar.' The crowd roared, 'Seth Makhan Lal Gupta *murdabad*!' – Death to Seth Makhan Lal Gupta!'

Ishwar Dutt let the crowd enjoy their triumph until he felt that it was possible to control them again. Then he held his hands high above his head and the 200,000 people below him fell silent.

'I have, as you know, paid for this victory with the life of my beloved son. You have come here to share in my grief, and it's only your love and support that have enabled me to endure this tragedy. I want this great rally to mark a new beginning for Uttar Pradesh. I want it to mark the end of *goonda raj* in the state and the beginning of the *raj* that great Indian, Mahatma Gandhi, the Father of Our Nation, gave his life for – a non-violent *raj*, a *raj* without corruption, a *raj* where justice rules. I appeal to you all: go home peacefully and start the great work which has been delayed too long – the work of building Mahatma Gandhi's India. You have shown where power lies, with the people. You must now use that power responsibly. All India will be watching the way we go home. This rally will be the start of a great movement to throw out this corrupt government and bring in the first honest administration you have ever known, but one act of revenge or violence and I will call off the movement, just as the Mahatma did when the police station in Chauri Chaura was attacked. Brothers and sisters, I appeal to you in his name. Forswear revenge. Follow the path of peace and non-violence.'

The crowd dispersed peacefully, and Ishwar Dutt returned to his village, where his small, ugly concrete house became the centre of political activity in Uttar Pradesh.

Ministers, accustomed to the smooth tarmacked streets of central Lucknow, were jolted and jarred as they drove down the brick road to his home. The red lights on the top of their cars, the symbols of VIP status, flashed officiously, and police in the jeeps leading the cavalcades gave bullock carts a passing thwack with their *lathis* to make sure they moved right off the road.

Ishwar Dutt refused the ministers' offers of cabinet posts in return for calling off his movement and supporting the government.

Dhoti-clad opposition politicians, emerging from the dust-covered, snub-nosed Hindustan Ambassadors, were surprised when Ishwar Dutt wasn't interested in their plans either. They tried to convince him that he could follow in the footsteps of Jayaprakash Narayan, or JP, whom Indians had regarded as the successor to Mahatma Gandhi. (He'd led the movement which had resulted in the downfall of Indira Gandhi.) They also promised that this time there would be no sordid squabbling over office, that they would provide a stable and an honest government.

But once Ishwar Dutt had achieved this immediate goal of taking revenge for the killing of his only son, he was overcome with grief and a sense of futility. No one could bring his son back, and the opposition politicians didn't care about that. They were just using him for their own ends and once they'd come to power they wouldn't bother with him. He remembered how Jayaprakash Narayan had been ignored when whose who'd claimed to be his followers eventually formed a government. You can't reform politics if you can't reform politicians, and even Mahatma Gandhi had not been able to do that. What impact had his own earlier successes made? A few officials and the odd one or two politicians had been temporarily embarrassed, but politics and the administration were as corrupt as ever.

When the leader of the opposition came himself to persuade the Gandhian to change his mind, Ishwar Dutt told him, 'You are wasting your time. My eyes have been opened. I see that the Ganges of corruption flows from the top of the Himalayas and I can't climb up there. I am no longer interested in politics.'

News of the collapse of the opposition movement reached Gupta in jail and he sent an emissary to the Chief Minister suggesting that in reward for past favours and in expectation of future payments he should be generous. But the emissary returned empty-handed. The High Command had not asked the Chief Minister to explain Gupta's arrest. The voters of eastern Uttar Pradesh had welcomed the end of the running war between his gang and Jang Bahadur's. 'So why,' the Chief Minister had asked, 'should he be released?'

The Chief Minister did, however, offer one concession. He agreed to order Jang Bahadur's arrest too, so that at least honours would be even. The Thakur gang leader was taken to the same jail as his rival. There they lived in comparative comfort: money will buy most things in an Indian jail. Jang Bahadur found little difficulty in making friends and even started to enjoy institutional life, in the way that many long-term hospital partients do. But Gupta found the loss of his authority very difficult to bear.

He sought a meeting with Jang Bahadur which the jail superintendent allowed in one of the prison offices. Gupta opened the conversation with a humility that surprised the Thakur.

'I have made mistakes, that's why we are both here. I should have talked to you instead of trying to finish you.'

'That would have been better, Sethji,' Jang Bahadur replied politely.

'Sometimes, sitting in the barracks in this jail, I have thought that maybe power made me mad. It's always better to share. One man can't have everything.'

'I agree, Sethji. I never intended to push you off your chair, I always accepted that you were the leader of Gopinagar. But, after all, we Thakurs have our pride, and how could I accept that everything should go to a Bania and we should have nothing?'

'Han, you are quite right,' said Makhan Lal Gupta thoughtfully.

There was an informal agreement that Jang Bahadur should be allowed to widen his activities, and then the cycle of revenge killings would end.

The two men sent a message to the Chief Minister telling him that they had made peace. They also promised substantial contributions to 'party funds' if their applications for bail were not opposed. Peace with a price paid seemed more attractive than peace without, and so the Chief Minister agreed.

When Ishwar Dutt read that the two Mafia leaders had been released, he turned to the friends sitting with him on his veranda and said, 'I told you there was no point in politics. I have sacrificed my son for nothing.'

TWO BROTHERS

Ajay Kumar shovelled yellow earth into a basket. A young girl picked up the basket and put it on her head. The Harijan boy watched her hips swing as she climbed up the steep embankment to throw the earth on to the village road they were building. Then seeing another girl approaching, he slammed his mattock into the hard ground to loosen more earth. After filling this basket he wiped his face with the end of the cloth tied loosely round his head, leant on the handle of the mattock and thought, 'It will go on like this all day. How will I ever make progress while my mind is divided between this labouring and studying? I feel the whole weight of the household is on my shoulders.'

The Principal of the school he was attending had recently warned him that if he continued to fall behind with his work, he would fail his exam and have to go back and do the year all over again. Ajay Kumar was shown no sympathy when he'd explained that there had been a problem at home, and he had to earn money to supplement the family income. He'd had to endure a lecture during which the Principal claimed that he himself, as a young boy, had studied all night by the light of a hurricane lamp after spending the whole day grazing cattle.

'*Saale*, he never did a day's hard work in his life,' Ajay Kumar thought. 'They're all the same these teachers, officials and politicians. They come and tell us it's shameful not to be educated, education is the key to the future – but they don't know what it's like to dig all day in the sun, the dust blinding your eyes and blocking your throat, or to be up to your knees in water, bent double, transplanting rice until your back aches so much you feel you'll never stand straight again. Then after that they think it's easy to just sit down and study. And what about the days at school I miss when my father threatens to beat me if I don't go out to work? How would the Principal suggest I catch up on the lessons I've not been able to attend? I suppose by paying him and his colleagues for private tuition. That's a joke, when I can't even afford to come to school.'

Ajay Kumar was brought back to even more immediate problems by one of the more elderly labourers. Seeing him still leaning on his mattock handle, she said, 'You're a fine young man. If you're tired, what do you think I am? That contractor doesn't pay us to stand around doing nothing – he measures every pinch of earth we carry. I've got to fill my stomach, so fill this basket.'

When the required amount of earth for the day had been shifted, Ajay Kumar walked back to his village, Haripur, through the yellow mustard fields. 'At least now it's cool,' he thought. 'By the time the mustard is ready to cut it will be hot, very hot, and then how will I labour and study? I have to get back to school.'

Ajay Kumar's father, Chand Ram, had different views. That evening, after eating *chapattis* and *daal* with raw onions in the small space fenced off by twigs behind his hut, he got up as usual to go and play cards with his friends. Ajay Kumar stood up and said, 'Father, I have something to say to you. I'm going to school from tomorrow. I am not going to do any more *mazdoori*.'

Chand Ram put his hand on his son's shoulder and said, '*Beta*, I understand. I am proud that you want to be educated, but what can we do? I've educated one son, and all I've got is trouble and expense. Labouring earns money, school doesn't, and you know we need the money.'

Then, turning away, Chand Ram bent down to enter the

hut, lifted the wooden bar across the door facing the lane and walked out.

Ajay Kumar asked his mother when his elder brother was returning, but she didn't know. Sudama had gone to Allahabad to take an entrance test for some job. No one in the family quite knew what job, except that it was said to be government service, the passport to security, income and influence sought by every educated villager.

'All right,' said Ajay Kumar, 'when Sudama gets back from Allahabad he can work, and then father can let me go back to school.'

'I don't know whether Sudama will agree to that,' said his mother Chameli anxiously. 'You know he's become very proud. If he only came back with a government job, then you could go to school again.'

'No hope of that, from what I've heard. He's aiming too high, and he doesn't have the money to bribe the *babus*. He should go for some private service.'

The trip to Allahabad was indeed not a great success. Sudama had been sent there by a clerk in the Ghazipur Employment Exchange who, for a fee, claimed to have engineered an introduction to a recruiting officer that would lead to a clerical job in the nationalized Poorvanchal Bank. The man had turned out to be not the recruiting officer but his clerk, who'd demanded money just to make sure Sudama's form reached the right desk. After that there was no guarantee. When Sudama had asked what hope he had the clerk, an arrogant young man dressed in fashionably baggy trousers and wearing trainers, replied, 'Depends on how much money you've got.'

'I've spent almost all my money just to get here, and now you want what little I've got left. How can I find money to pay for a job? I paid the man in the employment exchange because he said you would help.'

'Employment exchange! They should be called *un*employment exchanges. If you haven't got any money, I suggest you forget about a job and go back to your village.'

Turning to one of his colleagues who was sitting reading a newspaper, picking his nose, the clerk asked, 'Did you hear that? What can you do with these people? They're so ignorant. It costs twenty thousand to have any hope of becoming a constable in the police, and fifty to be a peon in a government office, and this man thinks he can become a clerk for nothing.'

But Sudama refused to accept defeat. 'I'm Scheduled Caste,' he said. 'I should get service from the special quota. If the officer knows that, he'll see me.'

'I'm telling you, you will not see any officer if you haven't got any money. Do you think there are no Harijans nowadays who can afford to pay for jobs? If you haven't got the bribe, you're wasting my time.' To make that abundantly clear the clerk shouted to a peon, 'Ram Kishan, call the next man.'

It was a long journey back to the village of Haripur. First there was the crowded unreserved carriage on the broad-gauge to Varanasi, then the change to the slow and dirty meter-gauge train to Ghazipur, used mainly by those who wanted to take advantage of the railways' failure to check tickets. Finally the bus to the tea shop where the track to Haripur joined the tarmac road. So Sudama had plenty of time to think over his experience. He should have known better. While studying at the degree college, he'd heard so often about the bribes necessary to get a job, but he'd never thought it would be quite so bad. He didn't know what he would do now, but he did know what he would not do. He was not going to face the humiliation of working alongside his contemporaries on embankments or in the fields. He'd mocked them for dropping out of school. He'd been arrogant and superior when things were going well. Now they'd get their own back when he had to come back to their level. How they would gloat.

Walking through the Dalit settlement, past women milking buffaloes tethered outside their huts, he came to the Pradhan's house. He wasn't just Pradhan of this settlement; he was Pradhan of the whole village of Haripur. In the last election the Harijans had for the first time stuck together to defeat the Bhumihar candidate. The Dalit Pradhan had not been able to cheat them because he was dependent on their support. He had seen to it that the Block Development Officer had sanctioned some development work for them. He'd even succeeded in getting electricity to their houses, but that wasn't much use because the power supply failed as soon as the sun went down. There was to be another council election soon, and the Pradhan was bound to win as all efforts to divide the Dalits had failed. He was their unanimous choice as the candidate again.

The Pradhan was sitting outside the new house he was building, discussing tactics for the election with Satya Kam Ram, an elderly member of the community who was widely respected for the number of young men like Sudama whom he'd persuaded to persevere with their education. He'd had a better start in life than most because his father had been in the police and had made sure he went to university, in days when that was rare for Scheduled Castes.

The Pradhan's new house was not the traditional plain rectangular construction. It was more like a bungalow and had stylish bow windows. There was even the beginning of a garden, a few red coxcombs and yellow marigolds. Palm squirrels scuttled along the branches of mango trees, chirruping shrilly. The three other more successful Harijan families lived in the same area of the village. Television masts marked their houses as being out of the ordinary.

When Sudama saw Satya Kam Ram sitting with the Pradhan, he walked over, stood in front of the old social worker and, without even greeting him or the Pradhan, said, 'You are the one who got me into all this trouble. All your talk about education being the only soap to wash away the differences between us and the higher castes. I believed it and look where it's got me – nowhere.'

'Sit down, sit down, calm yourself,' said Satya Kam Ram, pointing to the *charpoy* on which he was sitting. 'What's the problem?'

Sudama, still standing, replied, 'I've just been to Allahabad where some bad-mannered, shameless clerk, probably with less education than I have, insulted me. He wouldn't listen when I asked to see the recruitment officer in the Poorvanchal Bank because I didn't have any money for bribes.'

The Pradhan remonstrated. 'You've no shame that you stand in front of a respected elder, that you shout so rudely at a man who has done so much for our community? If you can't make the best of your education, that's your fault, not his. Look at me and my family – look at what education has done for us.'

Satya Kam Ram put his hand on the Pradhan's knee to calm him saying, 'Leave him, Pradhanji. I can understand his anger.' Then, turning to Sudama, he said, 'You go home now. I'll come to your family tomorrow and we will see what should be done.'

Sudama turned round and walked away without saying another word.

The next evening, as Satya Kam Ram approached the hut where Sudama lived with his family, he heard loud and angry shouting. Sudama was bawling at his father, 'I got government scholarships. What have you ever done for me, you miser?'

Chand Ram was trying to calm his son. 'No, *beta*, no. Don't shout at me. I just said that if you can't get a job, you will have to work in the fields again.'

'You're pitiable. You just lie down under everything and take what you get. I'm not going to end up like you, dependent on greedy farmers who don't pay you the proper wage and corrupt contractors who cheat you.'

Satya Kam Ram hurried into the small yard to put an end to this row. 'Sudama,' he said firmly, 'you have no right to speak to your father like this. He has made sacrifices for you – after all, he could have sent you out to work as a child. Sit down and we'll discuss this problem calmly.'

'I'm not doing mud work. I have got my honour to save,' said Sudama in a surly voice.

When everyone was sitting on *charpoys*, Satya Kam Ram asked Sudama, 'Do you think you are the only boy in this *basti* to get a degree? Do you know there are at least nine BAs and two MAs? A few have got jobs; the others haven't behaved like spoilt children. Some have gone away to find work. Others are labouring here.'

Chand Ram said, 'He won't do any labour. I never tried to stop him getting educated, in fact I was proud of him. But in my heart I thought it would do no good. My father advised against it. Before he died he told me, "If your son gets a little education, he's out of your hands, and if he gets more educa-tion, he's out of the house." He warned me that these educated boys don't care what happens to their fathers in old age. They just feel ashamed of us because we can only sign with our thumbs.'

Satya Kam Ram turned to Sudama. 'Will you work?' he asked.

'Why should I? You told me that the only way to lift up my family was to get educated, and now you are saying I should go back to labouring. Where's that ever got anyone?'

'You got a second-class degree. I will try to get you a job as a teacher with one of the schools run by a Harijan committee.'

'I don't want to be a teacher. I went to the degree college because I was told it was a passport to an office job.'

'If you don't work, I will recommend to your father that he throw you out of the house.'

'I'll go before I'm thrown out.'

'Don't let me hear such a thing,' moaned Chameli, holding

THE HEART OF INDIA

her hands over her ears. 'My son being thrown out of my house. I'll never see him again. *Beta*, why are you so obstinate? Work a little until we find you some service. Satya Kam Ram will help you, I'm sure.'

'Of course I will,' the old man said, 'if you will help yourself.'

'I'm not going to do any labouring,' muttered Sudama, adamant that he would not work with the other members of his community who were uneducated. He had his pride. He was prepared to go to Ghazipur and find work provided his father gave him some money to get started. Chand Ram told his younger son to hand over the small savings he had made from his labouring, saying, 'Now I'm afraid the question doesn't even arise of your going back to school.'

'But I've only got another half year to complete my Intermediate,' Ajay Kumar protested.

'Then what will you do? Fail to get a job and borrow money from me. This education is meant to make us better off but it seems to ruin me.'

'Don't despair, Chand Ram,' Satya Kam Ram intervened. 'I can arrange for a scholarship for the Welfare Fund to see that you do not lose out if your younger son finishes his education. By the time he does that, I am sure Sudama will be set up and sending you money regularly.'

'When I was young my father ruled his house,' grumbled Chand Ram. 'Now it seems that all power has been taken out of my hands. Do what you want. Leave your mother and me to starve.'

So it was agreed that Ajay Kumar could go back to school provided he handed over his small savings to his elder brother. Sudama would leave for Ghazipur in search of work. Satya Kam Ram was reasonably satisfied. At least he had prevented one of the brightest Dalit boys from dropping out of school. That would have been a real set-back to his work. Many other parents would have used Ajay Kumar's example to justify not sending their children to school. There was still far too much opposition to education among the poorest members of the community whose needs were so immediate that they wanted their children to start earning as early as possible. In India, in spite of all the laws which were meant to protect children, that was still far too early.

There was a young man from the settlement who had found a job as an assistant to the proprietor of a small chemist's shop in Ghazipur. That seemed just about acceptable to Sudama – at least it wasn't labouring and required some degree of literacy. So when he reached Ghazipur bus station the next day he set off down the long, narrow road which was the main bazaar. It ran along the banks of the Ganges, but there was barely a gap in the buildings which flanked both sides of the road, commercial pressures having taken precedence over aesthetics, and so Sudama didn't catch a glimpse of the sacred river. He looked at the shop names, Raja Lamp House, Shakti Traders, Kushwaha Medical Stores. That wasn't the name he remembered, and he didn't think the proprietor of the shop where his friend worked was a Khushwaha by caste. He walked past the district hospital and the police station. The road got even narrower. There was a shop selling musical instruments and a branch of Bata, the shoe manufacturer. He stopped at a *paan* stall to ask whether there was another chemist nearby. The *paan-wallah* grunted, 'There are a lot of medicine shops,' without even bothering to look up from the green leaves he was plastering with lime. Sudama walked on past the town hall with its ornate arched verandas. He didn't want to waste any of his money by sitting down at a tea shop, usually the best place for gathering information, so on he walked. Just as he was coming to the end of the bazaar he recognized another young man from his settlement sitting in a rickshaw resting his legs on the handle-bar. 'Chotu Ram,' he said.

The rickshaw puller looked up uncertainly, '*Arre*, Sudama, Chand Ram's son. What are you doing here?'

'I am looking for Ram Kishore, the man from our village who works in a chemist's shop. Do you know him?'

'Very well. He's a good man. He doesn't look down on us rickshaw pullers. Get in – I'll take you there.'

'But I don't have the fare. Tell me and I'll walk.'

'Don't worry. There's not much business at this time of the day, as you can see, and it isn't far.'

So Sudama climbed into the rickshaw and within a few minutes he reached Om Prakash, Pharmacy. Ram Kishore was standing behind the counter which faced the street. Business was slack for him too because the doctor who had rented the next shop was not in his surgery. He greeted the rickshaw puller and then, recognizing Sudama, he said, '*Arre*, you too. I had heard that you were going to get a job in Allahabad. What are you doing in this little town?'

Sudama looked down at the ground and mumbled, 'That didn't work out. Too much corruption.'

'I understand. These government jobs are very difficult. That's why I've come here. Even with a science degree I couldn't get a job, although when the District Magistrate came to lecture at our college he said there was a shortage of Scheduled Castes for technical jobs. These officials lie, of course, or maybe they would rather not fill our quota if they can't find SCs who can pay the bribes.'

'I'm only an arts student. Can you help me to find a job like yours?'

'It's not easy. I was very lucky. The owner of this shop had just been cheated by his assistant. I just happened to come here for some medicine, which he hadn't got, and when I suggested an alternative, the chemist asked me how I knew so much. I told him I was a science graduate and for some reason he took to me. It was just luck.'

'So there's no system.'

'System? You mean getting jobs through contacts?'

'Yes.'

'Not for us because our *biradaris* are very poor, and no one has any jobs to offer. Our people are not in business. That's why most of our young men who come here end up like Chotu Ram, pulling rickshaws or doing cleaning work.'

'Yes,' said Chotu Ram encouragingly. 'You won't be the first graduate to end up pulling a rickshaw.'

Although he couldn't hold out much hope or offer any useful advice, Ram Kishore did invite Sudama to share his room while he looked around. He also promised to ask his proprietor whether any other shopkeepers needed an assistant.

It wasn't long before Sudama found out the truth. He went from shop to shop asking, 'Do you have a job?' but met with nothing but disinterest expressed abruptly and rudely. His money was running out and he couldn't expect Ram Kishore to feed as well as house him. So within a few days he drifted back to the street corner where he had found Chotu Ram.

The rickshaw puller welcomed Sudama. 'How are you getting on? Any luck?'

'Nothing yet.'

'Any chances?'

'Not really.'

'I told you so.'

Sudama then changed the subject and asked in a deliberately casual tone, 'Those graduates you were talking about who pull rickshaws – is that really true?'

'Yes, of course. I'll introduce you to one if you come here early tomorrow morning when he hires his rickshaw.'

'Maybe I will,' said Sudama. But he was still unwilling to concede the possibility that he might be reduced to an occupation so far beneath the dignity of a graduate. He went out again in search of a job people would regard as dignified. But he got nowhere and the money he had taken from his younger brother ran out. So eventually he was forced to swallow his pride and return to Chotu Ram, who took him to the rickshaw proprietor and lent him ten rupees for the first day's hire.

Sudama stationed himself at Chotu Ram's corner to wait for a passenger. There were two or three other rickshaw pullers hanging about who took no notice of him. Chotu Ram himself went off to a family whose children he took to school every day. The others soon found passengers, leaving Sudama on his own.

He didn't have to wait long before two men dressed in ill-fitting suits and carrying plastic briefcases climbed into his rickshaw and demanded to be taken to the District Magistrate's office. Fortunately this was one place that Sudama did know, but it was a long haul. The two men were heavy, and he had to stand on the pedals to get the rickshaw moving. As soon as he got up any speed he was forced to stop because he lacked the skill to negotiate his way through the traffic. Other rickshaw pullers slid through the gaps between bullock carts and *tongas*. They swerved skilfully to avoid scooters coming at them head on. They drove pedestrians out of the way by ringing their bell incessantly and shouting, 'Get out of the way! Give me the road!'

Sudama's passengers became impatient. 'Eh, rickshaw-wallah,' one said, 'we want to get to the DM's office today, not tomorrow. Get a move on.'

Sudama stood up again and pressed hard on the pedals. The rickshaw gained momentum and picked up speed because it was going slightly downhill. Sudama sat down and pedalled vigorously. Suddenly a scooter pulled out from behind a buffalo cart. Sudama clasped the brakes of the rickshaw, but nothing happened. He swerved violently, ran into a pothole and the rickshaw capsized. The scooter drove on. A crowd materialized as if from nowhere and surrounded the rickshaw. Sudama and the passengers had been thrown on to the road. After staring at them for a few minutes, some of the crowd came forward to help the two passengers get up. No one paid any attention to Sudama. The passengers started shouting abuse at him. He rose to his feet and stood in front of them menacingly, with his hands on his hips. 'Why are you calling me foul names? It wasn't my fault. It was the fault of that scooter-wallah. If you want to abuse anyone, abuse him.'

One of the passengers appealed to the crowd. 'Look at the shamelessness of these rickshaw pullers. They nearly kill their passengers and then fight with them.'

A policeman appeared and, without bothering to find out what had happened, told the two passengers to be on their way. He would deal with Sudama.

The policeman took him down a side alley and demanded he hand over all the money he'd earned. When the policeman refused to believe he had none, Sudama began untying his *lungi* saying angrily, 'I'll strip naked to show you.' The policeman recognized that Sudama was angry enough to carry out his threat and said, 'All right, all right. Get in your rickshaw and get out of here before I arrest you.'

Sudama pedalled off, the policeman giving the rickshaw a thwack with his *lathi* to help it on its way.

Not every ride was as disastrous as that first one, but Sudama could not reconcile himself to pulling a rickshaw. He accepted Chotu Ram's offer of ganja to lighten the burden on his mind. He used to smoke it of an evening, sitting around with the other rickshaw pullers. One night they were joined by a man whose hair was matted with dust. Neither his *lungi* nor his shirt had seen soap for many days. His eyes were red and dull, and he had a twitch under one. Seeing the rickshaw pullers smoking their *chilum*, he remarked, 'That's not real intoxication. I'll show you something which makes *ganja* seem as intoxicating as mother's milk.' He produced some paper screwed into a small ball from under his shirt. After he had unwrapped it carefully, he sprinkled a pinch of powder on each of their pipes. Then, getting up to go, he said, 'That's real intoxication. If you want any more, I'll be here tomorrow.'

The next evening the man with the powder was back again. Chotu Ram refused to allow him to sprinkle any on his *ganja*. 'I know what that is,' he said. 'It's heroin. Once you get addicted to that intoxication, you can't give it up. You spend all your money, and then you die. I'm quite happy with *ganja*; we've always smoked it in the village and it's done no harm.'

'Nonsense,' said the man with the powder. 'This isn't heroin. It's an intoxicant I take every day, and I'm still alive.'

'Just,' said Chotu Ram, who was not convinced. But Sudama couldn't resist the relief the new intoxicant provided. His sense of failure because he had fallen so low, his anger against society which had so humiliated him, his suspicion that everyone was mocking him, all seemed to disappear miraculously under the influence of that intoxication. He did not feel part of the sordid world of rickshaw pullers. He had no cares.

The habit soon got a grip on Sudama. Every day he would go to the rundown area on the outskirts of the town where the members of the Mallah caste lived. They were by tradition boatmen and fishermen but had recently managed to corner the new trade in drugs. He would buy the powder and then retire to a mango grove beyond the Mallah colony. There he would place a pinch of powder on a piece of silver paper torn from a cigarette packet, light a match under it and inhale through a narrow tube of paper he'd rolled. There would be a lighted *bidi* by his side, and he would draw on it greedily as soon as he had inhaled all the fumes from the powder. His daily dose cost about fifteen rupees and he was earning as much as fifty as a rickshaw puller, so he could manage financially. In fact, he was even saving money.

One evening Sudama decided to go home for a holiday. He needed a rest from rickshaw pulling and wanted to show his father and that self-righteous meddler Satya Kam Ram that he could survive without their help. He would pay back his brother's loan just to teach the family to respect him. A rest from the intoxication would be no bad thing either. He realized that it wasn't doing him any good. He seemed to need to smoke more and more and was also finding it increasingly difficult to cope with the after-effects.

Sudama smoked that evening but the next morning he

was full of the resolve of the drunkard with a terrible hangover who says, 'Never again.' On his way to the bus station, he walked past the government factory built by the British more than one hundred years ago to produce opium for the China trade. He saw brown monkeys sitting on top of the high walls swaying gently. They had drunk themelves into a stupor on the waste which came out of the factory drains. Sudama shouted at them, '*Nashekhor*, you'll wake up with your head spinning, I know, that's why you won't see me in *nasha* again.'

Still, by the time the bus reached the point where the mud track to Haripur met the main road, Sudama was feeling restless. His whole body was crying out for a smoke. 'I'll just have one more,' he thought. 'I just need this one to get me through the tension of going back to the village. Once I'm settled at home everything will be peaceful and I won't feel the need for it.' He walked towards his village until he came on a field of *arhar daal*. Scuttling between the tall plants until he was well hidden from the mud track, he squatted on his haunches and performed the ritual which had become so much part of his life.

The drug took effect rapidly. Sudama felt very much himself again. He decided to go back to the tea-shop on the main road to gossip and learn the news of the village so that he would be prepared for any eventuality when he got home.

There was the usual group of travellers sitting around the shack where tea and a few snacks kept in old-fashioned glass bottles were purveyed. Some travellers were waiting for the bus to take them away, some gathering their strength before they walked back to their villages, some hoping to get a lift in a bullock cart or perhaps even the trailer of a tractor. A holy man with a finely drawn ascetic face, his forehead smeared with grey sandalwood paste and a red *tika* down the middle, sat silently sipping tea from a thick glass. He had long grey hair down to his shoulders and a wispy beard, but he was clearly no mendicant. His blue turban and long, flowing white *kurta* were spotlessly clean, and he had neither a staff by his side nor a begging bowl.

'Move over, Baba,' said Sudama, sitting down beside the man of God. 'Where are you going?'

'I've just come. I have to walk to the Markhandeji Math.'

'Oh, yes? That's just beyond my village. What's happening there?'

The man of God was clearly not at all anxious to continue this conversation. He wanted to be left to himself, but, being polite and mild, he told Sudama, 'There's a Hari Kirtan going on throughout the day and the night. It's lasted fourteen months so far. I take part, four hours every day and four hours every night.'

Sudama laughed cheerfully, saying, 'My village is called after Hari. It certainly needs someone to pray for it.'

The holy man stood up before Sudama could introduce a new subject or put another question, and asked the young boy who served the tea and did the washing up to lift a tin trunk on to his head. The boy couldn't manage, so Sudama picked it up and put it on the old man's head, making sure that a newspaper was firmly wedged between the trunk and the turban. The old man adjusted the trunk slightly and walked off without another word.

'Strange that people like him still exist,' Sudama said to the tea-shop proprietor. 'In these days, when money counts for everything, you'd think they would be chasing after it too.'

'Oh, don't take them for what they say they are,' the proprietor replied cynically, dropping a lump of fresh ginger into the tea boiling in a smoke-blackened saucepan. 'They don't have a bad life at all. Do you think he'd be able to carry a trunk on his head at his age if he'd ever felt the pain of an empty belly? Anyhow, what do you want? Just tea?'

'Yes, tea, but with plenty of sugar and *masala*.'

'You'll get the sugar you are entitled to. Can't afford to give it away.'

'You are the son of one of the Harijans from Haripur,

aren't you?' asked a farmer, whose stomach not even the voluminous *kurta* he was wearing could conceal.

'Yes, and you are Kabir Rai – my father and my brother have worked on your land, and most of the money they should have earned has gone into that belly of yours.'

The farmer sat bolt-upright. His small eyes popped out of his face. His head shot forward. The veins in his bull neck throbbed. 'Shameless bastard,' he roared. 'You wait until you want work from anyone in our community. I'll make sure you don't get it, and don't let your father or brother come near me again. What's their name? Ram . . . some Ram . . . anyhow I'll remember . . .'

Sudama interrupted him rudely, 'Oh, be quiet. I don't need your work. I'm a graduate and doing very nicely, not an illiterate, oafish farmer like you.'

'Did you hear? Did you hear?' the farmer cried out. 'I'm not sitting here to be insulted.' Leaping to his feet, he picked up his staff and, turning to the proprietor, said, 'You should choose your customers. If you allow rude, shameless men like this one to insult decent people, you will not have any. Wait until I tell my people about this.'

The proprietor scrabbled off the clay stove on which he had been squatting and bent down to touch the farmer's feet, pleading with him, 'Rai Sahib, please forgive me. I don't know this man. He's not regular here. It's the first time I have seen him. It's not my fault. I'm not to blame.'

'Then throw him out,' the farmer demanded.

The proprietor ordered Sudama out. He stood up, stared at the farmer with a look of contempt and walked off.

The sun was setting. A train of carts returning from the market, sacks draped over the bullocks to keep out the early evening chill, turned down the mud track to Haripur. Sudama knew the state of that track, and calculated that he would get home more quickly and more comfortably by walking rather than asking for a lift.

It was dark by the time he reached the family hut. His

mother was scouring the dishes after the evening meal. Seeing her son, her eyes sparkled, and the moonlight erased the lines from her face, making her as beautiful as she had once been. She leapt up like a young woman and embraced Sudama, jabbering excitedly. He patted her on the shoulder, trying to calm her, and eventually asked where the men were. 'Oh, your father's playing cards as usual. Ajay is inside studying. It makes your father so angry. He says it's a waste of money, the oil he uses in the lantern.'

Sudama pushed open the door of the hut and peered in. 'Don't waste your time, *bhaiya*. You'll just end up a rickshaw puller like me. Education isn't going to get you anywhere. Get out with the other boys and enjoy yourself.'

His brother looked up from his books and said, 'So it's true, what we heard. You are pulling a rickshaw.'

'Yes, and I suppose the whole *basti* is laughing about it. That should teach you not to have high ideas. Anyhow it's very hard work, and I'm tired. Get me a *charpoy* and a quilt.'

Chameli tried to persuade her son to have some food but he refused. He wanted to get to sleep. The journey had been tiring and the row in the tea shop, for all his appearance of indifference, had unnerved him. He wanted to get to sleep before his father returned in case there was another row. Leave that one for the morning.

The concept of taking a holiday was unknown to Chand Ram. He worked every day he could get employment. The days he couldn't he spent worrying about where the next rupee was to come from. But he didn't want an argument and so he didn't complain about his eldest son even though he loafed around on a *charpoy* all day, making it clear that he was too superior to work with his father.

One evening when Sudama was asleep Chameli asked her husband, 'Do you notice anything peculiar about Sudama?'

'No. Except that he does not show me any respect, but I suppose that's what I have to expect because I am uneducated.'

'Maybe there's nothing to worry about, and I'm being stupid. I do wonder, though, why he does not take a bath. He used to be so clean. He's always wandering off into the field too. I don't know what he does there.'

'They learn dirty habits in cities. I wish he'd work here in the village. After all what is so grand about being a rickshaw puller? If only he wasn't so worried about his standing, he'd see that my work is no more demeaning than being a rickshaw-wallah.'

On the first morning he was back, Sudama had said he would repay the money he took to go to Ghazipur. But that hadn't happened. Sudama had spent his money on visits to the nearby town of Yusufpur. After a fortnight, without showing any sign of returning to his work in Ghazipur, he became very listless. There were no more trips into town. His money ran out. He just lay on his *charpoy* staring listlessly at the passers-by in the narrow alley. His nose ran, his eyes watered and he scratched himself so much that he drew blood in places.

Eventually his mother summoned the courage to ask, 'Are you ill?'

'Sort of,' he replied.

'What's the matter?'

'They call it "sickness" in Ghazipur.'

His mother took a step back and asked anxiously, 'You mean, you've been with dirty women?'

Sudama was becoming irritated by this conversation. 'No,' he said, 'I don't mean that. Sickness can only be cured by regular medicine, and that medicine is very expensive. We can't afford to buy it.'

When his mother asked how expensive, an idea came into her son's mind. 'Money can't buy it, at least not the sort of money we have. Only gold.'

His mother asked whether the medicine really would heal him, and he assured her that it would. She didn't have any gold but she did have a little silver. She went into the hut with Sudama following her, crossed to the far corner and unlocked a wooden box hidden behind a sack of grain. She took out a package wrapped in cloth, untied it and brought out a broad silver bangle. 'Will this do?' she asked shyly.

'Yes,' said her son, grabbing the bangle and stuffing it into his pocket.

'Don't let your father know, whatever you do. He'll die of shame if he knows I have sold my last piece of jewellery,' Chameli warned, locking the box, hiding it behind the sacks and tying the key to the end of her *sari*.

That same evening Chand Ram found out the real reason for his son's illness. At first, although he was infuriated by his son's laziness, he had not taken the matter very seriously. But when Sudama became ill his father had started to worry. Sickness would be very expensive if his wife insisted on taking him to a doctor, and he wouldn't have the heart to refuse her. So after his evening meal he set out to consult Satya Kam Ram, almost universally recognized as the wisest member of the community.

He walked along the narrow paths through the *basti* with the mud huts pressing in on either side. There was hardly any moon, but it was an open, clear sky and the occasional lantern provided a little additional light. Loud film music from radio sets disturbed the peace of the evening. A dog yelped when Chand Ram nearly fell over it, but he reached the old man's brick-built house without any more serious inconvenience. Satya Kam Ram was sitting outside, holding court and purveying advice as usual. Chand Ram waited until the group broke up and then said, 'Baba, I must have a private word with you.'

The old man invited Chand Ram into the one room of his house, fumbled around until he found a match to light the wick stuffed into the neck of a bottle of oil and then motioned Chand Ram to sit on a *charpoy*. 'Why are you so worried?' he asked. 'Your sons again?'

Chand Ram rubbed his hands together and looked down at

the ground, unable to decide how to explain his problem. After a long pause he looked up slowly and said, 'It seems as though Sudama has come back from Ghazipur ill.'

'What's the matter?'

'It's difficult to explain. He's very lazy. He changes a lot. Sometimes he's very happy; sometimes he's not angry so much as irritable. It wasn't so bad when he was going into the town most days. But since he's stopped, he just lies on the *charpoy* all day. He says he has "sickness" but won't say what that is.'

'Is his mood very down now?'

'Yes. He doesn't even bother to have a bath. His hair is filthy. He hardly speaks. My wife is very worried. I can't afford a doctor, but I know she will want one.'

Satya Kam Ram recognized what was wrong with the young man. The district had always been known for its opium because of the factory in Ghazipur, but for several years now heroin had been spreading in the villages and towns of the district. Its impact, the old social worker had noticed, was far more vicious. People said heroin had started with the Sikh extremists in Punjab. They had been the ones to first smuggle it across the border. Satya Kam Ram had known too many cases of heroin addiction to be in any doubt about the symptoms Chand Ram had described. He told the labourer as much.

Chand Ram was appalled. 'He takes heroin?'

'Yes, it seems so. All the signs are there.'

'But that's a very dangerous intoxicant, isn't it? It can't be stopped I've heard, and people die from it.'

'Dangerous it is, certainly, and I'm very worried about the spread of this habit in our community, but I know one man who gave it up and he has occasionally been able to help others too. You stay at home tomorrow and I'll come and talk to the boy.'

The next morning when Chand Ram returned from the fields where he had emptied his bowels, he said to his wife, 'The news about Sudama is very bad.'

'What do you mean?'

'Satya Kam Ram says he's taking heroin.'

Chameli burst into tears. 'Taking heroin,' she sobbed, 'and I've given him my jewellery to buy it with.'

'You've what?'

'I've given him my jewellery. I've given him my jewellery,' repeated Chameli, like a gramophone record which had got stuck.

Chand Ram collapsed on to a *charpoy*, holding his head in his hands and moaning, 'Ram, Ram, save us, save us.'

At that moment Ajay Kumar came back. It took him some time to get any sense out of his parents, but when he did eventually find out exactly what had happened, he asked where his elder brother was. Chameli said he'd left for Yusuf-pur early in the morning, telling her he was going to buy the medicine for his sickness.

Ajay Kumar was livid. '*Saale*,' he said. 'He's too proud to work, but he's not too proud to steal from us. He can go right back where he's come from. I am not going to be made the laughing stock of the village because my brother has become a *nashekhor*.'

His mother pleaded with him, but Ajay Kumar was ada-mant. He was not going to allow his elder brother back in the house. Chand Ram was overcome by this latest disaster and made no attempt to influence his son's decision.

Ajay Kumar didn't care what happened to his elder brother provided it didn't happen in Haripur. So instead of going to school he walked to the main road to wait for his brother to return.

He stood on the opposite side of the road from the tea-shop for several hours before an Uttar Pradesh Roadways bus drew up, its green-and-cream livery faded and its bodywork bearing the scars of many a minor collision. Sudama stepped down. He was surprised to see his younger brother and asked whether anything was wrong. 'A lot,' replied Ajay grimly. 'Walk down the road, and I'll tell you.'

Sudama feared that his theft of the family savings might have been discovered and he didn't know how his younger brother would take it. He was very stern, very determined, and had nothing of Sudama's fecklessness. To postpone the encounter he was dreading, Sudama suggested that they first have a cup of tea. He hoped that while drinking tea he might be able to soften Ajay a little. Although Ajay, knowing where the money had come from to pay for the tea, was reluctant, he eventually agreed. But when Sudama showed his face under the low beam which held up the tattered thatch of the tea-shop, the proprietor shouted, 'Get out! I'm not having you here annoying my customers.'

Sudama retreated hurriedly. Ajay Kumar asked, 'What was that all about?'

'Oh, just some row I had with a fat oaf of a Bhumihar when I first arrived back from Ghazipur.'

'You mean you had a public quarrel in the tea-shop?'

Sudama, clearly embarrassed, looked down, scraped the dusty verge of the road with the toe of his shoe and mumbled, 'It wasn't my fault.'

'Is there no limit to the shame you will bring on the family?' Ajay asked, grabbing his brother by the elbow and leading him up the road. When he thought they had walked far enough from the bus stop to ensure that no one would see them talking, Ajay took his brother into a mango grove, where they sat in the deep shade. He told Sudama that Satya Kam Ram knew everything. 'It'll be all round the village already that you took your mother's only silver bangle and sold it in Yusufpur to buy drugs. If you come back, you won't be able to hold your head up for shame, and there's bound to be a fight between you and Father, which will make us even more notorious. So you are not coming back.'

'Who says?' asked Sudama aggressively.

'I do, and I'll knock you about so badly you won't be able to get back to the village if you don't climb on the next bus out of here.'

Sudama collapsed. 'Don't hit me,' he pleaded. 'I'm so weak I couldn't take it. I'll go.'

So they walked back, and when the next bus came Ajay saw his brother on to it without so much as wishing him luck. Two weeks later his mother received a brown postcard from her elder son saying that he was now living in a slum in Delhi, pulling a rickshaw. Then nothing more was heard of him.

Shortly after dispatching his brother, Ajay Kumar passed the exams to get into a degree college, but he didn't have the heart to suggest to his father that he should go there, so he began to work in the village. He very rarely thought about his brother. Chand Ram showed little sign of concern either. But Chameli never reconciled herself to the disappearance of her son. She fretted and refused to eat. The lines on her face deepened. Her cheeks, which had once been full, sank as though she were toothless. Her *saris* might have been threadbare, but they had always been spotlessly clean; now she gave no thought to her appearance. Her husband Chand Ram worried about her, but what could he do? There'd been no more news of Sudama after that one postcard. Chameli kept on begging him to bring his elder son back home, but how could he? He'd never been beyond Yusufpur, and he'd heard that Delhi was a vast city like a thousand Yusufpurs. He would never be able to find his son there.

Eventually Chameli became so weak that Chand Ram told his younger son something would have to be done. Ajay Kumar resented his brother's arrogance. He did not see why his mother was grieving for a waster who had tricked her into giving away her jewellery. After all, he, Ajay, had been the one who had sacrificed his education. He had never insulted his father by saying it was demeaning to work with him. So at first he was reluctant to go to Delhi. But eventually his mother persuaded him.

He went off to see Satya Kam Ram, who advised him to travel to Delhi in second-class, unreserved railway carriages, where it was rare for a ticket collector to enter.

On arrival in the capital he made contact with a friend of the old social worker who had become the headman of a gang of municipal sweepers near New Delhi Railway Station.

The headman directed Ajay to the circular railway that went from New Delhi Station to Nizamuddin, the area where Sudama had said in his postcard he'd had been living. Arriving at the small, comparatively uncrowded station, Ajay walked to the end of the platform and along the railway line to avoid the ticket collector at the official exit. To his left were a cluster of small, one-room shacks which had sprung up around a Mughal monument just outside the high walls of Humayun's tomb. The path between the rows of huts was even narrower than any in his village. He asked a woman squatting outside her door, scouring her cooking pans, where the slum he wanted was. She didn't know and suggested he asked one of the stall-holders outside the station. A fruit-seller there told him to walk to an old bridge spanning what was once a river but was now a wide, open drain, and go into the slums running along its banks. Someone in those slums should know about his brother.

Looking down from the bridge, Ajay was appalled. His village was poor, but it was at least reasonably clean and orderly. Here he saw a smoky inferno of sordid wooden shacks, crudely nailed together and providing little protection from the wind or the rain, crowded so close to each other that some seemed about to slip down the bank into the pools of stagnant water on the edges of the drain. Black pigs nosed around in the garbage. Women washed at hand-pumps set right by the roadside. As if the horns of drivers, impatient with the congestion caused by the stalls which had spilled into the road, weren't enough to deafen Ajay, every few minutes a railway-engine driver would blast off with his brassy hooter.

Ajay was terrified at the thought of leaving the main road and entering those cramped warrens where men and women must surely live like animals, fighting to preserve their territory from encroachment and ready to attack any stranger. But he hadn't come this far to fail at the final stage, so he turned into one of the narrow paths running through the slums.

The smoke from the numberless wood fires stung his eyes as he peered into the shacks he passed. He was struck by the number of television sets he saw; squalor didn't necessarily mean poverty, apparently. He had expected hostility, or at least suspicion, but did not sense it. No one asked what he was doing; no one challenged him. The women were too busy getting on with their lives, the men with entertaining themselves, many playing cards as his father did, and strangers were of no interest to the worldly-wise children of the slums. Eventually he came to a small space where a man was repairing cycle rickshaws. He asked him whether he had heard of Sudama. The rickshaw repairer couldn't help but suggested that Ajay return to the station. 'There are a lot of rickshaw pullers there, waiting for passengers. Maybe they will know something about your brother.'

At the station a young Bengali sitting in his rickshaw waiting for a passenger did remember Ajay's brother. He remembered him because he'd been so well educated. 'He didn't last long,' the rickshaw puller said. 'He was taking drugs. Some can take drugs and do this hard work, but he couldn't, and I don't know what happened to him.'

'How can I find out?' Ajay asked.

The rickshaw puller pointed to another young man and suggested, 'Ask him. He takes smack and may take you to where it's sold. They might know.'

The young man thought that Ajay was another addict needing a source of drugs and willingly agreed to take him, hoping for a commission.

He led Ajay back into the slums, to one of the few brick-built shacks. The door was shut, but he hammered on it shouting, 'Krishan Lal, open up. Here's someone needing some stuff.'

A middle-aged man came out, buttoning up a brightly coloured silk shirt which just met across his pot-belly, rubbing his eyes and running his fingers through his hair. He was clearly displeased at having been woken from his sleep. 'Don't make such a racket,' he said angrily. 'I have enough trouble with the police already without you announcing my business to all comers.'

Ajay did not want to get into trouble with the police either, so he explained, 'I haven't come to buy. I was told you might know what happened to my brother Sudama. He came here from Ghazipur.'

'Oh, that arrogant bastard. He was a no-gooder. Died owing me money. Now you get out – and you too,' he said, turning to the rickshaw puller. 'Don't you go giving my name to any stray passer-by, or you'll be in real trouble.'

The two men moved off sharply, the rickshaw puller now upbraiding Ajay for wasting his time and getting him into difficulties with the drug supplier. Ajay just wanted to get out of the slum and go home. He didn't doubt the word of the drug supplier because he didn't see how Sudama could have survived in such squalor. There seemed no point in making further inquiries.

He reached the bus stop nearest the village after a tiring twenty-four-hour journey. It had been impossible to sleep in the crowded compartment, and Ajay had been thinking of his future. He knew his father would take Sudama's death as the final proof that education ended in disaster. But to Ajay it meant something else. If Sudama had found a decent job, he would have been able to help them all rise above the status of agricultural labourers. Now Ajay Kumar knew only he could do that, and he was determined that his father should not stop him.

As he approached the Dalit settlement he saw the smoke from the evening fires hanging like a pall over the huts. He smelt the burning cow dung, so much more comforting than the acrid smells of the slums. He skirted around the outside of the settlement until he came to the path leading to Satya Kam Ram's house. When he reached it he begged the old man to come with him to help break the news to his mother.

Chameli was crouching over her clay stove, stirring *daal*. When she saw her son and the old social worker approaching she knew the news was bad. If it had been good, Ajay would have come straight home. 'He's dead,' she said. 'You don't need to tell me.'

'Yes, he's dead,' Ajay replied.

Chameli stood up, wiped her hands on the side of her *sari* and said, 'I hope you and your father are satisfied.'

Neighbours were already gathering. News of a tragedy passes from mouth to mouth in a village faster than any sound wave can carry it. Women burst into tears and embraced Chameli, but she pushed them away. 'How can it be that a mother isn't weeping when her son dies?' they asked each other.

Chameli looked at Ajay and said, 'You drove my son away because you were ashamed of him, although all he wanted was to get a good job to help you.

'I can look after myself,' retorted Ajay. 'I will get a job. I have the guts, unlike Sudama.'

VILLAGE STRIKE

The shrill voices of his women labourers were still ringing in the ears of Brajbhushan Rai as he sat cross-legged on a *charpoy*, waiting for his breakfast. It was about ten o'clock in the morning, and the farmer from the Bhumihar caste had just come back from his paddy fields without reaching agreement with the women on how much they should be paid for transplanting rice seedlings. The labourers were demanding the monstrous sum of sixteen rupees per day, which was perilously near the minimum wage ordained by the government. To obey any government order was an insult to a Bhumihar, who always regarded his pride as even more precious than his pocket. What was worse, in recent years the women had bargained hard but had settled for something less than their original demand, enabling him to claim a victory and save his face, or *izzat*, but this year they wouldn't reduce their claim by a single *paisa*.

There was no comfort for him at home. His mother banged the breakfast tray down and then, standing back, arms akimbo, squawked, 'You haven't fixed those work-shy women, have you? It's written all over your face that you haven't. You are a disgrace to your father. If he'd been alive, he would have soon had them in the fields at the rate he was prepared to pay them, and that would have been no more than a *seer* of *khesari*. You are offering them real money, and they say that's not enough. You've got a *lathi* lying by your *charpoy*. Why don't you pick it up and use it? Drive them into the fields.'

Blocking his ears, Brajbhushan shouted, '*Bas, bas*! Keep quiet! What with you and those labourers, I've had enough of women. It's not just the neighbours – the whole village can hear you shrieking like a parrot. You'll even let the Harijans know about our problems. Haven't you any shame?'

'Shame? Shame?' shrieked the old lady. 'You dare to speak to me of shame? I never expected to see a son of your father with so little courage. If anyone ever dared to suggest that Babu Digvijay Rai had any cause for shame, he would break his skull. He was the leader of the Bhumihars in this village, and nobody ever challenged that. You,' she sneered, 'you don't even look like a leader. When did you last have a shave? Weeks ago. Get your face cleaned up. Make yourself look like a man, and then those women will accept whatever you offer.'

Brajbhushan's father had been the *sarpanch*, or head of the council, of Latari village for many years. He had seen to it that the council was dominated by his caste, Bhumihars, who claimed to be Brahmins but did not assume priestly prerogatives. They were, as Brajbhushan's father used to say, 'ploughers rather than prayers'. He had always claimed that the Bhumihars ruled all along the banks of the Ganges, from Benares to the borders of Bengal. He'd bullied Brajbhushan, his only son, just as he'd bullied the whole village, leaving Brajbhushan without the self-confidence of a leader but with the aggression of insecurity. Brajbhushan's wife had died after giving birth to his second son. She had stood up to her mother-in-law, but now Brajbhushan, although in name head of the joint family, had, in fact, surrendered that office to his mother.

When Brajbhushan eventually managed to escape from the storm raging in the *zenana haveli* to the comparative peace of what was known as the 'gate' (the few small rooms the men of the family could call their own), he slumped down on a *charpoy* under a neem tree just outside the veranda. His servant squatted below him, wearing just a stained loin-cloth tied tightly between his legs. The loin-cloth had been beaten against the *dhobi*'s washing-stone so often it was almost transparent. Brajbhushan shouted at his servant, 'Get off your haunches and get over to where the *nau* lives, as quickly as possible. Tell him I want him here at once. It's a disgrace that he hasn't been for days on end and that I should have to send for him.'

Actually, Brajbhushan had been quite happy to give his face a bit of a rest. The *nau*, or barber, employed a cut-throat razor which was not always as sharp as it should be and economized by not using soap, so shaving could be a painful process.

The servant returned, not with the barber but with his son, who instead of squatting humbly in front of Brajbhushan stood before him, with a surly look on his face, and asked abruptly, 'You sent for my father?'

'Yes. He hasn't been to see me for many days now. You can tell by the state of my beard.'

'How much will you pay him for a shave?'

'Pay!' exploded the Bhumihar. 'He and you know very well what the tradition is. Those who give the village service like you *naus* get your annual payment in grain. You have plenty to eat and some left over to sell.'

'That was so,' said the truculent young *nau*, 'but we've decided that we want to be paid in cash, and on the spot. The days of so-called gifts are over.'

'You can't just decide to break our village traditions like that. It needs a decision of the council to make such changes and the *sarpanch* is, as you know, my cousin–brother, so go back to your father and tell him to get over here immediately, or I will send someone to put him right – and you too. I have never heard such nonsense. Who do you think rules in this village: the *naus* or the Bhumihars? Get out, *saale*, and get that old man here.'

The young *nau* turned and walked away, leaving Brajbhushan uncertain about the outcome of the argument. Normally if you gave someone like a barber a good tongue-lashing, that did the job, but the young *nau* had walked off with remarkable assurance and without making the usual grovelling apology. Perhaps he should have had a taste of the *lathi*. That would have taught him where the power lay. Maybe Brajbhushan's mother was right. It could be that he was too soft, although it wasn't so easy to wield the *lathi* as it had been in his father's day. The politicians had given the lower castes a voice, say what you like about them. Anyhow, he couldn't suffer the humiliation of going to the *nau*'s hut and administering the thrashing now. News of that would get all round the village. He must just wait and hope that the old *nau* would bring his son to his senses and point out the obvious – that the family couldn't live in the village unless they accepted the Bhumihar *raj*.

One day went by, two days, three, and still there was no sign of the barber or, indeed, his son. Brajbhushan's position was becoming more and more difficult. The stubble had now grown well beyond the limit allowed to a Bhumihar, but he couldn't explain to his mother or anyone else that a *nau* had made the outrageous demand that he should be paid cash for a shave. He didn't feel at all confident about shaving himself, and anyway there was no privacy in his home to allow him to take such a revolutionary step in secret. If he went to the nearby town and came back shaved, questions would be asked too.

Gradually, however, it dawned on Brajbhushan that he might not be alone. He began to notice an unusual amount of stubble on other Bhumihar jowls too. It looked as though the *nau*'s strike was spreading, so Brajbhushan was not surprised when a meeting of the *biradari* was called. It came as a great relief. He had been carrying a guilty secret. Now the load was lifted off his back. The *biradari* would take over. He said to his mother, 'We'll show the bastards, you'll see.'

But that stern old lady was not fully convinced. 'I don't know whether today's men have the courage to do what has to be done – beat them until they whine like curs, which is what they are. Talk, talk seems to be the modern way, and it will just encourage them. Beta, make sure that you at least go into the *biradari* meeting with a *lathi* in your hand.'

Brajbhushan was one of the first to speak at the *biradari* meeting, which was held on the terrace outside the house of the *sarpanch*, Shiv Kumar Rai. The curly fringe of grey hair surrounding Brajbhushan's bald pate was dishevelled. The grey stubble on his cheeks contrasted with his black eyebrows. His eyes were red with anger. The sleeves of his *kurta* were rolled up. In short, he had the look of a man rearing for action as he demanded from the meeting, 'How many more insults can we swallow? I tell you, too much has happened. There will be no end to all this until we make them understand that we rule this village, and there is only one way to do that – the *lathi*. I, for one, am ready to pick up my *lathi*. It's the only medicine I know which will cure their impudence.'

Not all the members of the *biradari* were in agreement. There were fears that the *naus* would register a police case against them, but those fears were quashed by the general view that the Bhumihars could afford to pay more for the support of the police than the *naus*, so the case would end up with the barbers being accused of assault.

It was decided that the attack should take place quickly, so that the *naus* didn't get to hear of their plans in advance and run away. Brajbhushan agreed to be the leader. Slogans were suggested, but no one came up with anything more imaginative than '*Bhumihar raj zindabad* – long live *Bhumihar* rule,' and it was felt that the attackers did not need this to keep their morale up as they marched to the *naus*' quarters – better to go in silence and maintain the advantage of secrecy.

Unfortunately, the Bhumihars' brawn was not matched by brain. They were not very good planners. They forgot that nothing is ever a secret in an Indian village and failed to notice that the *sarpanch*'s servant had slipped away when he heard about the decision to attack. So it happened that as the brave Bhumihars led by Brajbushan, who was determined to restore his reputation in his home, were walking in single file down a path leading to the barbers' huts, they found their way blocked by a ferocious, half-starved dog on a long rope tied to a peg in the ground. Behind the dog was a none too amiable bull, similarly tethered. The Bhumihars held a council of war. The lane was too narrow to by-pass the barbers' defences. They could go through the mud huts and cramped courtyards crowded together on one side of the lane, but it would be beneath their dignity, and they might even get lost in that maze. So they decided to clamber along the bank of the *garhai* on the other edge of the lane. It was a crater excavated by the villagers for mud to build their huts. Bamboos and other bushes were sprouting from its banks now because mud was used less often in house contruction. Brick had taken its place.

Brajbhushan, using his *lathi* to support himself, proceeded gingerly along the bank, which the first monsoon shower had made very slippery. He kept quite near to the top to avoid the steeper part of the slope – too near, in fact, because he misjudged the length of rope securing the dog. The ferocious animal leaped at him, missing his arm but catching the end of his *kurta*. Brajbhushan kicked the dog viciously, but his other foot slipped from under him and he rolled down the bank into a pool of stagnant water at the bottom of the *garhai*. The other Bhumihars ran for it, leaving Brajbhushan with the indignity of having to scramble up the bank on his hands and knees under the gaze of the satisfied but silent *naus* and members of what the Bhumihars regarded as the lower castes who had assembled to watch the spectacle. So eager was Brajbhushan to escape this humiliation that he left his *lathi*, the symbol of Bhumihar authority with which he had believed such mighty works would be wrought, entangled in a bush half-way down the bank.

The *biradari* assembled again the next day. The *sarpanch* had not joined the attacking party himself. His role had been as a general back at headquarters, but he had received a full

report of the inglorious action. He looked angrily at Brajbhushan and said, 'After all that boasting about your *lathi* you
made a fool of yourself and made us all look fools too. It's said
that Thakurs have fight but no brains, Brahmins have brains
but no fight, only Bhumihars have both. Yesterday you made
it clear to the whole village that Bhumihars have neither.
Now what do you propose?'

Brajbhushan sat silently, his eyes downcast. Eventually a
younger member of the *biradari*, wearing a vest and *dhoti*, who
described himself as a youth leader, the first step on the
ladder to political fame and fortune, said, 'We politicians
always believe in doing caste calculations. You can't win an
election on your own, so you have to join hands with other
castes. My calculation this time is that we have to join hands
with the Brahmins. After all, they want to see the lower castes
taught a lesson just as much as we do, and if you think we
lack brains, they don't.'

The *sarpanch* replied, 'Hanuman Prasad, you don't seem to
me to be very good at doing these sums you are talking about.
You've changed political parties more often than I've eaten
hot *jalebis*, yet your career seems to be going nowhere. Never
forget, a Brahmin looks as pure and peaceful as a white egret
standing on one leg, but, like the egret, he is in reality always
on the look-out to stab a fish. I never trust Brahmins.'

But, while any formal alliance was rejected, it was agreed
to consult Pandit Ram Kishore Dwivedi, who had a reputation for cunning that was unusual even in a Brahmin.

Dwivedi, with his pointed face, sharp nose and small,
bright eyes, had the look of a fox about him. He was only
about forty. His hair, still black, shone with oil; he wore an
immaculately tied white *dhoti*; his hairless chest was bare
except for his sacred thread. He had feigned reluctance to
involve himself in the affairs of the Bhumihars when the
sarpanch had summoned him, but in reality he was delighted
to have the chance to demonstrate that they couldn't get on
without Brahmins. To make his point, he insisted on a meeting

of the *biradari*. He refused to give advice privately to the *sarpanch*.

Just as the meeting was about to start a shout went up, 'Wait! Wait! Bhishamji is coming!' Emerging from one of the narrow lanes could be seen the figure of an old man bent double over his stick, hobbling towards the meeting. He was Bhisham Narayan Singh, the oldest of all the Bhumihars in the village. The *sarpanch* moved over to make room for the patriarch on his *charpoy*, but the old man refused to sit down. Pointing his stick at the Brahmin, he said, 'I don't accept this. I have been to meetings of the *biradari* for eighty years, and I have never known someone from another caste to attend. This is shameful, and no good will come of it. We Bhumihars have always sorted out our own affairs without help from anyone else.'

The Brahmin looked at the old man scornfully and replied, 'I never asked to come to your meeting. If you don't want me, I'll go. In your days, Bhishamji, if a Brahmin was insulted, he would climb a tree and threaten to throw himself down until he received a suitable apology. You know how deep the belief used to be that you must not insult a Brahmin, yet now you are treating me as an unwelcome guest. What greater insult can there be than that?'

The old man folded his hands in front of his bowed head and said, 'Forgive me, forgive me. I never thought I was insulting a Brahmin. It's very stupid of me. I didn't think straight in my anger because the traditions of my *biradari* are very dear to me. I did not think of you as a guest. I should have done.'

The Brahmin turned to the *sarpanch* and said, 'I am surprised that the elders of your community can behave in this way to a Brahmin. This must be why some young Bhumihars are now even saying, "We are Brahmins too, and we don't need anyone else to perform our rituals." Some of you have forgotten that it's your sacred duty to give us alms. The only time you worry about us is at funerals, when you are afraid that if the Brahmins are angry, the dead man will be unhappy in his next life. Is it any wonder that the barbers don't respect you any longer if you don't respect the Brahmins? If you no longer accept the old way that society used to work in the village, with every caste knowing its duty, how can you expect the barbers to?'

There was a murmur of 'That's true, that's true,' from the *biradari*, and the *sarpanch* said, 'Panditji, we have taken this very unusual step of asking you to our meeting because of the respect we have for Brahmins, and I can assure you there has never been a time, nor can there ever be, when Bhumihars say there's no need for Brahmins. If respect for Brahmins is not there, then our society will collapse. Accept my assurance that we have the utmost respect for your community, but how can we restore the proper relationship between us and the *naus*?'

'Not by beating them up,' replied the Brahmin. 'You are very lucky that Brajbhushan fell into the *garhai* and the rest of you ran away. This government has been elected by the backward castes. Our sort of people are not ruling any more. The Chief Minister is now a backward, so is our MLA and so is the *thanedar*. You could have been in jail for a very long time if you'd given the *naus* a thrashing.'

The Brahmin tried to convince the Bhumihars that the only answer was to pay the *naus* in cash instead of in kind. He argued that under the caste system everyone had a right to be paid for their work. If the sweepers were not given enough to live on, the whole system would collapse because there would be no one to do their job. The same went for the barbers. All they were demanding was a different form of payment. Better to agree to that than have the *naus* leave the village and there be no one to shave, cut hair and massage. The Brahmin also reminded the *biradari* that *naus* played important roles in the ceremonies that marked a man's passage through life, including death. Without them, religion in the village would collapse too.

The *biradari* had expected a clever solution to their dilemma, not a simple one, but they were reluctant to reject the Brahmin's advice outright for fear of offending him again, and so tea was called for, and the Brahmin was assured from all sides that his views would be considered most seriously. But after he had left, the *biradari* firmly rejected the proposal to pay barbers in cash.

It was Brajbhushan Rai who came up with a strategy. He proposed that all the *biradari* should go to the nearest *qasba* and have a hair-cut and shave there. That, he was sure, would bring the village *naus* to their right minds because they would see that their livelihood was threatened. Some doubt was expressed about the sort of haircut the Bhumihars would get. One elderly Bhumihar told Brajbhushan, 'I don't want to come back looking like that son of yours who goes to college with his hair all over the place and hanging over his eyes. We Bhumihars should always have our hair cropped. That makes you look like a man, not a woman.'

Hanuman Prasad, the youth leader, said, 'Come on, dada, you could never look like a woman. You don't have enough hair on your head, and your buffalo face would give you away anyhow. I've been to saloons and they have photographs of all sorts of hair cuts so you can choose to come out with a head as bald as a pumpkin or looking like Amitabh Bacchan – that's who Brajbhushan's son thinks he looks like.'

The next day the Bhumihars set off in tractors and on bicycles to the small town of Nasimganj. A hyperactive MLA had once galvanized the local administration into building a mud road for much of the way, but lethargy soon overtook the local bureaucracy again and the road was now gently disintegrating.

The convoy stopped at the first saloon they came to. It was nothing more than a small shack on the side of the main road running through the town. The young barber was doing good business. There was one customer in the chair and two sitting waiting. Brajbhushan threw down his cycle and strode up to the barber to announce that the Bhumihars of Latari village wanted shaves and haircuts immediately. The barber seemed unimpressed and, without turning from his task, told Brajbhushan the *biradari* would have to wait. The Bhumihar's hands shot out. He yanked the customer out of the barber's chair, hurled him on to the muddy roadside, sat down himself and ordered, 'Bastard, now cut my hair and don't ever think a *chutiya* of a *nau* like you can insult a Bhumihar.'

The barber ran out of the saloon shouting, 'Save me! Save me! I am being killed!' His customer, who was still lying in the mud, feigned serious injury and shouted, 'I am dying! I have been beaten to death!' A crowd gathered as if from nowhere. Everyone was talking at once, each anxious to express his own views on the incident, but no one was at all interested in finding out what had happened. Very soon the atmosphere became distinctly hostile to Brajbhushan. Sensing this, his friends faded into the background, leaving him to fend for himself. Bluster failed, and so the Bhumihar tried to win sympathy, but in all the shouting that no one could even hear him plead that he had been insulted. Brajbhushan was only saved from a thorough beating by the timely arrival of a police jeep.

The police quickly assessed that Brajbhushan was the 'fat chicken'. They took him away, leaving the barber and his customer behind because they clearly did not have the wherewithal to pay a worthwhile bribe. In the police station Brajbhushan was ordered to sit down in front of a sub-inspector whose belly was bulging over his leather belt. He was told that a First Information Report would be lodged against him, alleging that he had been guilty, under section 146 of the Indian Penal Code, of creating a riot, under section 159 of affray, under section 355 of assault and under the catch-all clause 263 for being a public nuisance. He would be held in the police lock-up that night and presented in the magistrate's court the next day. In view of the seriousness of the offences the police would oppose bail, and the magistrate, who didn't like people making trouble for him, would almost certainly consign him to the district jail, some thirty miles away.

Brajbhushan demanded that the barber be called in to be interrogated, but the sub-inspector said there was no need for that. He would say exactly what was required of him in court, and there would be other witnesses too who would tell the magistrate exactly what the police told them to say.

Then suddenly the sub-inspector was struck by an interesting thought.

'*Nau*, did you say?'

'Yes, the *nau* who started it all by insulting me. You see, it was his fault, Inspector Sahib, you must understand, a man of your status. How would you feel if you were insulted by a mere *nau*?'

'You committed a crime against a *nau*. Ah, now, that's *really* serious,' the police officer said, leaning back in his chair, massaging his belly and smiling with satisfaction. 'You have committed an atrocity against one of the Lower and Scheduled Castes, and that's one of the worst charges you can have against you. Even if we were to think of a different road, that would be very difficult now because if a police officer is booked for not reporting an offence under the Scheduled Caste and Scheduled Tribes Atrocities Act, it's regarded as a very serious dereliction of duty.'

'Different road? What different road do you mean?' asked Brajbhushan.

'Well, I can tell you that in your case it won't just mean tea and snacks.'

'You mean to say – You are suggesting that I pay a bribe?'

'If you must state the obvious.'

'But I can't,' said an even more agitated Brajbhushan. 'My *biradari* would never forgive me. They might even order *hookah pani bund*. We Bhumihars are rulers, and we only bribe you police to take action against our enemies, especially the lower castes. It would be against my honour to offer money to save myself.'

'It would be against my honour not to take a bribe, and a big one too, from a man apparently as important as you. I suggest five thousand rupees and then there would be no damage to my honour.'

After some bargaining the sum was reduced slightly, but it was still a substantial amount for a farmer. The sub-inspector took the small sum of money that Brajbhushan was carrying as a deposit and warned that a force would pay a visit to Latari and he would suffer the humiliation of being taken away in handcuffs if the balance was not paid within a week. The sub-inspector also noted in the station diary that there had been a minor scuffle outside a barber's saloon, but no one was prepared to lodge a First Information Report, and so he'd dismissed both sides with cautions. He smiled as he made the entry, happy with the money and also happy to have fooled the Bhumihar – *naus* were not Scheduled Castes and did not come under the Atrocities Act.

Brajbhushan was a much sobered man. He didn't want to risk any further humiliation, so he decided not to go back to the saloon to see if his bicycle was still there. Instead he skirted round the edge of Nasimganj and walked back to his village, reaching home well after dark.

Once again there was no comfort for him at home. The whole village, including his mother, although she kept *purdah* and never went outside the walls of the women's quarters, had heard of the shame that had befallen Brajbhushan. What is more, the situation on the domestic front had deteriorated. Apparently the *dhobis* were now demanding money too. The *dhobi* had come that morning with his donkey, carrying two bundles of clean clothes slung across his back, but the donkey had left the house without his usual load of dirty clothes.

When Brajbhushan's mother brought him his dinner she said sarcastically, 'You keep on telling me your *sarpanch* and your *biradari* meetings will fix these people who don't know their place, but it seems to me that it's you who are being fixed.' She turned and walked away before her son could find anything to say in reply.

Having failed to cow the *naus*, and needing to teach the *dhobis* a lesson too, the Bhumihar *biradari* decided to go to a neighbouring village and ask them to send *dhobis* and *naus* to their rescue. To avoid a third public humiliation, it was decided that only the *sarpanch* should go. He would say that he was just going to pay a fraternal call on the *sarpanch* of the other village to discuss politics and other interests in common between the two elders.

So Shiv Kumar Rai, *sarpanch* of Latari village, draped a white cotton cloth around his shoulders and set off on his tractor.

Laxman Singh, the *sarpanch* of Dukhdera village, was not surprised to see him. After the essential politenesses had been observed he said, 'You will have come to see me to talk about the misbehaviour of your *naus* and *dhobis*.'

Shiv Kumar was surprised, 'So you know everything? How can that be?'

'Well, the news was not on the BBC, if that's what you are worried about, but even without radio and television, news like this always spreads like jungle fire.'

'Yes, that's true, and since you know all about our problem, I won't waste your time. I have come with this purpose: to ask you to join in our struggle because you must be afraid that this misbehaviour will spread to your village too, and only if we Bhumihars stand together can that disaster be averted.'

Shiv Kumar then put forward his proposal that *dhobis* and *naus* should be sent from Dukhdera to his village to break the strike. But it was not well received. Laxman Singh retained tight control over Dukhdera, and he was not going to allow his *naus* and *dhobis* to get first-hand experience of what was happening in Latari village.

'Remember the ber and the banana tree,' he said, quoting

a well-known couplet by the poet Rahim. 'If they stand side by side, the ber's thorns will tear the soft banana leaves. I have kept my *naus* soft. You've let yours grow thorns.'

So yet another strategy of the Bhumihars of Latari failed. As the *sarpanch* approached the village pond he saw black buffaloes wallowing in the muddy water, snorting contentedly. Labourers, their day's work over, were washing in the water spouting from the pipe of a tubewell. Ponies, their legs tied together to prevent them from wandering too far, were grazing on what remained of the common land, and a lame donkey walked towards him crabwise, rather like the buses, with their twisted chassis, which charged, sideways on, down the main road to Ghazipur.

'Everything,' the *sarpanch* thought, 'seems so normal and peaceful. Who would think that the whole foundation of our society is threatened?'

But as he drew nearer to the area where the Bhumihars lived he smelt the sickly stench of rotting flesh. Something else was wrong, he realized. When he reached his home he was informed that another disaster had befallen Brajbhushan.

One of his cows, which had been sick for some time without benefit of a vet, had died in a stall adjacent to his gate. His servant had been sent to call those sweepers whose traditional job it was to remove the carcasses of dead farm animals to a field outside the village. There they would skin the animal and leave its flesh to be eaten by vultures, dogs and jackals. The sweepers had arrived but had refused to remove the carcass unless Brajbhushan paid them what he regarded as an outrageous sum of money. The Bhumihar threatened *lathis* and much more, but the sweepers stood their ground. Their leader said, 'We don't see why we shouldn't have a strike too, and if you can't make the *naus* and the *dhobis* do your work, why should we unless we are satisfied with what we get in return?'

Brajbhushan's tempestuous temper overcame him. This was

one insult too much. Without a thought for all the words of caution he had heard about attacking the scheduled castes, he raised his *lathi* and began to belabour one of the sweepers about the shoulders. Suddenly there was a thwack across his arms and his hands fell away. One of the Bhumihar's sons had heard the sounds of the altercation and had run across just in time to save his father from committing murder. The sweepers ran for their lives with Brajbhushan's son shouting after them, 'Get out, you bastards! Get out. The next time I will let him kill you.'

That still left the problem of the cow, which was reported to the *sarpanch*. Calling meetings of the *biradari* had solved nothing so far, but still the village elder could think of no alternative.

When the leading members of the Bhumihar community gathered yet again in an emergency session of the *biradari* council, they took an even more serious view of the scavengers' revolt. It wasn't that one of their community had almost committed murder. Murder was comparatively commonplace. No, what upset them was that the revolt might now spread throughout the entire Harijan community. Then where would they get the labour to work their fields and look after their livestock?

The *sarpanch* said, '*Naus* are always troublemakers. I wasn't all that surprised when the *dhobis* followed their example – after all, many of them are now making good money in laundries – but I never expected those who are nothing but scavengers to react like this. I have always said,' he continued, misquoting the saint Kabir, 'that Harijans are one community who can tolerate anything. They are like the earth: however much you dig it up, it bears it; however much the rivers flood, the trees on the banks, they will survive. But now it seems that's not true.'

The meeting went round and round in circles. Violence was considered again, this time burning down huts to set an example, but Brajbhushan pointed out that the new *thanedar* was only interested in 'very fat money, or touching the MLA's feet'. He wouldn't side with them, nor would the MLA, who belonged to a backward caste. The Brahmin was discussed, but it was generally agreed that he would only repeat his advice to settle. That was considered too, but even the stench from the cow's carcass, the flies and the threat of disease they represented could not persuade the *biradari* that pride had to be swallowed. So the meeting was adjourned.

When Brajbhushan reached home with his two sons after the meeting they were surprised to find the door of the women's *haveli* locked. Brajbhushan rattled the door and shouted, 'What nonsense is this? Come on, open up.' This provoked a verbal barrage from the other side of the door. Brajbhushan's mother shouted, 'You men can't enter through the door until the disgrace on our house is lifted, and you get rid of that cow's carcass.'

The daughters-in-law of the house yelled, 'No food, no bed, until you shave and put on clean clothes.'

One son, who was with Brajbhushan, shouted, 'Shut your mouths. If you don't let us in, I will beat your bones into chaff.'

The other banged on the door with his fists and yelled, 'Open this door or I'll break it down and break open your heads.'

Brajbhushan beat the door too, adding to the uproar by shouting, 'This is shameful, shameful! Open up. Open the door.'

But all the bravado and all the threats were of no avail. Eventually the men decided that they had been defeated yet again, and Brajbhushan called out querulously, 'At least you might explain what you mean by all this.'

'We are on strike too,' his mother replied.

It wasn't just the Bhumihar men who had been planning strategies to defeat the *naus* and *dhobis*. Brajbhushan's mother had been plotting with other Bhumihar women behind the walls of her *zenana*. At first she had been as adamant with the women as she had been with her son. 'Go,' she told the youngsters, 'and put some bone in your men's cocks.' But remembering her son's narrow escape from jail, she decided that perhaps a little finesse was required. As the men had consulted the Brahmin, Ram Kishore Dwivedi, she called his wife, who was just as direct.

'Your men have been fools,' she said. 'They didn't treat the *naus* with proper caution. Everyone knows that old saying: "Of all the birds that fly, the craftiest is the crow. The *nau* is the most cunning of men who walk below." Your Bhumihar men think brawn baffles brains, but it doesn't. It's the other way round, and that's why you underestimated your enemy.'

'We all accept that our men are very stupid, but what can we do about it?' asked Brajbhushan's mother.

'You have no alternative − get your men to settle for the best terms they can negotiate before the *naus* turn the whole village against you and you find you have to come out of your *purdah* and transplant rice yourselves.'

When Brajbhushan's mother asked how they could force their men to see the sense of compromise, the Brahmin's wife pointed out that women too provided services which could be withdrawn.

Brajbhushan's mother asked, 'You mean cooking food?'

'Is that all you do?'

'What else?'

Some of the younger women started to giggle, and the Brahmin's wife, pointing at them, said, 'They know what I mean, but perhaps it's too long ago since you provided any other service than cooking food for you to remember.'

'Ah, yes,' the old lady said, 'now I understand. The meaning is that we should have a *bistara bund* − a ban on bed.' Everyone burst out laughing.

One younger woman said, 'That's all very well. You haven't got a man demanding to go to bed with you. He's long dead. Some of us will get a sound thrashing if we refuse.'

'How can you be beaten if you don't allow your men into the house?' said the Brahmin's wife with a smile.

That was how Brajbhushan and his sons came to find themselves hammering on the door of the *haveli*. They didn't know whether the strike was limited to their women, or whether it was a case of 'all out', and so they decided to keep their shame to themselves, and crept quietly across to the gate. There they brought out their *charpoys* and lay down uncomfortably close to the stall in which the cow had died. No one brought them their evening meal.

The next morning the three men woke up as usual, washed their mouths out, and then sat disconsolately on the edge of their *charpoys*. One of Brajbhushan's sons groaned, 'I don't feel like going into the fields this morning to have my motion.'

'That's not surprising,' replied his brother. 'What you don't put in, you can't force out.'

Brajbhushan sighed. 'I can't even go into Nasimganj to have breakfast in a hotel in case that bastard *thanedar* sees me. I still haven't collected the money to pay him. That will be the final insult if he comes and takes me away in chains.'

Another group of Bhumihar men walked past the gate chewing neem twigs to clean their teeth. Brajbhushan called out, 'Ram, Ram, did you have a good night?'

'Yes,' replied one of them. 'If you call trying to sleep with your belly rumbling and your balls aching a good night.'

'So it happened to you too?'

'Yes. Come on, let's go and see the *sarpanch* to find out if he's got any ideas about this one.'

The *sarpanch* was already surrounded by angry members of the *biradari* threatening a no-confidence motion against him if he couldn't resolve the crisis. The situation was going from bad to worse. The *sarpanch* had now learnt that all the village knew their wives were on strike. Once again servants had been the messengers. Their stories had been so improbable that at first they had been accused of spreading rumours, but then their reports had been confirmed by reports from other villagers who had seen that the doors of Bhumihar *zenanas* were indeed firmly shut.

When Ram Kishore Dwivedi heard the news he hurried through his morning ablutions and rituals with unusual alacrity and set off in the direction of the Bhumihar homes. He walked over to the gathering outside the *sarpanch*'s house he walked over, bowed his head low in an exaggerated gesture of respect, folded his hands and said, '*Namaste*, Laxman Singhji. I have heard that you rejected my advice. Perhaps you were quite right. Maybe it wouldn't have been a good thing to surrender to those impudent *naus*. No one knows where that would have led. Everything is all right now, isn't it?'

'All right?' fumed the *sarpanch*. 'All right? You know perfectly well that nothing is right. I can see from that sly look on your face. What have you come here for – to mock us? Why don't you go away and leave us to our misery?'

'*Sarpanchji*,' said the Brahmin in tones of mock surprise, 'I never expected to hear you talking like that, a man who is so resourceful that he can rule this village, a friend of *thanedars*, an adviser to big political leaders. You have often told me how great a man you are. Surely such a man can't be at a loss just to deal with a lot of women?'

'So you have heard.'

'Well, yes. I have heard that there was no consolation for Bhumihar men in their beds last night, but how can I believe such a thing? The next rumour we will be hearing, I suppose, is that your women have taken to the servants for comfort. After all, you are always boasting about how passionate your women are.'

The Bhumihars were growing increasingly angry, and some suggested that the Brahmin should be thrown out, but when he reminded them that earlier attempts at violence had not exactly helped their cause, they restrained themselves. The Brahmin then turned to the *sarpanch* and said, 'Shiv Kumarji,

I can see that you still think you know best and so there's no point in my staying here. I will be off so that the breakfast my wife is cooking for me won't get cold.'

As the Brahmin walked away one of the Bhumihars shouted after him, 'That witch of a wife of yours may be able to cook you food, but I bet she can't do anything for you in bed.'

Hungry and with nowhere to get a meal, the Bhumihars eventually decided the only option was to reopen negotiations with their women. But when they reassembled no one had any progress to report. The women had all been adamant. Brajbhushan was, however, able to throw light on how the strike had started. His mother had told him of the intervention of the Brahmin's wife. Some of the Bhumihars were all for going to threaten Dwivedi with a thrashing if he didn't tell his wife to get the strike called off, but the *sarpanch* was of a different mind.

'Now,' he said, 'we have the high castes as well as the low castes against us, but at last I see how it has all happened, how stupid we have been. We didn't realize that we had forgotten our status. Just because we are always proud of the fact that by birth and tradition we are the only caste which has brains and brawn, we thought we were as clever as the Brahmins. I should say we thought we were more clever than they.'

'So what do we do now?' Brajbhushan asked.

'I'm going to call Panditji and apologize to him for not knowing our place,' replied the *sarpanch*. 'Then I'll tell him to settle all this nonsense.'

'But that's an intolerable humiliation.'

'It's people like you, with more pride than brains, who have brought it on us,' said the *sarpanch*, standing up and walking towards the quarter of the village where Dwivedi lived.

That was the only wise decision that the Bhumihar leader took. He calculated, rightly, that the Brahmin would be a much more skilled negotiator than any Bhumihar – a negotiator who, after all, had an identical interest in keeping the price of village services as low as possible.

TWICE BORN

'There are those who like parties and those who don't. My wife is one who certainly does,' thought Ramadhar Upadhyaya, standing on the edge of the gathering on the lawn of the Mohammed Bagh Club in Lucknow, watching his wife Usha listening attentively to Seth Ramdas, the son of one of the biggest industrialists of Lucknow. In the semi-darkness, outside the pool of light from the coloured bulbs strung over bushes and the lamps discreetly shaded behind branches, he stared at the garish *saris*, the contrived hair styles and ostentatious jewellery brought out by the élite of the capital of Uttar Pradesh to celebrate the traditional spring festival of Holi. 'Where's India's aesthetic sense gone?' he asked himself. 'Usha is the only one with any style.'

There certainly was nothing vulgar about his wife. She wore a plain dark-red silk *sari*, elegantly tied to show off her hips. Her long black hair was pulled off her forehead and ran straight down her back. On her fingers she wore just the gold ring he'd given her when they married, and around her neck a gold chain with one smoky topaz set in a pendant. She was tall, well built but carried no fat, with the strong, almost male features which yet remain so female in fine-looking Sikh women.

'Introduce me to your husband,' said Seth Ramdas. 'We industrialists can never know too many IAS officers.'

Usha laughed, saying, 'You've got the wrong man. Ramadhar is not exactly sociable, and he hates all the *sifarish* and *chaplusi* which goes on at functions like this.'

'Well, that will make a difference. Most of these bureaucrats are only too anxious to tell you how important they are, and to suggest the favours they may be able to do for you. Let's go and find him.'

They made their way past the group which had gathered round the Chief Secretary, with the industrialist pausing to exchange his half-empty glass of whisky for a full one from the tray of a club waiter. Ramadhar saw them approaching but did not move. When the couple reached him, Usha said, 'Come, stop looking down your long nose at those of us who are enjoying the party. Meet a friend, Seth Ramdas. You must have heard of him.'

Her husband folded his hands politely and said, '*Namaste*, Sethji.'

The businessman replied, 'I don't know how we've never met before. I come across most of the IAS crowd.'

Ramadhar said, 'I am not fond of gatherings like this one.'

'Well, your wife certainly is!'

'Someone has to be.' Usha laughed. 'Otherwise we would be social outcasts.'

Conversation at the Club's Holi party this year was dominated by discussion of the destruction of the mosque at Ayodhya less than a hundred miles away. It had been pulled down a few months previously by militant Hindus who had broken through the security cordon at a vast rally, swarmed all over the building and dismantled it stone by stone. They were supporters of the BJP, the Hindu party spearheading the campaign to build a temple on the Ayodhya site. They claimed that the Mughals had destroyed an earlier temple, and maintained that the site was the birthplace of the God Rama. Before Ayodhya it was not done to discuss religion in the Mohammed Bagh Club. The civil servants who dominated the membership were officially committed to secularism. But at this party Ramadhar had heard a senior colleague tell an army officer, 'The Muslims have got what they deserve.' Another civil servant had agreed with a businessman who said, 'It was time that we Hindus showed we wouldn't take everything lying down.' A police officer had suggested that India should become a Hindu state.

The Prime Minister, who had originally been bitterly criticized for failing to live up to his commitment to preserve the mosque, was now, as far as Ramadhar could tell, widely regarded as a cunning old fox who had realized that sentiment in the country favoured its destruction. There were some civil servants who were openly showing their political colours by criticizing the Prime Minister for dismissing the BJP government in Uttar Pradesh after the demolition of the mosque.

Seth Ramdas came from a family which firmly believed that their riches were the answer to the prayers they'd addressed to the Goddess Lakshmi. He also regarded the BJP as the party of his trading caste. Although, like any wise businessman, he would back all parties with any chance of passing the post first in an electoral race, his contribution to the BJP in the last election had been particularly generous. He knew by his name that Upadhyaya was a Brahmin, and assumed therefore that he would be in favour of the demolition.

'I think we Hindus had every right to destroy that structure,' he said. 'After all, the Muslims hardly left a single temple standing in this part of India, and now they're crying because we pull down one mosque. About time we Hindus stood up for ourselves. More and more people are saying that.'

'I'm not,' said Ramadhar.

'But you are a Brahmin. Surely you must approve of the slogan "Say with pride you're a Hindu." Ayodhya is all about that, about making us Indians proud.'

'I have enough pride to have no time for religion. It's for those who are so weak-minded they need some external prop. Anyhow most of what passes for Hinduism isn't even religion: it's superstition.'

Anxious to bring down the temperature, Usha said in a

conciliatory voice, 'But even you still wear your sacred thread.'

'It's useful to tie my keys to,' replied her husband and walked away.

That wasn't the reason for his wearing the sacred thread. He had never told even Usha why he did. He'd never told her about the university vacation when his grandfather had seen him wash under the handpump in the courtyard of their small family house and had noticed that there was no sacred thread over his left shoulder. The old man had said nothing, but that evening he did not come for his meal. He wasn't in his room either. Eventually Ramadhar's father had found him lying on a *charpoy* under a peepul tree outside the compound. He'd asked anxiously whether he was ill. The old man had replied, 'Not ill in my body but sick at heart. I never thought I would live to see the day when my grandson rejected his *janeo*. How can I eat with such an irreligious person? That's why I can't join you in the meal. I have decided − I will fast until he wears the thread again.'

Ramadhar's father had run back to the house, grabbed his son by the elbow and dragged him to the tree. Pointing at the old man lying on the *charpoy*, he'd said, 'There, you see the suffering you have caused by your arrogance and disrespect? Now your grandfather is going to die. He says he can't eat in this house, and you know that he will not eat in any other house because that's against his belief, so he'll die and then will you be happy? Will you say you've done enough?'

As a child Ramadhar had, like so many other children, been fonder of his grandfather than of his father. In spite of his deep respect for tradition, it had been the old man who had supported Ramadhar when he announced that he did not want to follow the family profession of *purohit*, and become the village priest, but wanted to go to university and join the civil service. When he'd seen the pain in his grandfather's eyes he'd realized how important religion could be. How principled was his rejection of religion? Did it really matter to him in the same way that faith mattered to his grandfather? Perhaps not, he thought. Maybe jettisoning his sacred thread had merely been a gesture. Anyhow, if he believed the thread could have no significance, why not wear it? It didn't have to mean that he believed in all it stood for.

So he had apologized to the old man and agreed to wear the *janeo* again. The cotton thread had been spun inside the house to prevent the neighbours from finding out that Ramadhar had flouted tradition in such a shameful way.

His grandfather was long dead and Ramadhar did not believe his spirit lived on, but for all his rationalism, for all his scorn of religion, he couldn't bring himself to discard his *janeo* now.

After another ten minutes or so Usha came over to Ramadhar again. Her long, black hair swung from side to side as she shook her head angrily, saying, 'If you can't be polite to anyone and are just going to stand here like a spoilt child, we'd better go. It's not doing you any good behaving like this in front of so many important people.'

'I never asked to come in the first place,' replied Ramadhar, turning and walking towards the driveway, leaving Usha to follow him.

The central government in Delhi had taken charge of Uttar Pradesh when the BJP administration was dismissed. Officially the central government was meant to provide a politically neutral caretaker administration until elections were held and the voters of Uttar Pradesh expressed their wishes again. But the central government was not neutral. It was in the hands of the Congress party, and so it came as no surprise to Ramadhar or any of his senior bureaucratic colleagues when civil servants and police officers appointed to influential posts by the BJP found themselves transferred. Inevitably they were replaced by officials considered to have Congress Party loyalities.

Ramadhar Upadhyaya had always been an inconvenient

officer, a stickler for the rule book, unwilling to make an exception for politicians of any party. The Governor therefore did not regard him as fit to be transferred to what he considered a 'sensitive post', but he could fill a hole left by a man required for special purposes. That was why, shortly after the Holi party, he received orders to be transferred from Lucknow to Gorakhpur as chairman of the Industrial Development Corporation.

Ramadhar knew that his new posting would put more strain on his marriage. Usha had made it quite clear that she'd had enough of what she regarded as petty, small-town life in his earlier career. She believed no one interesting ever lived in the smaller towns of the state. They all gravitated to the capital, Lucknow. But Ramadhar made no effort to get his posting order changed.

As both Ramadhar and his wife had feared, the old bungalow in Gorakhpur, left behind by the British administration, did not prove to be a happy home. Usha made no effort to make new friends, and rejected all attempts to drag her into the endless gossip and card games which passed for social life among the wives of the other officials posted in Gorakhpur. As the wife of a senior IAS officer, she enjoyed considerable status, but not the supreme position. That belonged to the Commissioner, which annoyed Usha too. She had considerable social skills but was not prepared to exercise them unless she was in a position at least of equality. At parties in Lucknow the pecking order didn't matter so much. Here in the limited bureaucratic circle of Gorakhpur it did. She had left her only son in a hostel so that he could continue his education in Lucknow and Usha used this as an excuse to spend much of her time there too, staying with friends.

Ramadhar was not surprised to find that his job, which was officially to promote industrial development, actually consisted of trying to prevent the government from making loans to so-called industrialists who would pocket the money instead of spending it on the projects it was intended for. The number of industries classified in his files as 'sick' bore evidence of his predecessors' failure to plug this waste of the state's slender resources, and it soon became clear to him that he was not likely to be any more effective. Frustrated professionally, he did find some solace in the company of the District Medical Officer, a man who, like Ramadhar, had an interest in philosophy. The two viewed the world very differently – the doctor was a religious man, Ramadhar certainly was not – but that, they found, made their dialogue all the more interesting.

One evening, sitting on the lawn of his bungalow, Ramadhar told the doctor, 'You know, I sometimes think the whole trouble with India is the rituals we believe in. They've become so important in our lives that they have become a reality. People can't separate ritual from reality. They don't even see the need to be realistic because they have convinced themselves the rituals will answer all their needs. Take my father – he spends hours every day praying, pouring Ganges water everywhere, blowing on conch shells, worshipping stones. What relationship can that have to reality?'

The doctor tipped his cane chair backwards to look up at the clear night sky. 'What do you see up there?' he asked. 'The moon, whose reality we know something about because we have actually been there. The stars, the planets, we know something about their reality too because of astronomy – more and more, in fact. Or do you see something of incredible beauty, something that has overawed man for as long as we know anything about him?'

'I accept that beauty is a reality, if that's what you mean.'

'No, I mean that there is so much beyond what you call reality. As a doctor, I know the physical body is not the end of the story. Not even the mind is the end. There is something beyond, and it's that something which appreciates beauty. The mind comes along and spoils it all by asking about the reality of that beauty.'

'So what's that got to do with ritual?'

'If you'd ever bothered to listen to the language of your father's rituals, and to understand their symbolism, you might realize they have a beauty which appeals, which gives strength, because it makes you aware that you're part of something infinitely greater than yourself – only a very small part but very much a part.'

This did strike home. Ramadhar had joined the civil service as a realist but at the same time an idealist. He believed the government was the only institution powerful enough to fulfil his ideal of creating an India where there were no rich but no poor either, where ancient superstitions had been replaced by modern realism, where the bonds of caste were broken and every citizen was free from discrimination. He'd married Usha because she'd been inspired by the same dream.

Her inspiration had not lasted long. The sacrifices she had to make after their son was born, when she'd given up work as a journalist and managed her household on the meagre earnings of an honest civil servant, had taught her that bread is more important than idealism. Ramadhar often wished that she hadn't been left money when her parents died. Then she might have gone back to journalism and been less discontented and easier to live with. As it was, whenever he suggested she might start work again, she dismissed the idea, saying, 'I've seen the impact of journalism. Do you think a thousand investigative reports about corruption are going to make any difference? One person in this family in a futile job is enough.' He couldn't argue with that. He had become all too convinced of the futility of his own work.

Confronted with the collapse of his idealism, Ramadhar still refused to consider what he regarded as the weak man's answer – fleeing to God in the face of the frustrations of life. But the doctor's concept of a part of the infinite being in each of us did hold some attraction for him. It might be a better answer than the manifest stupidity of taking oneself too seriously. It was a way of suppressing the uncomfortable ego. And it needn't, as he knew from his reading of Hindu philosophy, mean you had to believe in anything as naïve as a personal God.

Usha didn't even have this spartan spiritual comfort. She became increasingly unhappy, realizing that she could not spend all her time with friends in Lucknow without giving rise to pernicious gossip about her marriage, but at the same time finding it quite impossible to adjust to life in Gorakhpur. Time and time again she argued with Ramadhar that he should swallow his pride and do some *sifarish* to get moved back to the capital.

She made no progress until a businessman in Gorakhpur applied for a loan to finance a high-tech factory for making computer chips. The businessman had no experience in this field, and as far as Ramadhar knew there were no trained workers available locally, so even if the project did take off, there would be no reduction in Gorakhpur's unemployment. What was worse, the businessman already had two failed projects to his debit. He blamed sudden changes in trading terms and labour unrest, but Ramadhar had seen evidence on his files to show that in both cases the money advanced by the government for the machinery had been spent elsewhere.

Ramadhar had written a stern note on the file containing all the paper which had built up around the businessman's latest proposal, and flatly refused to approve a loan. He'd been visited by a local Congress leader, who'd warned him that his decision would not be well received in Lucknow, but he refused to budge. He'd been called back to the capital for a meeting with the Industry Secretary, who'd suggested that it would make life much easier for everyone if his note was removed from the file, and new and more conciliatory advice given. Ramadhar had told the Secretary that he would require a written order before he did that. Eventually he was telephoned by the Chief Secretary, the head of the state's civil service, who told Ramadhar that the government required him to change his note. Ramadhar said he would need to have a written order.

When he told this to Usha she burst out in anger. 'You are an obstinate fool! You had the ear of the Chief Secretary and you could have done a deal to get yourself back to Lucknow and all you did was stand on your stupid principles. What do you think you will achieve? All that will happen will be that you'll be transferred to some even more God-forsaken place than this and someone else will be sent here who'll find reasons for disagreeing with your note. So what good will your principles do anyone but you and your wretched pride?'

Ramadhar knew that Usha's prognosis might be all too accurate. There really wasn't any point in going on like this. He could keep up the fight by leaking the story to the press or the opposition, but that would just throw up a lot of dust, and once it had settled the loan would be granted anyway.

'You realize that if I do a deal on this, it will be a denial of all I've ever stood for?' he asked his wife.

Usha got up from her chair, came and knelt in front of her husband, took his hand in hers and said, 'My love, I know how much you've suffered, but honestly it's just no good standing up for principles when no one else does. It gets you nowhere. The world's made differently and we have to accept that. Please, for my sake and for the sake of our son, understand that.'

Ramadhar ran his fingers through her long shiny hair, 'You really want this?'

'Yes.'

'All right. I surrender.'

Usha shot up, threw her arms around him and, for the first time for many months, kissed him lightly on the lips. Then, holding his face between her hands, she said, 'You won't regret it. I know that sounds like the dialogue of a corny Bombay movie, but you won't, I promise you.'

The Chief Secretary was only too happy to strike a deal

and Ramadhar moved back to Lucknow, this time as an Officer on Special Duty, a job which was known in the service as 'Officer with Sod-all to Do'.

Compromising the principles he had upheld throughout his career destroyed what little interest Ramadhar still had in the IAS. He knew that he would now just tread water until he retired, and after that – what? Well, he'd have his books, but nothing much else. He and Usha would probably drift further apart, and he did not anticipate a close relationship with his son, who'd inherited his mother's gregariousness. Remembering that he'd never had time for anything but work as he slogged his way from village primary school, through the government high school in the nearby town to Allahabad University, and from there into the prestigious IAS, he regarded his son's facility at passing exams without any apparent effort as talent misused. Remembering the loneliness of a village boy among the sophisticated students of Allahabad, he was suspicious, perhaps even envious, of the ease with which his son made friends. There was a lack of seriousness about the boy. He seemed to assume that as the son of an IAS officer he had no need to worry about his future in an India where privileged birth still counted for so much.

There was one alternative for his retirement which Ramadhar never even considered – a return to his village. He'd put all that behind him when he married Usha. He very rarely even visited his home, contenting himself with writing to let his father know when he was posted in case there was an emergency. It came as a surprise therefore when his personal assistant brought him a postcard written in his father's still neat handwriting. The contents were very simple: 'My dear son, I am writing to let you know that Sunara is very ill. You must come quickly to see her before she dies.'

Ramadhar rarely thought of the woman he'd married on his father's instructions before he'd gone to university. He sent some money back each month to care for her, but that was as far as it went. When he'd fallen in love with Usha, he'd justified his relationship on the grounds that his first marriage had been part of the archaic rural culture which he believed India had to shake off if it was to become a modern nation. The marriage had been an involuntary union, so he owed nothing beyond his duty to keep his wife. When it came to his second marriage he didn't even tell his father until the wedding was over, and then he only wrote to him.

But now he had lost so much of the certainty of his youth. When he heard his first wife was dying he wondered whether that marriage had merely been a contract to see that he provided for her. He knew how much Sunara had wanted a child but he'd refused to consider it. He'd blighted her whole life. Could he really fail her again? Could he afford to lose this chance to redeem his neglect? He could, of course. It would be just another step on the path he'd chosen when he'd married Usha and written off his first wife. Why open up all that again at this last moment? It was possible that he might disturb Sunara by going back before she died. Better perhaps to let her die as she had lived, accepting what life had given her. He didn't know. He was not sure.

He rang Usha and said he was coming back to the flat at once because he had something urgent to discuss with her. When he unlocked the door of his flat and called, 'Usha, where are you?' she came out of the kitchen where she'd been supervising preparations for a lunch she was giving for her friends. Her hands covered with flour, she said irritably, 'Ramadhar, I hope this isn't going to take too long. I'm awfully busy.'

'I'm sorry. I had to talk to you. Something dreadful has happened. Sunara's dying.'

Usha's attitude changed immediately. 'Oh, you poor thing,' she said. 'Of course you were right to come back at once. Sit down. We must discuss this.'

Ramadhar sat down opposite Usha with his eyes cast down, staring at his feet. 'I don't know what to do,' he mumbled, almost to himself. 'Part of me says I should go.

Part of me says I shouldn't. She's nothing to do with me any longer.'

'Look at me,' Usha said firmly. 'You must go. There's no doubt about it.'

'But why do you, of all people, say that? You are my real wife. She means nothing to me. Surely you want it that way too.'

'I say it because I have had everything and she's had nothing. She's never even tried to interfere in our lives. She's never made any claim on you. You can't leave her at a time like this.'

This wasn't the first time Usha had surprised Ramadhar. Nowadays he tended to think of her as a disappointment, a woman he'd married as a partner in his struggle to fulfil his ideals but who'd become nothing more than a social butterfly. He often wondered whether she even cared for him any longer. Then suddenly she would show how mature she was and convince him that she did care deeply. He realized that she was right. He must go back to his village.

Dr Saxena, who had become Ramadhar's friend in Gorakhpur, had also been posted back to the capital. He was not over-employed and readily agreed to go with Ramadhar to his village to see if there was anything which could be done about his wife. Ramadhar was too scrupulous about government rules to take his official car on this private journey, so the two men caught the train to Varanasi and from there they hired a taxi to the village. They drove past the small country school where Ramadhar had started his education, and overtook a white egret stalking majestically along the embankment of the canal which ran beside the road. The first sight of the village was the large house and mango grove of the former *zamindars*. Ramadhar's father was still their family priest, although they'd taken to the modern way of life when it came to agriculture. Two combine harvesters were parked outside the house. Sheaves of rice that had been cut and threshed were laid out to dry in front of them. Ramadhar noticed the men who had come with the harvesters were Sikhs. 'That symbolizes the backwardness of our state,' he said to the doctor. 'Sikhs from Punjab come here with their machines. Our labour has to go to Punjab to do whatever manual work is required there.'

Ramadhar told the taxi driver to go on to the main bazaar. He wanted to walk through the village so that he had time to collect his thoughts before he met his father. The two men got out opposite a branch of the Kashi Gramin Bank. As they walked through the bazaar Ramadhar said to Dr Saxena, 'This shows there has been some progress in our state, if you call it progress. When I was a boy there were a few shops selling just the most basic items. Now the bazaar would do justice to any small town. There are shops selling almost anything any customer could want, and there's another bank. There seem to be plenty of members of your *biradari* practising every sort of medicine, and the chemists to go with them.'

'Both, I fear, robbing the public,' said the doctor. 'The over-prescription that goes on in a place like this is scandalous. Going to a doctor here would be a bit like sending your car to a mechanic. The last state is usually worse than the first.'

All this commercial activity was inevitably accompanied by Hindi film music played at a decibel level which certainly constituted noise pollution.

Some things had not changed. There was an elderly *baba* in a deep sleep on the plinth of the porch of the Ram Janaki temple, his long white beard flowing down his chest, rising and falling rhythmically with the regular movement of his breathing. The sound of the Muslim clergyman calling the faithful to prayer could be heard from the mosque just down the lane. As the two men walked past they looked in through the doors and saw several Muslim men washing their feet in preparation for prayers. 'The Hindu–Muslim tension everyone has been talking about since Ayodhya doesn't seem to have got as far as your village,' the doctor said.

'A lot of exaggeration by journalists,' Ramadhar said almost as though he was talking to himself. 'I can't really blame Usha for not wanting to join that rabble again.'

Soon after the mosque, they entered the old part of the village. This hadn't changed much since Ramadhar's child-hood. Brick and concrete boxes, functional but ugly, had not come this far. The villagers here still lived in mud houses with thatched roofs. Their walls had been replastered with cow dung and mud for the festival of Diwali, and there were dotted patterns painted in white lime and earth colours on their light-brown walls. Green creepers with yellow flowers, which would eventually mature into bottle gourds, spread over the roofs of the huts. The village news service was as active as ever too. As the doctor and Ramadhar passed a well where two women were drawing water in buckets, they overheard one say to the other, '*Panditji*'s son has come back, the *dehijar*. What's the point of his coming now?'

They walked on through the shade of a bamboo grove and came to open land. There Ramadhar saw his home, set apart from the rest of the village, near the *zamindars*' house. The two men had walked almost a complete circle since they had left the taxi. Ramadhar could no longer postpone the meeting with his father, which he feared he would not be able to carry off with any dignity.

The doctor waited outside while Ramadhar pushed open the double door that led into the small courtyard around which his father had built his new house. The old man was sitting quietly beside a *charpoy*, occasionally fanning flies off the face of Sunara, Ramadhar's wife, with his hand. His hair, with the small knot tied at the back, was now white and thinner than Ramadhar remembered. His eyes were even more deep-set, and he'd lost two front teeth. His face was softer, less certain, than it had been. Sunara was asleep on the *charpoy*, her cheeks so sunken that her face seemed to have collapsed. The old man looked up and, seeing his son, smiled. 'I knew you would come.'

Ramadhar bowed down to touch his father's feet and then

sat on the ground beside his stool. He asked, 'Is there any hope?'

His father shook his head.

'What is it?'

'It's my fault. I took her to one of those fake doctors in the bazaar. I should have known better. He said she had some infection, I think it was, and kept on giving her medicine. It wasn't for a long time that I realized he wasn't giving the right medicine. Then I took her to the district hospital, where the doctors were very helpful, may God bless them. They kept her in the hospital for some time and I stayed with her, but in the end they told me she had cancer and that the kindest thing would be to bring her home to die. They even arranged transport for us to get home.'

The old man paused and turned to look at his daughter-in-law, choking back his tears. When he had regained control of himself, he went on, 'She's such a good woman. She's been so good to me, and I have killed her because of my neglect. That's what the government doctors said, and they were good people. They did their best, may God bless them.'

Ramadhar had never seen his father so moved. He'd taken his wife's death with calm detachment, appearing to his son almost arrogant about the inner strength he possessed, but this time that strength seemed to have deserted him.

After a brief silence Ramadhar asked, 'Did she ever call for me?'

'I suggested it, but she said you were not to be bothered. You were a big man who had enough to worry about with your work. I didn't tell her I'd written to you.'

'Because you feared I wouldn't come?'

'I hoped you would and I haven't been disappointed. Now my only hope is that she will recover enough to recognize you. It will mean a lot to her.'

'I hope we can do better than that. I've brought a very good doctor with me.'

Ramadhar called Dr Saxena. He examined Sunara thoroughly and then asked to see the papers from the hospital. They confirmed his diagnosis, so he turned to the old man and asked, 'What do you want me to say?'

'The truth.'

'There is nothing I can do.'

'When will she die?'

'Maybe today, maybe tomorrow. Not much longer. I will wait outside.'

The two men sat staring at the woman lying on the *charpoy*. Ramadhar wanted to know what his father had meant by 'neglect', but he couldn't ask for fear of appearing to be critical. After a while the old man turned to him and smiled. 'I'm glad you've come. I've got my pride, but it would have been difficult to get through this on my own, especially as the doctors said it was my fault, although I didn't do it deliberately. I was careless.'

'How can it be your fault? You have always looked after Sunara as though she was your own daughter.'

'The doctors said if I had brought her to them earlier, she could have been cured, but I just went on taking her to that bogus doctor in the bazaar, although I could see she was not being cured. It wasn't a question of money. It was just, I suppose, that I didn't want to make all the effort of going into the town. I'm getting old, and it would have interfered with my *puja*.'

Ramadhar got up and started pacing round the courtyard. He had barely given his wife a second thought for so many years and now here he was suddenly overcome with remorse. How could his father be expected to realize that she was so ill? It was he who had been negligent – negligent all his life. His wife hadn't allowed him to be called because she thought he wouldn't care. She probably hadn't wanted to face that final humiliation. Why should she think anything else? But if he had come earlier, he would have seen that she should be taken straight to the government hospital and would have used his influence as an IAS officer to make sure she got the best possible treatment. Now it was too late.

Ramadhar went out to talk to his friend. The doctor offered to stay but Ramadhar said, 'You've given up a lot of your time, and there's nothing you can do now. It's better for me to be on my own with Father. I've got a great deal to face up to.'

The doctor understood that his presence might inhibit the tears which Ramadhar needed to shed, and so he walked back to the bazaar to find the taxi.

Ramadhar returned to the courtyard and sat down beside his father, putting his arm round his shoulder. 'Father,' he said, 'you must not grieve. She would never say that you'd neglected her. I am the one who has been neglectful. I'll go inside and have a wash and then sit with her in case she wakes. I want to speak to her. Anyhow you must have a rest.'

Some women from the village came to the door asking after Sunara and made as if to come in. Ramadhar joined his hands and said, 'It's very kind of you to come, but I've not seen my father or my wife for a long time. Please leave us to be on our own.' The women stood staring at Sunara. Ramadhar repeated, 'We are very grateful for your kindness and concern, but please leave us for now.'

'But surely some other relatives have come?' asked one of the women.

'No,' said Ramadhar. 'My father has called only me.'

The women walked away muttering among themselves about this strange *pandit* and his son. Sickness and death were normally occasions for a gathering of the family and of the village.

Ramadhar sat beside the *charpoy* until the ripe yellow rice waiting to be harvested glowed in the sunset and he felt the slight chill of an autumn evening. Fearing that his wife would get cold, he called for his father's servant and they carried the *charpoy* into the house. Putting it down again, they gave Sunara a jolt which woke her. She looked at Ramadhar, smiled, but said nothing. He couldn't tell whether she'd recognized him or not. He switched on the light, a naked bulb, in the hope that this would keep her awake. After a few minutes her eyes closed again, and her head fell forward. Ramadhar switched off the light.

Ramadhar stayed by his wife's bed. He wanted to be with her when she died, and he didn't think that could be far away. The night wore on, the silence punctuated from time to time by the barking of dogs who never seemed to sleep. At four o'clock Ramadhar heard his father start his rituals. As he listened to the low murmur of the Sanskrit prayers, he felt an urge to join his father. Sunara was breathing quite regularly. There didn't seem to be any immediate danger of her passing away. If he were to take part in the *puja*, it would mean so much to his father, who was suffering from grief and a sense of guilt. So he stood up, making as little noise as possible, and walked to the next room.

Through the open doorway he saw his father sitting cross-legged on a low wooden stool, wearing a *dhoti*. His chest was bare except for a thin, saffron-coloured cotton cloth covering his shoulders and printed all over with the name of the God Ram. In front of him was a small square table no higher than his stool. On it were a round steel *thali* or tray, two brass lamps full of *ghi*, a small water pot with a long thin spout, several other utensils, two brass bells and a pile of orange marigolds, purple bougainvillaea and white tuberose flowers sprinkled with red rose petals.

His father picked up a marigold flower and put it in the small *thali*. After adding a few grains of rice and a smear of sandalwood paste, he poured Ganges water into the *thali*, reciting mantras dedicating this offering to the sun. Then the old man held out his arms with the palms of his hands facing upwards, slowly brought his hands together and folded them in a *namaskar*. This was the preparation for the Gayatri Mantra.

'*Om bhurbhuvah svaha tatsaviturvarenyam bhargo devasy dhimahi,*' his father chanted, and Ramadhar found himself joining in, '*dhiyo yo nah prachodayat.*' He had refused to learn Sanskrit but he knew this, the most familiar of mantras, a prayer to the sun as the image of light, the image of the bliss of true understanding.

He remembered his conversations with the doctor in Gorakhpur. The death of his wife was all too real, but what was the reality behind it? How could life make any sense if this was all it came to in the end? But it wasn't, according to his father. He had now moved on to the *Tarpan*, that part of his daily ritual when he prayed for his ancestors. He'd moved his sacred thread to his right shoulder and was pouring water from the brass pot with a thin spout. He held it in his right hand, with his left hand supporting his outstretched arm under the elbow. He prayed that this offering would satisfy past members of the family, and named them individually, going back to his great-grandparents. Ramadhar found himself thinking Sunara would soon be mentioned in these prayers because she was his wife, whereas Usha would not be remembered. Maybe she could be now? She wouldn't want to be mentioned in such a ritual, so why was he worrying? But it seemed to matter to him somehow – perhaps because she was the mother of his son.

His father completed the *puja* with an *aarti*, circling a brass lamp in front of a coloured picture of the black goddess Vindhyachal with one hand and ringing a bell vigorously with the other. The smell of the *ghi* burning in the saucers of the lamp filled the room, and smoke enveloped the goddess.

Eventually he finished the last of the mantras and picked up a sweet topped with a *tulsi* leaf and a rose petal, and offered it diffidently to his son. Ramadhar remembered with embarrassment the time when he had refused to accept *prasad*, food which had been sanctified by being offered to the gods. This time he accepted the offering.

When the rituals were complete, the two men returned to

the room where Sunara was lying. Her eyes were open and turned towards them as they sat beside her bed, but she was too weak to speak. The old man said, 'She must go soon. We really should lie her on the earth now.'

'But then she'll know we have given up hope.'

'I've been with many people when they die, and if they are like Sunara, if they believe, they want to die in the way their forefathers did. But if you'd prefer we will leave her on the *charpoy*.'

'No, I've no right to decide. You know her, you understand her, and you know how to help people to die.'

So the old man went into the courtyard and cleaned a space, purifying it with Ganges water. Then Ramadhar and the servant carried the *charpoy* out, lifted Sunara gently and laid her on the ground, with her head pointing south, the home of Yama, the Lord of the Dead. The old man sat cross-legged beside her and recited verses from the Gita, leaning over so that he was speaking right into her ear. He put *kush* grass into her palm and sprinkled water over it, symbolizing the gift of a cow. Sunara seemed to smile and then closed her eyes. Her breathing became weaker and weaker, and she slowly faded away. The old man said, 'She's left us.'

Ramadhar's father went back to his room to prepare for the rites which had to be performed immediately after death. Ramadhar sat silently. His eyes were full of tears, but he couldn't cry. When he heard the sound of weeping from his father's room, he got up and walked out of the courtyard. He didn't want the old man to know he'd heard him grieving. Eventually the weeping stopped and his father came out and sat beside Sunara. Ramadhar returned and sat with him while he recited mantras, pouring water drop by drop into Sunara's mouth and placing *tulsi* leaves inside it. Then suddenly the old man broke down again, sobbing. 'I know I shouldn't weep. Many tears burn the dead. But I can't help it. She was so good. She cared for me when I had no one else, even though we had treated her so badly.' Ramadhar knew he couldn't comfort his father. He could only wait until the storm passed.

Eventually the old man wiped his eyes and began the mantras once more. But then he faltered. He started again but couldn't go on. He pushed the *thali* aside, bowed his head and said in little more than a whisper, 'What's the use? She has shown that all my *pujas*, all my prayers, have been to no avail. I should accept her death, but I can't. In spite of all my learning, I don't have knowledge.'

'At least you've sought,' Ramadhar replied.

The old man did not seem to hear his son. He muttered to himself as though no one was there, 'I should have remembered the words of the Gita: "One among thousands desires to know Him, and even among those who are desirous to know, one perhaps can actually know."'

Ramadhar took his father's hand and said, 'Don't despair now. Keep on down your road. There is only one other road and I have trodden it. I have been arrogant enough to think I could change the world. The only knowledge I have is of the futility of believing in man.'

The old man laid his hands on his son's head and smiled, saying, 'Maybe I will find the strength to continue my journey. Her death may not be the end, which I fear, but a beginning, because it has brought you to the realization of the truth. The great Ramakrishna said, "The idea of an individual ego is like putting some Ganga water in a pot and calling it the Ganga." Now maybe you will break the pot and flow into the Ganga.'

BEYOND *PURDAH*

Suraiya was not a woman who liked to think that anyone had got the better of her, especially not domestic servants. The cooks who arrived in the household each year to prepare the evening meals during these ten days of Moharram always upset her. She knew they were cheats and that there was nothing she could do about it because the elder women of the family always defended them. But that didn't stop her dipping a ladle into the yellow-brown *kichara* − a gruel of several different types of grain and meat − bubbling vigorously in a smoke-blackened pot. She lifted the ladle and poured the liquid back slowly, leaving one small piece of meat in the bottom. Tasting it, she asked sharply, 'What sort of meat is this? It's still tough after cooking for five hours. The butcher must have given this goat away. It must have been born when my grandfather was young.'

The cook paid no attention. His colleagues, who were kneading great mounds of dough, peeling potatoes and preparing the *tandoors* in which the sweet, red-topped *roghani rotis*, the favourite bread of the family, would be baked, paid no attention either. Suraiya moved away, muttering to herself about thieving which got worse every year.

The sight in the pillared hall which formed the largest room of the main house didn't please her either. It was dusk and there was, as usual, an electricity cut. The hall was lit by the bright white light of hissing Petromax lamps. Almost every branch of the family of the late Taluqdar Taqi Miyan had come home for Moharram, the most important occasion of their year. There were children running wild, gossiping mothers, garrulous grannies and great-grannies too. There seemed to be women everywhere. All wore black or white mourning dress in memory of the martyrdom of the Prophet Mohammad's grandson Imam Husain at the battle of Karbala, but the atmosphere seemed anything but funereal. The women still had plenty to talk about, even though they'd been together for six days already. There was occasional laughter too, although this was officially frowned on during the anniversary of Imam Husain's martyrdom. Imam Husain had been killed at Karbala by the army of the man who claimed to be Caliph, or head of the faith of Islam. The great schism in Islam between Shias and Sunnis had sprung from this battle and the dispute over the Caliphate.

'It's so typical of the lackadaisical ways of our Shia families,' Suraiya thought. 'No wonder our fortunes have fallen so low when these women just lie around gossiping as though nothing had changed since the days their men prospered merely by collecting rents from their lands. The way our men are going, we won't have the money to finance these Moharram reunions soon.'

Suraiya made her way across the crowded floor to a corner where a group of slender young girls were standing practising one of the laments which concluded the many *majlises*, or assemblies, held during Moharram to mourn the martyrdom of Imam Husain. Her daughter stood in the centre, holding a notebook of lyrics, which the girls were reciting to a new tune they'd learned in Victoria Street in Lucknow. As they chanted, they beat their chests with their open palms in time to the meter of the verse.

Suraiya interrupted. 'That's enough, *beti*, get ready to go to the *majlis*. We must arrive before there's such a crowd there's no room for us.'

'We're just coming,' replied her daughter, launching into another verse.

Suraiya moved over to her husband's eldest aunt, who was

lying against a cushion talking to another elderly woman. 'Bari Phuphi,' she said, 'they will listen only to you. Help me get everyone organized. We must leave for the Inner Village.'

The old lady took Suraiya's hand and said, 'Be patient. All in good time. When did we ever turn up to their *majlis* on time?'

Suraiya pulled her hand away impatiently and walked off. Bari Phuphi shook her head sadly, saying, 'What a pass we have come to. Look at that Suraiya – she has cut her hair, and now her husband, my nephew Asghar, doesn't even insist that she covers her head when she goes out. I remember the days when the men used to insist on strict *purdah*. Now they just sit around gossiping about their wretched politics.'

Munni Baji, an old lady with thick spectacles askew across her nose, spoke out with remarkable clarity, seeing that she didn't have a tooth in her head. 'They were much better days when there were no politics because of the British rule. Everyone talks about freedom but the freedom we have is destruction.' Getting into her stride, Munni Baji went on, 'That Suraiya, she's one of these new free women. They say they've freed us women, but I don't want their freedom. The fun we used to have when we had proper *purdah* – that was when we really enjoyed ourselves. There was so much happening in the house, so many friends, such a big family, so much fun, so much affection. We never had any work to do. We were never alone.'

Another elderly member of the family, wrapped in a shawl in spite of the summer heat, agreed. 'Even the food doesn't taste the same now. Then we used to sit around the stove and eat. Chickens, whole goats, were slaughtered and cooked on cow dung, which really gives a taste. What sort of taste can you get sitting around a table?'

'And the prices! Then ten people could eat three meals for one silver rupee, now you get nothing for a bundle of one-hundred rupee notes. They're nothing more than dirty paper,' said Munni Baji.

Eventually Bari Phuphi called over to the girls. 'Come on, get ready to go. We are getting late for the *majlis*.'

One tradition which survived among the descendants of Taluqdar Taqi Miyan was obedience to Bari Phuphi, and so the women gathered in the courtyard.

Munni Baji grumbled, 'I suppose we have to walk all through the *basti* and cross that crowded bazaar, and down alongside that filthy pond where the butchers live. In the old days we weren't even allowed to cross to the house on the other side of the lane unless we were carried from one court-yard to another in a *doli*, with its sides curtained.'

Bari Phuphi replied irritably, 'I know. When my mother travelled by train, the whole carriage was reserved for her. All its windows were blacked out, and they used to put up a corridor of curtains on the platform so that no one could see her getting on to the train. But those days have gone, and now we just have to walk, so there's no point in grumbling.'

They walked in single file, all except Suraiya draped in black *burqas* which made them almost invisible in the limited light of a new moon. Nevertheless they hugged the side of the narrow lane to make themselves even more inconspicuous. They moved like ghosts across the main road, diving into the darkness behind the brightly lit stalls of the bazaar. As they approached the big house they held their noses to block the foul stench from the quarters of the village butchers. At the gate of the big house which had been built by Taluqdar Saddan Miyan two hundred years before, they found the great wooden gates had been left open for them. They crossed the courtyard and passed through what had once been the kitchens into the *zenana* or women's quarters. Grass and weeds were growing out of the crumbling walls which surrounded this courtyard. The roofs of all the rooms had fallen in except for one small hall used as an *imambara*, or house of the Imam, where tall *tazias*, replicas of the Imam's tomb made of bamboo and coloured paper, were arrayed. The hall was crowded with the women of the Inner Village's family and their neighbours.

The women descendants of Taluqdar Taqi Miyan clambered over the congregation of the *majlis*, who were sitting on the white sheets spread over the floor, listening intently to an elegy of the poet Anis. Suraiya tripped over a woman, who scolded, 'Is this any time to arrive? At least sometimes try to be punctual.' Eventually she squeezed herself in between two members of the other family. An elderly woman was sitting on a chair draped in black, reciting the poet Anis' description of the suffering of the women and infant children at Karbala, denied water by the Imam's enemies for many days. As the couplets told of the children's thirst, their hunger and their fear, her voice rose, and she rocked back and forth, sometimes looking down at her book to remind herself of the words, sometimes looking up at the congregation and from time to time dabbing the tears from her eyes with a lace handkerchief. When the elegy had ended the whole congregation stood and a group of women chanted a lament, each verse ending with the refrain

> Listen to the strains of mourning,
> See how cruelly heroes die.
> Homes are looted, camps are burning,
> Innocent children cry.

As the lament concluded, the women began to beat their breasts in unison to cries of '*Ya* Husain! *Ya* Husain!', mourning the martyred Imam. Their voices rose, the tempo quickened, reached a climax, then suddenly died away. The *majlis* was over. Some women sat down again, while others reached for their *burqas*. One woman moved among the congregation distributing sweets which had been blessed. Then the congregation dispersed.

Outside the hall a group of women belonging to Taluqdar Saddan Miyan's family started to discuss the big *majlis* they had attended with their menfolk that morning.

'The man who recited came all the way from Delhi again this year.'

'Yes. He's a very important officer in the IAS.'

'He's a Hindu but that's good. It just shows that there's really no enmity between us Shias and Hindus. It's the politicians who cause all the problems.'

'In my grandfather's time a Kannauj Brahmin would come here to recite.'

Suraiya, listening to the women boasting about their family's *majlis*, became impatient. There was a traditional rivalry between the two leading families of Mohammadpur. Each liked to claim that their *majlis* had attracted the largest congregations and the most important guests. Suraiya said in a loud voice, 'I suppose your Pakistani relative made a big impact too?'

'Yes, he comes all the way from Karachi,' said one of the women.

'None of our family went to Pakistan at Partition,' replied Suraiya disdainfully.

'If someone went to Pakistan, that doesn't mean they are not members of the family. It's very right that they should come home for Moharram.'

'If they had such a great desire to go to Pakistan and break up their family, then they should stay there.'

By this time a small crowd had gathered and some were muttering against Suraiya, suggesting that if she wanted to insult their *majlis*, she and her whole family could stay at home. Bari Phuphi pulled Suraiya away, saying, 'Why are you always set on fighting? Learn a little self-control, a little modesty, a little sympathy for others. I don't know why Asghar doesn't control you.'

As they walked away Suraiya muttered, 'I don't see why we should sit down with Pakistanis when you are always saying it was the creation of that *kambakht* country which destroyed us.'

'You have so little understanding. Don't you know that the

majlis doesn't belong to that Pakistani? It belongs to Imam Husain – every *majlis* does.'

Suraiya knew that in theory every *majlis* belonged to the Imam, but at the same time she also knew that a *majlis* reflected the status of a family. The Inner Gate family had done everything that Suraiya disapproved of. They had neglected their lands; they had allowed their home to fall into disrepair; they had in effect deserted Mohammadpur. But at the same time many of them had prospered in Lucknow, Delhi, Karachi and other big cities as lawyers, journalists and university teachers. They were able to come back for Moharram each year and resume their position as members of the leading Shia family, treating Suraiya's family like country bumpkins. The smart Inner Village gentlemen from the cities showed no respect to her menfolk, although they were the ones who maintained the Shia presence in Mohammadpur throughout the year. What reward did her family get? They no longer had the rents from twenty villages to live on. They had to survive on the land left to them after the government had wreaked havoc by abolishing the *zamindari* system. What was worse, they couldn't possibly work the land themselves – that would have been beneath their dignity – and agricultural workers were now conscious of their rights. Their demands grew every year, but the fields didn't produce any more. Something would have to be done.

Shortly after Moharram the crisis broke. Asghar told Suraiya he was going to Azamgarh, the district headquarters, to see an agent about selling some of their land. His wife was horrified. 'That's all the capital we have,' she said.

'I have to pay our debts,' muttered her husband shamefacedly.

'That's the path to ruin. You sell first one field, run up more debts, then sell another until we have nothing left.'

'What else can I do? If I don't get this burden of interest off my back, the bank will take all our land anyhow.'

'I don't know what else you can do, but you will not sell one *bigha* of our land, that I promise you.'

Asghar shrugged his shoulders and walked away to join the men of the family sitting in the courtyard discussing the various *majlises* they had attended.

Suraiya sat for some time on her own, becoming more and more angry. Why were the men of her family so feckless? They took great pride in retaining the old feudal traditions, but they wouldn't lift a finger to provide the means to continue that way of life. Asghar himself had been quite successful in politics as long as the big leaders had valued his contacts, as a former landlord. But, like a fool, he had never made any money out of politics. He'd basked in the glory that his political contacts gave him. He'd been delighted when people said, 'Asghar is a big man. He can fix it for us.' But he'd regarded it as beneath the dignity of a Taluqdar to take money for the favours he did. What an idiot he'd been. Now politics had been taken over by the people the Taluqdars had always looked down on. Asghar was out.

Watching the men basking idly in the sun enraged Suraiya. She shouted to her husband, 'Come inside. I have something to say to you.'

The other men laughed. 'Go on, Asghar. The boss is calling you.'

'It's a good thing he's got a boss,' yelled Suraiya. 'Someone has to do something about you loafers. I'm going to see that there's at least one man in this family.'

Asghar got up and went indoors. His wife sat cross-legged on a wooden bed. He slumped into a chair and began to roll yet another cigarette.

'Do you want our family to be like the Inner Gate's?' she asked. 'Do you want our house to collapse like theirs?'

'No, of course I don't, but what can we do?'

'I'll tell you what we can do. You can go out and earn your living, start a business.'

'Business!' exclaimed Asghar, as though the proposal was preposterous.

'Yes, there's a clear path forward. Those crude contractors

and their *goondas* have pushed you out of politics. They've decided they don't need you now that you've helped them make the money to buy votes. Now it's up to you to beat them at their own game.'

'What do you mean? That I should become a contractor?'

'Yes, just that.'

Asghar was appalled. 'That's ridiculous. Our family has never been in business. It's beneath our dignity, alien to our whole nature.'

'What will happen to your dignity if we have to spread our hands before others for money?' She paused, looked him straight in the eye and continued, 'If you won't go in for contracting, can you tell me what else you intend to do to save the family?'

Asghar couldn't believe his ears. It was bad enough having a wife who humiliated him in front of the other men of the family in the way Suraiya did, but if she was now going to start a campaign to get him into business, that would be intolerable. He stubbed out his cigarette, got up and walked out of the house saying, 'Now you've crossed all limits.'

'Just you see,' Suraiya shouted after him.

Suraiya beat her forehead with her hands in frustration. What could she do? There was no way of getting her husband to do anything. He would just sit around and watch the family go to ruin. She couldn't save them. It was unthinkable that a woman of Taluqdar Taqi Miyan's family should work. All she could think of doing was to seek advice outside the family.

Through Asghar's political work Suraiya had become friendly with Tara Ahmed, one of the few Muslim women who was prominent in the Congress Party. She arranged to meet her in Lucknow.

The leader lived in a large official bungalow in Mall Avenue. The security guard at the gate stopped Suraiya, saying, 'You can't come in without an appointment.'

'I know,' said Suraiya. 'That's why I have one.'

The security guard was taken aback. He had assumed that Suraiya was just another of the hapless petitioners he took a delight in bullying. Without further questioning he let her in.

Tara Ahmed was not a politician who valued only those who could be useful to her. She had been fond of Asghar and had enjoyed coming to his home when she was in that area, so she welcomed Suraiya into her house.

When Suraiya explained her problem Tara Ahmed said, 'That's easy. Why don't we get Asghar back into politics? The Congress urgently needs help with the Muslim vote.'

'That wouldn't help,' replied Suraiya. 'He never made any money out of politics.'

'Why don't you go into politics?'

'Me?'

'Yes, you. I'm a Muslim woman, a wife, and I'm in politics, so why not you?'

'Asghar would never allow me to be seen in public making speeches and all that.'

Tara Ahmed tried to persuade her at least to consider politics, but Suraiya was adamant. She knew that was unrealistic, and she hadn't come all the way to Lucknow for advice which would not help her. Then Tara Ahmed suggested she should go into business. She promised to put opportunities her way and pointed out that business could be done from home. But Suraiya was still not convinced. If Asghar regarded it as beneath his dignity to be in business, what on earth would he say about his wife?

Tara Ahmed leant forward, took both Suraiya's hands in her own and said, 'I understand you, please believe that. But you know that there is nothing you can do with Asghar. He's never going to make money. Surely, then, you are the only one who can help? I remember the opposition I had from my family, but I overcame it because I was determined, and I have never regretted that. I promise you, from my own experience, it's only taking the decision that is hard. Very soon Asghar will come to accept it. If you are determined, he will have to.'

'Of course, you're right. If I don't do something, no one will. But what you are asking is very difficult. It goes against all the traditions of our family, and it's the family I'm trying to save.'

'I understand, but what won't a dying person do? At least go home and think about it, and remember that I can help you if you do decide to go ahead. Think of me as someone you can rely on for support in everything.'

Suraiya was moved by the politician's obvious affection for her. She trusted her. But she herself would be the one who had to take the decision and face the consequences, and she was far from convinced that she even wanted to flout the family traditions.

On the train journey back home Suraiya thought about the possibility of going into business. It was not her ability that worried her. It was all that she would have to surrender. She did not observe strict *purdah*. She had a reputation as a rebel in the family. But she was not really a rebel at all. She loved the family, all its branches, and she couldn't do anything which might cause a rift, like breaking away from the traditional role of a wife. Supposing, because of her, the family didn't all gather for Moharram next year? What would be the point of making money to save the family if the very way she earned the money destroyed it?

When Bari Phuphi ruled out the proposal that she should go into business, Suraiya thought that was the end of the matter. There could be no question of any woman in the family going against Bari Phuphi. It was unthinkable.

But the very next day a report of a shameful incident in the bazaar reached Suraiya. Apparently a shop-keeper had abused Asghar, shouting at him about people who pretended to be aristocrats but in reality didn't have the money to pay their debts. A crowd had gathered and had grown quite hostile. Unfavourable comparison had been made with the

Inner Village family members, who threw their money around when they came back for Moharram. Suraiya was livid. She went to look for her husband and found him, as usual, sitting with his cousins and friends in the courtyard. Forgetting all decorum, she stood over him and shouted, 'You never told me we owed money in the bazaar too!'

This was too much even for the mild Asghar. 'Don't you dare insult me in front of my friends,' he shouted back.

'I will insult you a lot more. Since you don't have the ability to provide for the family, I will. See how you like that.' And, turning on her heels, she walked away.

When she had calmed down Suraiya realized what she had done. She'd committed herself in front of all the family. If she now went back on her word, she would become a laughing stock.

Then she thought, 'The words just seemed to come out of my mouth. I didn't really speak them myself. Maybe it was fate deciding for me. I can't say they were the words of God – it would be blasphemy – but maybe it was meant to happen.'

That thought, more even than the consequences of not carrying out her threat, gave Suraiya the strength to defy tradition.

A few weeks later Asghar was not a little concerned to observe Hukum Chand, the defeated Congress candidate in the last election, walk into the courtyard. He folded his hands politely in greeting to the men and asked whether Suraiya was in. The men pointed to the house.

After an hour or so the Hindu emerged with a broad smile on his face, paid his respects again and walked off. He'd been delighted with the deal that Suraiya had offered. She would deliver Muslim votes to him if he helped her to become a contractor. Not only would that mean his political career would recover, but he would also be able to damage his opponent's business interests. Hukum Chand took contracts from the Public Works Department, which ruled him out of the Irrigation Department. That had become the virtual monopoly of his opponent, but now Suraiya would, he was sure, prove a formidable rival.

There was no difficulty in persuading the Irrigation Engineer that putting all his eggs in one basket did not make sound business sense, so he was the next visitor to invade what Asghar thought was his sanctuary – his home. The engineer arrived with an elderly man wearing a *dhoti* and silk *kurta*, whom he introduced as the *munshi*. He would provide and supervise the labourers for Suraiya's business. He would also make sure that no more work was done than was absolutely necessary to allow the engineer to certify that the contract had been completed. That would mean fat profits to be shared for all the work which should have been done but wasn't and for all the supplies which should have been supplied but weren't.

Before long there was a marked improvement in the family's finances, but naturally Asghar was not happy about this. Suraiya was an attractive woman, and perhaps this was the reason that the Irrigation Engineer and Hukum Chand found it necessary to call on her regularly. Asghar was kept out of their business meetings, but after they were over he found ashtrays full and glasses which smelt of cheap Indian whisky. Nothing could be kept a secret in Mohammadpur, and the *basti* was soon alive with rumours about drinking sessions and worse in Asghar's house where, until recently, no man outside their family circle had been allowed to enter.

The rumours crossed the road to the few inhabitants of the Inner Gate who still lived in the dilapidated ruins of their ancestral homes. Matters reached such a pass that the *maulvi* preached against the iniquity of unchaperoned women holding long meetings with men who weren't even Muslims. No name was mentioned, but the congregation at Friday prayers knew who the sinner was.

Eventually Bari Phuphi decided that a meeting of all the senior relatives living in Mohammadpur had to be called. The *maulvi* was invited too. He was a young man with a straggly beard and a small black bruise marking the place where his forehead touched the floor of the mosque five times a day in prayer. He'd qualified as an *alim*, an approved teacher and preacher, in Lucknow. In Bari Phuphi's younger days there had been no Shia *maulvi* in Mohammadpur. They had been called from Lucknow for special occasions, but elderly and pious Muslims had performed the ceremonies for the dead and for the earlier stages of life that the faithful passed through. Now the younger generation had lost this knowledge and, besides, Iranian money had considerably increased the number of young men passing out of theological colleges, all of whom needed employment.

Bari Phuphi would have preferred not to have this pious stranger interfering in what was a family matter. The *maulvi*, however, was too raw to appreciate the old lady's feelings and launched into a direct attack on Suraiya and Asghar too.

Suraiya cut him short, saying, 'I don't have any desire to hear myself insulted. It's up to God, not you, to judge me and my work. He has the contract for forgiveness, *sahib*, not you.'

One of the younger uncles put a hand over his mouth to stifle his laughter, but a more elderly relative protested, 'You shouldn't talk like that to the *maulvi*. Since he came here he has established an Islamic atmosphere in the *basti*. Many people come for Friday prayers, and he's right to protest when he finds sin spoiling that atmosphere.'

'Sin!' scoffed Suraiya. 'Can you only find sin in my house? Is everyone else washed with milk, they're so pure? Just look at the history of this family. Taqi Miyan didn't rule his villages by bothering about sin.'

Bari Phuphi was very unhappy about the way the meeting was going. Of course Suraiya should be censured and the family name protected, but this was not the way to do it. Without looking at the *maulvi*, she said, 'It's better that we discuss this within the family, Maulvi Sahib, if you would give us leave. This is not something you need to bother yourself with just now.'

The *maulvi* started to protest that it certainly was, but he was cut short by Suraiya, who said, 'In this family we listen to Bari Phuphi. You can go.'

Some of the men looked distinctly unhappy at this snub to the *maulvi*, but they said nothing. The man of God stood up, smoothed down his *kurta*, adjusted his round cap and walked out with his head held high. He was not going to let this insult to the dignity of his office pass. Suraiya was entirely wrong. He was entirely right. She must be punished.

Then Bari Phuphi took charge of the meeting. She spoke of the tradition of *purdah*, saying it was an honourable tradition which respected the modesty of women. It was mistaken to believe that women in *purdah* were oppressed. If she had been cowed, why was she so respected? When Suraiya said it was necessary for her to break *purdah* to save the family finances, Bari Phuphi had to agree that it was indeed a shame that her husband couldn't provide the wherewithal for the family to live as they should. However, she went on to say, even poverty was to be preferred to dishonour. Suraiya maintained that a woman could do business if her husband did not object. Everyone turned to look at Asghar, but he sat silently staring down at the floor.

'Please tell them,' said Suraiya. 'Do you object to my earning money?'

Asghar still did not reply. Bari Phuphi, exasperated by his weakness, said, 'I'm not surprised that Suraiya's running wild with a husband like that. He couldn't tether a goat, let alone control a frisky woman.'

'I didn't ask her to work,' mumbled Asghar. 'She insisted. She's my wife, but she's your niece. You arranged for me to marry her, so you control her.'

'I never thought I'd see a human being your size as helpless as an infant,' said Bari Phuphi. She reached for her stick, levered herself to her feet and, turning to Suraiya, said, 'You are the only man here.' Then she hobbled out of the room. The men dispersed without a word.

In his sermon on the next Friday the *maulvi* worked himself up into a lather of righteous indignation, inveighing against those who did not respect the learning of the clergy, women who practised immorality, men who allowed them to do so, defiance of God and many other grave, grave sins, all of which he knew would be ascribed to Suraiya. That evening two of the elders of the Taqi Miyan family went to the new house the faithful had built for the *maulvi* and implored him not to humiliate their family again. The *maulvi* was insistent. 'How can I allow such sin to go unpunished?' he asked. 'It will undo all the good I have done in improving the atmosphere here.'

The elders had no answer to that. They were very pious themselves and thoroughly disapproved of all these goings on. Assu Miyan rubbed the back of his bald pate and pleaded, 'Maulvi Sahib, we have thought and thought, but how can we do anything if Asghar doesn't take his wife in hand?'

'Compel him to. Threaten him.'

'To say that is one thing, but to do it another.'

'Suraiya is very fond of Moharram and proud of her *majlis* of the Eighth Day, I'm told.'

'That she is.'

'Well, tell her that you'll boycott her *majlis* next year. I'll make sure the Inner Village does.'

'It will be difficult for us to boycott the *majlis* of a member of our own family, and you know about our old rivalry with the Inner Village. But on a matter as great as this, I suppose we should be able to forget our differences.'

On their way home the two men passed three *burqa*-clad women making their way back from the bus stand.

'It's such a shame on us,' Assu Miyan said. 'In the old days the lower-caste families did not have the time to bother with *purdah*, nor the money either. Now they are the ones who are observing *purdah*, while our women are breaking it.'

'Yes,' replied his cousin, 'our family fought for independence in the Congress Party, but that same party destroyed us by taking our land away. It's the lower castes, who made no sacrifices for Independence, who have benefited from it. Now I wonder why we ever fought the British. We *zamindar* families were much better off under them.'

'But there's one thing, I tell you. Let the lower castes all wear *purdah*. It'll be generations before their women have the glow of genuine modesty on their cheeks, the glow our women have.'

The butchers were the other topic of conversation among the Shias of Mohammadpur. Someone had to sell meat to the carnivorous Muslims, but the trouble was that the Hindus would not allow the butchers to slaughter their buffaloes except in the privacy of their small houses. They couldn't sell the meat in the bazaar either. Customers had to come to the butchers' doors. This hadn't presented any problems as long as only rich Muslims could afford to eat meat regularly, but now almost everyone earned enough money to buy buffalo meat, and the number of butchers had increased to meet the demand. Unfortunately, their huts had sprung up on one side of a large pond in the middle of a *basti* of Shias and near the crumbling old house of the Inner Village family. The butchers chopped their meat on wooden stumps outside their huts. They piled up the bones in the corners of their yards and puddles of drying blood stained the ground. White scavenger vultures, their ruffs grubby with dust, kept the banks of the pond reasonably clean, but much of the butchers' waste found its way into the pond. The stench grew worse each summer.

Various efforts had been made to move the butchers to the outskirts of the small town. Land had even been offered to them, but they had refused to go. Although Muslims by faith, they were not notably pious, realizing that wealthier people regarded them with disdain, and so they were immune to threats from the *mullah* or pressure from the big families. They had played their politics cleverly, managing to offer their votes to the winner in the last State Assembly election, who now regarded them as a vote-bank to be protected from attempts to move them. This meant the health hazard they represented went unremarked by any official.

The influential members of the family of the Inner Gate no longer lived in Mohammadpur and were not over-worried about the problems of the few cousins left behind. They kept a useful eye on the family mansion, but that was all. That was why it was not with any great expectations that Sajid, one of the cousins in Mohammadpur, wrote to his great-aunt, Asimun Dadi, informing her of the death of his young son. The boy had died of an undiagnosed illness which the doctor said had probably been caused by the unhygienic conditions of the neighbourhood. Sajid asked his great-aunt request her influential sons to have the butchers moved.

Asimun Dadi was staying in Delhi with her eldest son, Irfan, a lawyer in the Supreme Court, when Sajid's letter arrived. That evening she showed him the letter and asked what he was going to do about it.

'Why do you bother, *Amman*?' he replied. 'We don't have any real connection with Mohammadpur any longer, so why should we trouble with every branch of your vast family? Those days have passed.'

'They may have gone for you, *beta*, but Mohammadpur is still somewhere very special for me. If the conditions there are so unhealthy, no one will stay for Moharram, and that's the only time the family gets together. You are a lawyer. Why don't you file a case?'

'Where is the time? And then it wouldn't do any good.' Hoping that was the end of the matter, Irfan walked over to the sideboard and poured himself a whisky and soda.

His mother was a great traveller, moving around the country staying with her many children. She was usually treated with the greatest respect wherever she went, but this was the one home where she knew she didn't count for much. Her eldest son was far too concerned about his career to bother about any relatives, and his wife practised in the Supreme

Court too. The children had been sent to boarding schools in the foothills of the Himalayas. But the more Asimun Dadi was ignored, the more determined she became to make her presence felt. She walked over to the sideboard where Irfan was standing with that obstinate look she knew so well, took the glass from him, put it down and led him back to his chair. Smiling gently, she asked, 'Do I often demand anything from you? I taught you religion and customs, so that you would know what they were. But after that I left you free to decide your own course in life, to adapt to the age you live in, didn't I?'

'You have been very tolerant, *Amman*, I agree,' acknowledged Irfan.

'Has it ever been the women of this family who have been opposed to change? Didn't your grandmother support your uncle when he wanted to be in films and your father said he must go into government service? When he first acted in a film, your grandfather refused to see it, but your grandmother told him, "You don't know what a great man my son is. If he has done something, it will be very good." She even went to a public cinema to see the film!'

'I know,' said Irfan irritably, 'and now you will tell me how you came out of *purdah* so that you could chose our school and make sure we were being taught well, but – '

'Yes,' interrupted the old lady, getting into her stride, 'and the whole family rose up in protest against me. I was told I was going English, that my children would grow up knowing nothing of their religion, that I was immoral. But if I hadn't stood up to that pressure, you wouldn't be here in Delhi with your smart house, your Supreme Court and your beautiful wife. You'd be back in Mohammadpur – a pauper trying to maintain the style of a Taluqdar.'

Irfan held up his hands to stem the torrent of words. 'All right, *Amman*, all right. When we go for Moharram this year I will see what can be done.'

'You must do, otherwise the whole family will be scattered

for ever. When everyone hears about that poor child dying and sees the filth and dirt, they will run away as if rats had taken over the place and plague had come. It will be just like Delhi in the last rains, when the plague rumour spread – everyone went mad. This year Moharram comes at the height of the hot weather, and that pond will stink.'

Asimun Dadi always went to Mohammadpur with her brother a few days before the rest of the family arrived for Moharram to make sure the few habitable parts of the old house were clean and that the kitchen was prepared for the cooks. That year she took her eldest son Irfan too.

It wasn't easy to keep anything secret in Mohammadpur, so Irfan soon heard of the plan to boycott Suraiya's *majlis*. He was not surprised therefore that one of the first who called to pay his respects to the family was the *maulvi*. Bowing obsequiously and salaaming, he asked after the welfare of various members of the family. Irfan called for two chairs to be brought out on to the patchy grass of the courtyard under the shade of a *neem* tree. Inviting him to sit down, Irfan said, 'I believe, *maulvi sahib*, that we have something to discuss.' It would have been polite for Irfan to engage the *maulvi* in small talk at least until the inevitable cups of tea were brought out, but he was in no mood for such formalities. 'I have heard that you want us to boycott Suraiya's *majlis*,' he went on.

The *maulvi* had been hoping to introduce the subject with a long prologue on the sinfulness of Suraiya and the disrepute she was bringing on the Shia community. He had been convinced that his eloquence and the monstrosity of her sins would convince Irfan that something had to be done. But he was put out by Irfan's direct approach and his well-planned strategy deteriorated into a nervous gabble. 'Yes, yes. You see, it's very bad, really very bad. She's behaving very badly. We are all getting a bad name. My work, which is so important, is suffering. It looks bad if I can't stop her. Already the Sunnis are laughing at us behind our backs.'

Irfan checked the torrent of words, saying, 'I know, *maulvi sahib*. I agree it's most undesirable. My mother also feels she's gone too far, but there is one problem – our family is most likely leaving Mohammadpur for good.'

'Leaving!' said the *maulvi*, sitting bolt-upright in his chair. 'That's not possible.'

'What is not possible in this world, *maulvi sahib*?'

'But why?'

'Because the filth is beyond endurance. The stench from that pond, produced by all the carrion left by the butchers, comes right up to here.'

'You are quite correct, of course. I have been trying to persuade them to go, but they are Sunnis, and they don't listen to me. They don't even follow their own *maulvi*. What can I do?'

'If you can't do anything, there won't be any members of my family here to boycott Suraiya's *majlis*. They'll all run when they see the conditions here. One child has already died. I am trying to persuade my mother to leave because I fear for her health.'

If the prominent visitors from the Inner Village deserted Mohammadpur for good, the consequences would be far more serious than just the collapse of the *maulvi*'s plan to punish Suraiya. It would be a major blow to the Shias, unbalancing the delicate relationship between the different communities of Mohammadpur. They would be reduced to an irrelevance, leaving them at the mercy of the Sunnis and Hindus. The Inner Village family had been the more important of the two Taluqdar families of Mohammadpur. It didn't matter that the lethargic Jaffar Miyan, who had been Taluqdar at the time of independence, had given away most of the family land. Birth, not wealth, granted prestige, and there was no doubt that the family of the Inner Village was still regarded by all communities in Mohammadpur as the leading family. This gave the Shias far more clout than their numerical position justified. Also, of course, it enhanced the *maulvi*'s prestige, although families of the Inner Village had never been great patrons of the clergy.

'But what have the butchers to do with me?' asked the *maulvi*.

'Quite simple,' replied Irfan briskly, making clear that, as far as he was concerned, the interview was over, 'You get rid of them and you have your boycott.'

The *maulvi* couldn't let matters rest there. 'You have the influence,' he pleaded. 'You live in Delhi. You have the *sifarish* with the big people. I'm merely a simple *maulvi*, living on the alms of the community.'

'It's not usual to find a *mullah* who is so humble,' replied Irfan in mock surprise. 'You people claim the right to rule nowadays, so rule.' Then, standing up, he bid the *maulvi* farewell and walked back to the house.

The *maulvi*'s head was bowed as he hurried back to his allies in the Taqi Miyan family. He didn't notice the crow-pheasant, with rust-red wings shining in the bright sunlight, strutting across the ground in front of him. 'Something has to be done quickly. Moharram is almost upon us,' he thought. He ignored the greetings of the women spinning outside the huts where their men sat weaving, their looms clacking with so many different noises it sounded as though every part must be going in a different direction and the whole must surely fall apart. 'I face a double disaster,' the Maulvi muttered. 'All the work I have done will be destroyed, and my face will be blackened with disgrace.' The sound of the *azaan* from the new Sunni mosque didn't this time prompt him to hurry back to his own mosque for prayers. He went straight to the house of the most trusted elder of the Taqi Miyan family.

The elder gathered the men of the family together. The *maulvi*'s news shocked them deeply. Although there was little love lost between the two former ruling families, Taqi Miyan's descendants knew how damaging it would be for the whole Shia community if the Inner Village was deserted. But what could they do?

One of the elders said, 'They have the brains. That's why they have been able to earn their bread in the cities, and that's why they don't care about Mohammadpur. Our problem is that we have never been good at using our brains. We have always fought with our *lathis*.'

Bari Phuphi, who had joined the conclave, remarked sourly, 'You can't even do that nowadays – Suraiya is stronger than any one of you.'

'You are boycotting her *majlis*. God forbid you should suggest approaching that sinner for help,' said the by now thoroughly alarmed *maulvi*.

'But she's the one with the political strength now,' Bari Phuphi said. 'She could probably get the butchers moved.'

The *maulvi* tugged at the lobes of his ears, saying, '*Tauba! Tauba!* God forbid that anyone should suggest such a thing.'

No one had any alternative, so the meeting broke up. The *maulvi* was grateful that he'd managed to head off any suggestion of asking for Suraiya's help or lifting the embargo on her *majlis*, but he was deeply worried. The departure of the Inner Village still threatened to deal an even bigger blow to the prestige of the Shia community and to his own standing.

Suraiya soon heard of this new development. Although no one was prepared to ask for her help, she saw no reason why she shouldn't offer it. Here, perhaps, was a chance to get her own back on the men of the family and that wretched *maulvi* who had persuaded them to shame her. She walked through the narrow lanes where the Taqi Miyan family lived and across the main street. When she reached the huge wooden entrance to the Inner Gate, she found it closed and the elderly watchman leaning against it, fast asleep. She woke him with the abrupt command, 'Tell Irfan Sahib I have come to see him.'

Looking up, the watchman saw Suraiya standing over him, wearing a smart dark-green *salwar qamiz*.

'What did you say?' he asked in surprise. 'Who do you want to see?'

'I've told you: Irfan *sahib*. Open the gate.'

This woman has no shame, thought the watchman. Coming here dressed like that and asking to see one of the men of the family. But he didn't want to pick a fight because he knew she came from a big family too, so he got to his feet, pulled back the bolt and opened the gate. Irfan was sitting in the courtyard and, to the watchman's surprise, got up to greet Suraiya as he saw her coming through the gateway. He led her on to the roof of the house, which overlooked some bedraggled guava trees, beds of summer vegetables and a dried-up well, all that remained of the family estates. 'You see this land?' said Irfan. 'We are thinking of selling it and knocking down the *haveli* because we can't keep it up. Many of us live away from here, and we can't maintain it.'

'Yes,' said Suraiya, 'I had heard that you want to leave Mohammadpur altogether.'

'News travels fast.'

'It's my business to know what's happening.'

Irfan was impressed, as Suraiya had been determined he should be. He spent so little time in Mohammadpur he might not have heard of her new-found power. He had to be convinced that she could deliver the bargain she was about to offer.

Suraiya spelt out that bargain in simple terms. Contractors financed politicians, so she now had considerable influence. She would use that influence to get the butchers moved from the pond, but only if Irfan and his family would come to her *majlis*.

'It won't be such easy work, you know, Suraiya. The MLA is backing the butchers.'

'What do you think will weigh more heavily with him – a few butchers' families or the women's vote?'

'But, according to the *maulvi*, all the women want you locked up.'

Suraiya laughed. 'What do you think the *maulvi* knows about women? He says they break *purdah* if they even look at him or any other man. I've learned one thing from being a contractor. There are two ways to get things done – one through heat and force and another through softness. It's the second that gives satisfaction. I have learned how to win people over using softness. Obviously, I don't have physical strength or bands of thugs, but I'm still a success.'

Irfan had a sneaking sympathy for Suraiya but, like a good lawyer, he demanded a foolproof guarantee before accepting her deal. She pointed out that he would have to trust her because there was no way of having the butchers moved out before Moharram. Not even she could make the government machinery move that fast. Realizing that he'd met his match but unwilling to acknowledge it, Irfan said that he would have to think the matter over.

Come Moharram Suraiya had still not heard anything from Irfan. The *maulvi* had no confirmation that the Inner Village family still intended to boycott Suraiya's *majlis*, but that didn't stop him informing her family that they did. With difficulty the men of Taqi Miyan's family had persuaded Bari Phuphi that she must abide by the boycott too. She eventually agreed because she could see no other way of bringing Suraiya back to the path of orthodoxy.

Suraiya gave the impression that she didn't care. On the evening before the *majlis* was due to take place in their *imambara*, her husband Asghar pleaded with her. 'There's still time to change your mind. Just say you'll give up your contracting and everyone will come to our *majlis*. If they don't, we will never be able to live down the shame. We'll have to leave the *basti*.'

'Will you take over the contracting then?' asked Suraiya.

'You know I can't.'

'All right. Then I'll learn to live with the disgrace they want to pile on my head – even though they should have looked at the dirt inside their own collars before criticizing me. I have spent my life in this village and I know very well what they all get up to. In any case, I don't eat their bread and am not answerable to them. If they want to waste their time worrying over me, let them. I'll not waste my time on them. Instead I'll use it to do my work.'

But for all her bravado Suraiya was very distressed. She feared that Irfan's silence meant he had rejected her offer and would boycott the *majlis*. She had begun to question the point of upsetting everyone so much. Her aim had been to earn enough to preserve the honour of her house and to allow them to stay in Mohammadpur with everyone acknowledging their status. If she was to be ostracized, she might as well forget Mohammadpur and go to the district headquarters, where she could continue her work much more conveniently. There, however, she would be no one very much, and certainly her family would count for nothing. She belonged in Mohammadpur.

The next morning her worst fears were confirmed. She sat waiting in the *imambara* for the congregation to join the renowned *alim* they had called from Lucknow, but only a few Hindu women had come to ask for favours from the *tazias* laid out in preparation for the great procession which was the culmination of Moharram. The whirring of two electric pedestal fans, circulating heat, was the only sound that broke the silence. Suraiya pulled the dividing curtain aside to see that the men's space was almost empty. There was only the *alim*, her husband and one or two family servants. The *alim* began to argue with Asghar, asking why he'd been brought all the way to Mohammadpur when there was no one to listen to him. He could have been addressing a mighty congregation somewhere else. There was no shortage of demand for his eloquence. Asghar knew that to be true by the fee he'd had to pay. Suraiya came from behind the *purdah* and tried to persuade the *alim* to stay, but this just made him more angry, '*Begum*,' he said, 'I was speaking with your husband. Return to your place.' Thereupon the *alim* gathered together his books, adjusted his immaculate turban and rose to depart.

At that moment the door of the *imambara* was pushed open

and in walked Irfan, followed by the entire male contingent of the Inner Village. Without saying a word, they sat down reverentially and waited for the *majlis* to start. The spy from the Taqi Miyan family, who had been watching the door of the *imambara* from behind a weaver's hut, moved off as fast as his dignity would allow to report this development to the men of the other branches of the family. There was consternation among them.

'Fools,' said Bari Phuphi as soon as the news reached her. 'Now it's we who are shamed, not Suraiya. Imagine what we will look like if we boycott a *majlis* of our own family and the Inner Village attend it.'

'But you agreed to the plan,' said one of her relatives querulously.

'Yes, and you said the Inner Village had too.'

Another cousin suggested that they call the *maulvi* to consult him. But he was told the clergyman had gone to a *majlis* in a neighbouring village. Bari Phuphi exploded. 'That wretched *maulvi*! Leave him to his own devices. He has drawn us into this mess. We should never have let an outsider interfere in our family affairs.' Then she stood up. 'You may do as you like,' she announced. 'We women are going to the *majlis*.'

Later that afternoon the *maulvi* called to inquire after the success of the boycott. A grim-faced Bari Phuphi told him, 'It was a very splendid *majlis*. The *imambara* was packed full. There wasn't room to put a sesame seed.'

'I would never have expected this of you,' burst out the *maulvi*. 'You have let your religion down. You have let me down.'

'Perhaps we have,' replied Bari Phuphi, 'but perhaps that will teach you to keep within certain limits. I never saw the need for a *maulvi* in Mohammadpur. For generations we had all been quite able to look after ourselves.'

On the tenth day of Moharram, the anniversary of Iman Husain's martyrdom, the men of Taqi Miyan's family, joined

by sundry other poorer Shias, took the *tazias* out of the
imambara. The flimsy bamboo structures wobbled precariously
on the mourners' shoulders as they marched down the narrow
lanes. Many of the houses lining them had been replastered
with cow dung and mud for Moharram. Hindu women
poured water from small pots on to the ground as the procession approached – their offering of respect for the martyrs
who had died thirsting. At the head of the procession Asghar
and his cousins took it in turns to chant laments, and the
refrains were picked up by the black-shirted young men
behind them who were beating their chests in time to the metre.
They beat themselves so hard that blood stained their shirts. All
the rest of Mohammadpur, Hindus and Muslims, wealthy and
poor, men and women, seemed to have left their homes, their
shops, their fields and their businesses, to watch the *tazias* pass
by in solemn mourning of the martyrdom of Imam Husain.

Occasionally the procession halted for a fragment of poetry
to be chanted or to disentangle one of the taller *tazias* caught
in overhead wires. When they reached the Inner Village, the
men of Saddan Miyan's family, their followers and their *tazias*
joined the procession. They all moved on through the lines of
spectators to a small square. There they halted. A group of
young boys, none older than eleven or twelve, bare-breasted
and wearing white trousers, started to flail their backs. The
thongs of their whips were chains, not leather. The tips were
knives, not knots. The chanting became more and more
frenzied. Men pressed in on all sides to see the blood oozing
from the cuts on the boys' bare backs and to sprinkle rosewater
on their wounds. The more pain the boys inflicted on
themselves, the more ecstatic they became.

Irfan noticed Suraiya among the women standing on the
steps of the mosque watching this frenzy. She saw him approaching, sheltering from the blistering sun under an umbrella, and called out, '*Arre*, Irfan *bhai*, you town people are
so precious you don't want the sun to darken your skins.'

The women covered their mouths to hide their smiles. Irfan

put down the umbrella and said, 'Well, it's been a good Moharram after all, Suraiya. I have kept my part of the deal. What about yours?

'You go back to Delhi, where you belong,' replied Suraiya. 'Leave me to look after Mohammadpur.'

GLOSSARY

aarti	a ceremony performed when worshipping a god – a lamp is circled in front of the idol
accha	good; all right, OK; (interjection) really!
alim	scholar – here religious scholar
arhar daal	the favourite lentil of eastern UP
arre	an exclamation
babu	title of respect; petty bureaucrat
badmash	man of bad character
Bania	a member of the trading caste
bas	enough
basti	settlement
behenchod	sister-fucker
beta	son
beti	daughter
bhai	brother
bhaiya	brother
bhang	an intoxicating drink made with ground leaves of cannabis
Bhangis	Sweepers. This is often used in a derogatory way
Bhumihar	member of an upper, landholding, caste
bidi	the poor man's smoke – tobacco wrapped in a leaf instead of cigarette paper
bigha	a measure of land varying in different regions from a quarter to over half an acre

bindi	a dot on the forehead, here on the forehead of a married woman
biradari	community, caste-fellows
Brahmin	a member of the priestly caste
brinjal	aubergine
burqa	the veil; generally a thin, black button-up coat worn with a headcovering and veil by Muslim women
Chamars	members of the Harijan caste whose traditional occupation is to work with leather
chamcha	lit. spoon; lickspittle, sycophant
chaplusi	flattery
charpoy	bed with a wooden frame typically strung with a thin rope made of grass
chilum	pipe
chutiya	cunt-born
daal	lentils
daan	gift; offerings; alms
dacoits	bandits
Dalit	lit. downtrodden, depressed; the name by which members of Harijan castes now prefer to be known
dehijar	term of abuse used by women about men
desi	here meaning country liquor
dhaba	roadside eating place
dhobi	a washerman; also used to describe the caste of washermen
dhoti	an unstitched lower garment, which is folded and wrapped round the body
Diwali	the Hindu festival of lights
faag	a traditional Holi song

ganja	cannabis
garhai	a pond formed when earth is excavated for building houses, etc.
ghat	here meaning a slope or flight of steps down to a river
ghi	clarified butter
godown	store, warehouse
goonda	thug
gujhias	sweet fried pastries shaped like miniature Cornish pasties
han	yes
Hari kirtan	devotional songs in praise of Vishnu
Harijan	lit. a person of God. A name popularized by Mahatma Gandhi for a person within the Hindu system but of a status well below the upper castes. They were formerly known as Untouchables. See Dalit
haveli	mansion
havildar	sergeant of police
Holi	the Hindu festival of colours
hookah pani bund	social boycott by refusing to share water or a smoke with some one
Humayun	the second Mughal Emperor
IAS	Indian Administrative Service, the élite corps which succeeded the Indian Civil Service of the British Raj
ikka	pony trap
imambara	house of the Imam, the building where Shia Muslims hold the mourning assemblies marking the anniversary of the martyrdom of the Prophet Muhammad's grandson, Imam Husain
izzat	honour, respect

jalebi	an Indian sweet, batter fried in squirly shapes and soaked in syrup
janeo	sacred thread
-ji	an honorific suffix
khadi	homespun cotton cloth popularized by Mahatma Gandhi
khesari	a poisonous lentil which cripples those who eat it regularly
kichara	a stew of meat and different kinds of grains
Krishna	one of the two most widely worshipped incarnations of the god Vishnu
kurta	loose-fitting shirt
Lakshmi	consort of Vishnu, goddess of wealth
lathi	staff
lingam	the emblem of Shiva, a phallus
lungi	a length of cloth wrapped around the waist and dropping to the ankles (unless folded up above the knees)
MLA	Member of the Legislative Assembly
madarchod	mother-fucker
majlis	mourning assembly
mantra	a sacred formula or verse
masala	spices
maulvi	a learned man; one learned in Islamic law
mazdoori	wages for manual labour
mela	a fair
Miyan	a title of respect for Muslims; slang for a Muslim
Moharram	The first month of the Muslim calendar. The anniversary of the martyrdom of Imam Husain falls in this month

munshi	writer, clerk; teacher; title of respect
munsif	a subordinate judge
nalban	cattle-shoer
namaste	a greeting
namaskar	a greeting
nasha	intoxication
nashekhor	addict, drunkard
nau	a member of the barber caste
paan	betel leaf
paisa	money; a hundredth of a rupee
pakora	a fried savoury snack
pandit	a respectful title for a Brahmin; a Brahmin priest
papardum	a thin, crisp snack made generally of pulses
paratha	fried Indian bread
pradhan	head of the village council
prasad	blessed food distributed after Hindu worship
puja	worship
pujari	a Hindu priest who performs ritual worship
pulao	rice cooked with vegetables or meat
purdah	curtain; veil
purohit	Hindu priest
raaga	a musical mode or sequence
raj	rule
roghani roti	bright, orange-topped bread made from a dough containing *ghi*
saale	brother-in-law; also a term of abuse
sadhu	Hindu ascetic
salwar qamiz	loose, baggy trousers worn under a long shirt
samosa	triangular fried pastry

sarkar	here a respectful title like 'Your Honour'; master, lord; landlord
sarpanch	head of the village council
Scheduled Caste	caste of traditionally low status, now entitled to certain benefits under the Indian Constitution
seer	a unit of weight, roughly two pounds
shikara	curvilinear tower of a Hindu temple
Shiva	the God of Destruction in the Hindu Trinity
sifarish	a recommendation
sindoor	vermilion, an auspicious colour; vermilion in the parting of a Hindu woman's hair proclaims her married status
tamasha	spectacle
tehsildar	an official responsible for the maintenance of land records and the collection of land revenue from a *tehsil*, the administrative area below a district
thali	tray, steel plate
thana	a police sub-district; the chief police station of that sub-district
thandai	a cooling drink
thanedar	the police officer in charge of a *thana*
thekas	lit. contracts; here shops selling liquor
tika	a mark in the centre of a Hindu forehead made using the thumb of the right hand moving upwards
tonga	a light, two-wheeled horse-driven vehicle
vakil	lawyer
Yadav	member of a now upwardly mobile caste, traditionally composed of small farmers and cattle-owners

yogi	Hindu ascetic
zamindar	major landowner
zarda	chewing tobacco
zenana	women's quarters within a family home
zulum	cruelty